THE INNSMOUTH HERITAGE

Borgo Press Books by BRIAN STABLEFORD

THE INNSMOUTH HERITAGE

AND OTHER SEQUELS

by

Brian Stableford

THE BORGO PRESS

An Imprint of Wildside Press LLC

MMIX

CONTENTS

INTRODUCTION

Writers of imaginative fiction are often asked where they get their ideas from. The fact is that they come from anywhere and everywhere, that the writerly state of mind involves living in an atmosphere that is as profusely-scattered with ideas as the cities of industrial England used to be with the smoke-particles that served as nuclei for the precipitation of smog. Literature is, after all, little more than a temporary weather-phenomenon, which flourished for a while when the climate was conductive and is now in the process of dying out, not because of the activation of any kind of Clear Air Act but merely because the intellectual air we breathe nowadays is too arid to support it. Most writers, however, find that sort of explanation too tedious, so they mostly manufacture shorter and wittier formulae for use as replies. I always say that I steal them, although I readily acknowledge that this is an empty boast. It is after all, great writers who steal; the rest of us merely borrow.

One of the side-effects of the historical growth of prose fiction, which became as profuse as an Amazonian rain forest in the nineteenth and twentieth centuries, although it will presumably dwindle away to a mere blasted heath in the twenty-first, is that the smoke-particles around which literary ideas might form were intensively recycled, recklessly multiplied in the meantime by a quasi-microbial process of fission. The easiest place for any modern writer to find ideas to steal, or merely borrow, is the work of other writers.

Unlike common-or-garden theft and borrowing, of course, literary appropriation is subject to a mutation rate so extreme that one might almost suspect the everpresence of some strange background radiation of the kind that was once mislabeled "inspiration". (Cynics, of course, might suggest that it is more akin to chemical pollution, but cynics have such dirty minds that one would naturally expect them to manifest such a preference.) At any rate, the literary recycling and reproduction of previously-owned ideas always involves a certain amount of alteration. The distinction between liter-

7

ary theft and literary borrowing is akin to that between beneficial and injurious mutation, the observed ratio being not dissimilar to that pertaining to biological mutation—although successive generations of fiction, not being subject to such rigorous processes of eliminative selection, tend to conserve far more deleterious mutations than successive generations of natural organisms.

The mutational processes to which recycled ideas are routinely subject are many and varied, but it is easy enough to identify some broad categories, the most important of which are extrapolation, inversion, perversion and subversion. The categories are, of course, far more distinct in theoretical terms than they ever are in quotidian practice; most actual transformations combine the elementary strategies in idiosyncratic ways. All the stories in this collection are extrapolations, that being inherent to the definition of a sequel, but all of them also feature a degree of perversion and subversion, and it is the degree and direction of these further adjustments that characterize me as a writer. I am, I fear, unassailably addicted to perversion and subversion, albeit in a purely literary sense. (In real life I am a run-of-the-mill recluse with hardly any personality at all.) Some readers—those in search of straightforward *hommages*, slavish pastiches, or further segments cut from the infinitely-repeating patterns that some successful literary series tend to become—might conceivably be disappointed by my notion of how sequels ought to be written. Hopefully, others won't.

The pattern formed by assembling these sequels inevitably provides some insight into my tastes as a reader, but cannot be taken as a straightforward indicator thereof. Collections of sequels to the works of famous writers are frequently commissioned nowadays in pursuit of marketing strategies, attempting to exploit the cachet attached to the names of writers whose modern celebrity is stubborn but regrettably posthumous. Some of the stories in this collection were written in response to invitations to submit to anthologies of that sort, and are thus representative of eccentric juxtapositions of market forces and my own inclinations.

"The Innsmouth Heritage" is a sequel to "The Shadow Over Innsmouth" by H. P. Lovecraft. It was commissioned for use in an anthology called *Shadows Over Innsmouth*, edited by Stephen Jones, but when the anthology initially failed to sell I redirected it to a specialist publisher of Lovecraftiana, Necronomicon Press, who issued it as a chapbook in 1992. The anthology eventually sold to Fedogan & Bremer, who published it in 1994.

"The Picture" is a sequel to *The Picture of Dorian Gray* by Oscar Wilde. It was first published in the second issue of *The Seventh Seal* in 2000.

"The Temptation of Saint Anthony" is a sequel to one of the items in the Golden Legend, assembled by Jacobus de Voragine, although earlier versions of the story predated that collection; it might better be regarded as an alternative version of the story reproduced by Voragine, and subsequently stolen or borrowed by many other artists and writers. It was first published in *The Secret History of Vampires* edited by Darrell Schweitzer, published by DAW in 2007.

"The Ugly Cygnet by Hans Realist Andersen" is a sequel to "The Ugly Duckling" by Hans Christian Andersen. It originally appeared in the fourth issue of *The Seventh Seal* in 2001.

"Art in the Blood" is an addition to the Sherlock Holmes series by Arthur Conan Doyle, although it combines the features of that series with those of H. P. Lovecraft's "Cthulhu Mythos," as per the brief of the anthology for which it was written, *Shadows Over Baker Street* edited by John Pelan and Michael Reaves, published by Del Rey in 2003.

"Mr. Brimstone and Dr. Treacle" is a sequel to *The Strange Case of Dr. Jekyll and Mr. Hyde* by Robert Louis Stevenson. It first appeared (under the pseudonym Francis Amery) in *Naked Truth* 6 (1996).

"Jehan Thun's Quest" is a sequel to "Maître Zacharius" by Jules Verne. It was written for *The Mammoth Book of New Jules Verne Adventures* edited by Mike Ashley and Eric Brown, published in the UK by Robinson and in the USA by Carroll & Graf in 2005.

"The Immortals of Atlantis" is, in some ultimate sense, a sequel to Plato's *Timaeus* and *Critias*, although it actually refers back to some of the multitudinous other sequels produced in the interim, especially those associated with the nineteenth century occult revival. It first appeared in *disLocations* edited by Ian Whates and published by the Newcon Press in 2007.

"Between the Chapters" is a sequel to the third chapter of *Genesis*, filling in the narrative gap which separates that chapter from the following one. It appears here for the first time.

"Three Versions of a Fable" is a sequel to "The Nightingale and the Rose" by Oscar Wilde, which was itself a calculatedly-perverted version of a story by Hans Christian Andersen. It first appeared in *Bats and Red Velvet* 14 (1995).

"The Titan Unwrecked; or, Futility Revisited" is a sequel to *Le Chevalier Ténèbre* by Paul Féval, which I translated into English as *Knightshade*; it is also a sequel to a hypothetical alternative version of a story by Morley Robertson that was originally called "Futility," although it is better known as "The Wreck of the Titan," and to similar alternative versions of the Allan Quatermain series by H. Rider Haggard and *Dracula* by Bram Stoker, as well as to the Rocambole series originated by Pierre-Alexis Ponson du Terrail and carried forward by other hands. As if that were not complication enough, it also features Lovecraftian elements closely akin to those featured in "The Innsmouth Heritage" and "Art in the Blood." It first appeared in *Tales of the Shadowmen*, edited by Jean-Marc and Randy Lofficier, published by Black Coat Press in 2005.

THE INNSMOUTH HERITAGE

The directions Ann had dictated over the phone allowed me to reach Innsmouth without too much difficulty; I doubt that I would have fared so well had I been forced to rely upon the map printed on the end-papers of her book or had I been forced to seek assistance along the way.

While descending from the precipitous ridge east of the town I was able to compare my own impressions of Innsmouth's appearance with the account given by Ann in her opening chapter. When she spoke to me on the phone she had told me that the book's description was "optimistic" and I could easily see why she had felt compelled to offer such a warning. Even the book had not dared to use the word "unspoiled", but Ann had done her best to imply that Innsmouth was full of what we in England would call "old world charm". Old the buildings certainly were, but charming they were not. The present inhabitants—mostly "incomers" or "part-timers", according to Ann—had apparently made what efforts they could to redeem the houses from dereliction and decay, but the renovated facades and the new paint only succeeded in making the village look garish as well as neglected.

It proved, mercifully, that one of the principal exceptions to this rule was the New Gilman House, where a room had been reserved for me. It was one of the few recent buildings in the village, dating back no further than the sixties. The lobby was tastefully decorated and furnished, and the desk-clerk was as attentive as one expects American desk-clerks to be.

"My name's Stevenson," I told him. "I believe Miss Eliot reserved a room for me."

"Best in the house, sir," he assured me. I was prepared to believe it—Ann owned the place. "You sound English, sir," he added, as he handed me a reservation card. "Is that where you know the boss from?"

"That's right," I said, diffidently. "Could you tell Miss Eliot that I'm here, do you think?"

"Sure thing," he replied. "You want me to help you with that bag?"

I shook my head, and made my own way up to my room. It was on the top floor, and it had what passed for a good view. Indeed, it would have been a very good view had it not been for the general dereliction of the waterfront houses, over whose roofs I had to look to see the ocean. Out towards the horizon I could see the white water where the breakers were tumbling over Devil Reef.

I was still looking out that way when Ann came in behind me. "David," she said. "It's good to see you."

I turned round a little awkwardly, and extended my hand to be shaken, feeling uncomfortably embarrassed.

"You don't look a day older," she said, hypocritically. It had been thirteen years since I last saw her.

"Well," I said, "I looked middle-aged even in my teens. But you look wonderful. Being a capitalist obviously suits you. How much of the town do you own?"

"Only about three-quarters," she said, with an airy wave of her slender hand. "Uncle Ned bought the land for peanuts back in the thirties, and now it's worth—peanuts. All his grand ambitions to 'put the place back on the map' came to nothing. He got tenants for some of the properties he fixed up, but they're most week-enders who live in the city and can't afford authentic status symbols. We get a few hundred tourists through during the season—curiosity-seekers, fishermen, people wanting to get away from it all, but it's hardly enough to keep the hotel going. That's why I wrote the book—but I guess I still had too much of the dry historian in me and not enough of the sensational journalist. I should have made more of all those old stories, but I couldn't get my conscience past the lack of hard evidence."

"That's what a university education does for you," I said. Ann and I had met at university in Manchester—the real Manchester, not the place to which fate and coincidence had now brought me—when she was studying history and I was studying biochemistry. We were good friends—in the literal rather than the euphemistic sense, alas—but we hadn't kept in touch afterwards, until she discovered by accident that I was in New Hampshire and had written to me, enclosing her book with news of her career as a woman of property. I had planned to come to see her even before I read the book, thus finding the excuse that made the prospect even more inviting.

As she watched me unpack, the expression in her grey eyes was quite inscrutable. Politeness aside, she really did look good—handsome rather than pretty, but clear of complexion and stately in manner.

"I suppose your coming over to the States is part of the infamous Brain Drain," she said. "Was it the dollars, or the research facilities that lured you away?"

"Both," I said. "Mostly the latter. Human geneticists aren't worth *that* much, and I haven't published enough to be regarded as a grand catch. I'm just a foot-soldier in the long campaign to map and understand the human genome."

"It beats being chief custodian of Innsmouth and its history," she said, so flatly as to leave no possibility of a polite contradiction.

I shrugged. "Well," I said, "If I get a paper out of this, it will put Innsmouth on the scientific map, at least—although I doubt that the hotel will get much business out of it. I can't imagine that there'll be a legion of geneticists following in my trail."

She sat down on the edge of the bed. "I'm afraid it might not be so easy," she said. "All that stuff in the book about the Innsmouth look is a bit out of date. Back in the twenties, when the population of the town was less than four hundred, it may well have been exactly the kind of inbred community you're looking for, but the post-war years brought in a couple of thousand outsiders. In spite of the tendency of the old families to keep to themselves, the majority married out. I've looked through the records, and most of the families that used to be important in the town are extinct—the Marshes, the Waites, the Gilmans. If it hadn't been for the English branch, I guess the Eliots would have died out too. The Innsmouth look still exists, but it's a thing of the past—you won't see more than a trace of it in anyone under forty."

"Age is immaterial," I assured her.

"That's not the only problem. Almost all of those who have the look are shy about it—or their relatives are. They tend to hide themselves away. It won't be easy to get them to co-operate."

"But you know who they are—you can introduce me."

"I know who some of them are, but that doesn't mean that I can help you much. I may be an Eliot, but to the old Innsmouthers I'm just another incomer, not to be trusted. There's only one person who could effectively act as an intermediary for you, and it won't be easy to persuade him to do it."

"Is he the fisherman you mentioned over the phone—Gideon Sargent?"

"That's right," she said. "He's one of the few lookers who doesn't hide himself away, although he shows the signs more clearly than anyone else I've seen. He's saner than most—got himself an education under the G.I. Bill after serving in the Pacific in '45—but he's not what you might call talkative. He won't hide, but he doesn't like being the visible archetype of the Innsmouth look—he resents tourists gawping at him as much as anyone would, and he always refuses to take them out to Devil Reef in his boat. He's always very polite to me, but I really can't say how he'll react to you. He's in his sixties now—never married."

"That's not so unusual," I observed. I was unmarried; so was Ann.

"Maybe not," she replied, with a slight laugh. "But I can't help harboring an unreasonable suspicion that the reason he never married is that he could never find a girl who looked fishy enough."

* * * * * * *

I thought this a cruel remark, though Ann obviously hadn't meant it to be. I thought it even crueler when I eventually saw Gideon Sargent, because I immediately jumped to the opposite conclusion: that no girl could possibly contemplate marrying him, because he looked too fishy by half.

The description that Ann had quoted in her book was accurate enough detail by detail—narrow head, flat nose, staring eyes, rough skin and baldness—but could not suffice to give an adequate impression of the eerie whole. The old man's tanned face put me in mind of a wizened koi carp, although I could not tell, at first—because his jacket collar was turned up—whether he had the gill-like markings on his neck that were the last and strangest of the stigmata of the Innsmouth folk.

Sargent was sitting on a canvas chair on the deck of his boat when we went to see him, patiently mending a fishing-net. He did not look up as we approached, but I had no doubt that he had seen us from afar and knew well enough that we were coming to see him.

"Hello, Gideon," said Ann, when we were close enough. "This is Dr. David Stevenson, a friend of mine from England. He lives in Manchester now, teaching college."

Still the old man didn't look up. "Don't do trips round the reef," he said, laconically. "You know that, Miss Ann."

"He's not a tourist, Gideon," she said. "He's a scientist. He'd like to talk to you."

"Why's that?" he asked, still without altering his attitude. "'Cause I'm a freak, I suppose?"

"No," said Ann, uncomfortably "of course not...."

I held up my hand to stop her, and said: "Yes, Mr. Sargent," I said. "That *is* why, after a manner of speaking. I'm a geneticist, and I'm interested in people who are physically unusual. I'd like to explain that to you, if I may."

Ann shook her head in annoyance, certain that I'd said the wrong thing, but the old man didn't seem offended.

"When I were a young'un," he commented, abstractedly, "there was a man offered Ma a hunnerd dollars for me. Wanned t'put me in a glass tank in some kinda sideshow. She said no. Blamed fool— hunnerd dollars was worth summin then." His accent was very odd, and certainly not what I'd come to think of as a typical New England accent. Although he slurred common words, he tended to take more trouble over longer ones, and I thought I could still perceive the lingering legacy of his education.

"Do you know what 'genetics' means, Mr. Sargent?" I asked. "I really would like to explain why it's important that I talk to you."

At last he looked up, and looked me in the eye. I was ready for it, and didn't flinch from the disconcerting stare.

"I know what genes are, Doc," he said, coolly. "I bin a little curious myself, y'know, to fin' out how I got to be this way. You gonna tell me? Or is that what y'wanner figure out?"

"It's what I want to figure out, Mr. Sargent," I told him, breathing a slight sigh of relief. "Can I come aboard?"

"Nope," he replied. "Taint convenient. You at the hotel?"

"Yes I am."

"See y'there t'night. Quarter of eight. You pay f'r the liquor."

"Okay," I said. "Thanks, Mr. Sargent. I appreciate it."

"Don' mention it," he said. "An' I *still* don' do trips to the reef. Or pose f'r Jap cameras—you mind me, now, Miss Ann."

"I mind you, Gideon," she answered, as we turned away.

As soon as we were out of earshot, she said: "You're honored, David. He's never come to the hotel before—and not because no one ever offered to buy him a drink before. He still remembers the old place, and he doesn't like what Uncle Ned put up in its place, any more than he likes all the colonists who moved in when the village was all-but-dead in the thirties."

We were passing an area of the waterfront that looked like a post-war bomb-site—or one of those areas in the real Manchester where they bulldozed the old slums but still haven't got round to building anything else instead.

"This is the part of the town that was torched, isn't it?" I said.

"Sure is," she replied. "Way back in '27. Nobody really knows how it happened, although there are plenty of wild stories. Gang warfare can be counted out—there was no substantial bootlegging hereabouts. Arson for arson's sake, probably. It's mostly mine now—Uncle Ned wanted to rebuild but never could raise the finance. I'd sell the land to any developer who'd take it on, but I'm not hopeful about my chances of getting rid of it."

"Did the navy really fire torpedoes into the trench beyond the reef?" I asked, remembering a story which she'd quoted in her book.

"Depth charges," she said. "I took the trouble to look up the documents, hoping there'd be something sensational behind it, but it seems that they were just testing them. There's very deep water out there—a crack in the continental shelf—and it was convenient for checking the pressure-triggers across the whole spectrum of settings. The navy didn't bother to ask the locals, or to tell them what was going on; the information was still classified then, I guess. It's not unnatural that the wacky stories about sea-monsters were able to flourish uncontradicted."

"Pity," I said, looking back at the crumbling jetties as we began to climb the shallow hill towards Washington Street. "I rather liked all that stuff about the Esoteric Order of Dagon conducting its hideous rites in the old Masonic Hall, and Obed Marsh's covenant with the forces of watery evil."

"The Esoteric Order of Dagon was real enough," she said. "But it's hard to find out what its rituals involved, or what its adherents actually believed, because it was careful not to produce or keep any records—not even sacred documents. It seems to have been one of a group of crazy quasi-gnostic cults which made a big thing about a book called the *Necronomicon*—they mostly died out at about the time the first fully-annotated translation was issued by the Miskatonic University Press. The whole point of being an esoteric sect is lost when your core text becomes exoteric, I guess.

"As for old Obed's fabulous adventures in the South Seas, almost all the extant accounts can be traced back to tales that used to be told by the town character back in the twenties—an old lush named Zadok Allen. I can't swear that every last detail originated in the dregs of a whisky bottle, but I'd be willing to bet my inheritance that Captain Marsh's career was a good deal less eventful than it seemed once Zadok had finished embroidering it."

"But the Marshes really did run a gold refinery hereabouts? And at least *some* of the so-called Innsmouth jewelry is real?"

"Oh sure—the refinery was the last relic of the town's industrial heyday, which petered out mid-nineteenth century after a big epidemic. I've looked at the account-books, though, and it did hardly any business for thirty-five or forty years before it closed down. It's gone now, of course. The few authentic surviving examples of the old Innsmouth jewelry are less beautiful and less exotic than rumor represents, but they're interesting enough—and certainly not local in origin. There are a couple of shops in town where they make 'genuine imitations' for tourists and other interested parties—one manufacturer swears blind that the originals were made by pre-Columbian Indians, the other that they were found by Old Obed during his travels. Take your pick."

I nodded, sagely, as if to say that it was what I'd suspected all along.

"What are you looking for, David?" she asked, suddenly. "You don't really think that there's anything in Zadok Allen's fantasies, do you? You surely can't seriously entertain the hypothesis that the old Innsmouthers were some kind of weird crossbreed with an alien race!"

I laughed. "No," I reassured her, with complete sincerely. "I don't believe that—nor do I believe that they're some kind of throwback to our phantom aquatic ancestors. You'd better sit in tonight when I explain the facts of life to old Gideon; the reality is likely to be far more prosaic than that, alas."

"Why *alas*?" she asked.

"Because what I'm looking for will only generate a paper. If the folklore quoted in your book were even half-true, it would be worth a Nobel Prize."

* * * * * *

Gideon Sargent presented himself at the hotel right on time. He was dressed in what I presumed was his Sunday best, but the ensemble included a roll-neck sweater, which kept the sides of his neck concealed. There were half a dozen people in the bar, and Gideon drew a couple of curious glances from the out-of-towners, but he was only a little self-conscious. He was used to carrying his stigmata.

He drank neat bourbon, but he drank slowly, like a man who had no intention of getting loaded. I asked a few questions to find out exactly how much he did know about genes, and it turned out that he really was familiar with the basics. I felt confident that I could give him a reasonably full explanation of my project.

"We've already begun the business of mapping the human genome," I told him. "The job will require the collective efforts of thousands of people in more than a hundred research centers, and even then it will take fifteen or twenty years, but we have the tools to do it. While we're doing it, we hope to get closer to the answers to certain basic problems.

"One of these problems is that we don't know how genes collaborate to produce a particular physical form. We know how they code for the protein building blocks, but we don't know much about the biochemical blueprint that instructs a growing embryo how to develop into a man instead of a whale or an ostrich. Now, this may seem odd, but one of the best ways of figuring out how things work is to study examples which have gone wrong, to see what's missing or distorted. By doing that, you can build up a picture of what's necessary in order for the job to be done properly. For that reason, geneticists are very interested in human mutations—I'm particularly interested in those which cause physical malformation.

"Unfortunately, physical mutants usually fall into a few well-defined categories, mostly associated with radical and fairly obvious disruptions of whole chromosomes. There are very few viable human variations that operate on a larger scale than changing the color of the skin, or the epicanthic fold that makes Oriental eyes distinctive. That's not entirely surprising, because those which have arisen in the past have mostly been eliminated from the gene-pool by natural selection, or diluted out of existence by hybridization. It's one of the ironies of our trade that, while molecular genetics was becoming sophisticated enough to make them significant, the highly inbred communities of the world were disappearing. All we have in America is a handful of religious communities whose accumulations of recessive genes aren't, for the most part, very interesting. As soon as I read Ann's book I realized that Innsmouth must have been a real genetic treasure-trove back in the twenties. I hope that there still might be time to recover some vital information."

Gideon didn't reply immediately, and for a moment or two I thought he hadn't understood. But then he said: "Not many people got the look any more. Some don' show it 'til they're older, but I don' see much sign of it comin' thru in anyone I see. Ain't no Marshes or Waites any more, and the only Eliots"—he paused to look at Ann—"are distant cousins o' the ones that settled here in the old days."

"But there are a few others, besides yourself, who show some of the signs, aren't there?" Ann put in.

"A few," Gideon admitted.

"And they'd co-operate with Dr. Stevenson—if you asked them to."

"Mebbe," he said. He seemed moodily thoughtful, as though something in the conversation had disturbed him. "But it's too late to do *us* any good, ain't it, Doc?"

I didn't have to ask what he meant. He meant that whatever understanding I might glean from my researches would only be of theoretical value. I wouldn't be able to help the Innsmouthers look normal.

It was, in any case, extremely unlikely that my work would lead to anything which could qualify as a "cure" for those afflicted with the Innsmouth stigmata, but there was really no longer any need for that. The Innsmouthers had taken care of the problem themselves. I remembered what I'd said about gross malformations being eliminated from the gene-pool by natural selection, and realized that I'd used the word "natural" in a rather euphemistic way—as many people do nowadays. The selective pressure would work both ways: the incomers who'd re-colonized Innsmouth after the war would have been just as reluctant to marry people who had the Innsmouth look as people who had the Innsmouth look would have been to pass it on to their children.

Gideon Sargent was certainly not the only looker who'd never married, and I was sure that he wouldn't have, even if there'd been a girl who looked like he did.

"I'm sorry, Gideon," I said. "It's a cruel irony that your ancestors had to suffer the burden of ignorance and superstition because genetics didn't exist, and that now genetics does exist, there's not much left for you to gain from a specific analysis of your condition. But let's not underestimate the value of understanding, Gabriel. It was because your forefathers lacked a true understanding that they felt compelled to invent the Esoteric Order of Dagon, to fill the vacuum of their ignorance and to maintain the pretence that there was something to be proud of in Innsmouth's plight. And that's why stories like the ones Zadok Allen used to tell gained such currency— because they provided a kind of excuse for it all. I'm truly sorry that I'm too late to serve your purposes, Gideon—I only hope that I'm not too late to serve mine. Will you help me?"

He looked at me with those big saucery eyes, so uncannily frightening in their innocence.

"Is there *anythin'* y'can do, Doc?" he asked. "Not about the bones, nor the eyes—I know we're stuck wi' *them*. But the dreams, Doc—can y'do anythin' about the dreams?"

I looked sideways at Ann, uncertainly. There *had* been something in her book about dreams, I recalled, but I hadn't paid much attention to it. It hadn't seemed to be part of the problem, as seen from a biochemist's point of view. Obviously Gideon saw things differently; to him they were the very heart of the problem, and it was because of them that he'd consented to hear me out.

"Everybody has dreams, Gideon," said Ann. "They don't mean anything."

He turned round to stare at her, in that same appalling fashion. "Do *you* have dreams, Miss Ann?" he asked, with seemingly tender concern.

Ann didn't answer, so I stepped into the breach again. "Tell me about the dreams, Gideon," I said. "I don't really know how they fit in."

He looked back at me, obviously surprised that I didn't know everything. After all, I was a doctor, wasn't I? I was the gene-wizard who knew what people were made of.

"All of us who got the look are dreamers," he said, in a painstakingly didactic fashion. "Taint the bones an' the eyes as kills us in the end—'tis the dreams that call us out to the reef an' bid us dive into the pit. Not many's as strong as me, Doc—I know I got the look as bad as any, an' had it all the time from bein' a kid, but us Sargents was allus less superstitious than the likes o' the Marshes, even if Obed's kin *did* have all the money 'fore it passed to Ned Eliot. My granpa ran the first motor-bus out o'here, tryin' to keep us connected to Arkham after the branch-line from Rowley was abandoned. It's the ones that *change* goes mad, Doc—they're the ones as starts believin'."

"Believing what, Gideon?" I asked, quietly.

"Believin' as the dreams is *true*...believin' in Dagon an' Cthulhu an' Pth'thya-l'yi...believin' as how they c'n breathe through their gills'n dive all the way to the bottom of the ocean to Y'ha-nthlei...believin' in the Deep Ones. That's what happens to the people wi' the look, Doc. Natural selection—ain't that what y'called it?"

I licked my lips. "*Everyone* with the look has these dreams?" I queried. If it were true, I realized, it *might* make the Innsmouth enigma more interesting. Physical malformation was one thing, but specific associated psychotropic effects was quite another. I was tempted to explain to Gideon that one of the *other* great unsolved questions about the way the genes worked was how they affected mind and behavior *via* the chemistry of the brain, but that would have meant taking the discussion out into deeper water than he could be expected to handle. There was, of course, a simpler and more probable explanation for the dreams, but, in confrontation with Gideon's quiet intensity, I couldn't help but wonder whether there might be something more profound here.

"The dreams allus go wi' the look," he insisted. "I had 'em all my life. Real horrors, sometimes—unearthly. Can't describe 'em, but take my word for it, Doc, you don' ever want to meet 'em. I'm way past carin' about the look, Doc, but if you could do summin 'bout the dreams...I'll dig up the others f'r ye. Every last one."

It would mean widening the tests, I knew, but I could see that it might be worth it. If the dreams *were* significant, at the biochemical level, I could have something really hot. Not a Nobel Prize, but a real reputation-maker. The implications of discovering a whole new class of hallucinogens were so awesome that I had difficulty pulling myself back down to earth. *First catch your hare*, I reminded myself, carefully.

"I can't make any promises, Gideon," I told him, trying hard to give the impression that I was being overly modest. "It's not easy to locate abnormal DNA, let alone map it and figure out exactly what it's doing. And I have to say that I have my reservations about the possibility of finding a *simple* answer, which might lend itself to some kind of straightforward treatment. But I'll do the best I can to find an explanation of the dreams, and, once we have an explanation, we'll be able to see what might be done to banish them. If you can get these people to agree to my taking blood and tissue-samples, I'll certainly do what I can."

"I c'n do it," he promised me. Then he stood up, obviously having said what he came to say, and heard what he'd hoped to hear. I put out my hand to shake his, but he didn't take it. Instead, he said: "Walk me to the shore, will y'Doc?"

I was almost as surprised by this as Ann was, but I agreed. As we went out, I told her that I'd be back in half an hour.

At first, we walked down the hill in silence. I began to wonder whether he really had anything to say to me, as I'd assumed, or whether it was just some curious whim that had inspired him to ask me to go with him. When we were within sight of the seafront, though, he suddenly said: "You known Miss Ann a long time?"

"Sixteen years," I told him, figuring that it wasn't worth wasting time on an explanation of the fact that we hadn't communicated at all for twelve-and-a-half out of the last thirteen.

"You marry her," he said, as though it were the most natural instruction in the world for one stranger to give another. "Take her to Manchester—or back to England, even better. Innsm'th's a bad place f'r them as owns it, even if they ain't got the look. Don' leave it to y'r kids...will it to the state or summin. I know you think I'm crazy, Doc, you bein' an educated man 'n' all, but I know Innsm'th—I got it in th' bones, th' blood an' th' dreams. Taint worth it. Take her away, Doc. Please."

I opened my mouth to answer, but he'd timed his speech to preclude that possibility. We were now in one of the narrow waterfront streets which had survived the great fire, and he was already pausing before one of the shabby hovels, opening the door.

"Can't invite y'in," he said, tersely. "Taint convenient. G'night, Doc."

Before I could say a single word, the door closed in my face.

* * * * * * *

Gideon was as good as his word. He knew where to find the remaining Innsmouthers who had the look, and he knew how to bully or cajole them into seeing me. A few he persuaded to come to the hotel; the rest I was permitted to visit in their homes—where some of them had been virtual prisoners for thirty years and more.

It took me a week to gather up my first set of samples and take them back to Manchester. Two weeks after that, I returned with more equipment, and took a further set of tissue specimens, some from the people I'd already seen, others—for the sake of comparison—from their unafflicted kinfolk. I threw myself into the project with great enthusiasm, despite that I still had a good deal of routine work to do, both as a research worker and in connection with my teaching. I made what passes in my business for rapid headway, but it wasn't rapid enough for the people of Innsmouth—not that there was ever any real possibility of making good my promise to find a way to banish their evil dreams.

Three months after our first meeting Gideon Sargent died in a freak storm, which blew up unexpectedly while he was fishing. His boat was smashed up on Devil Reef, and what was left of it was later recovered—including Gideon's body. The inquest confirmed that he had died of a broken neck, and that the rest of his many injuries had been inflicted after death while the boat was tossed about on and around the reef.

Gideon was the first of my sample to die, but he wasn't the last. As the year crept on I lost four more, all of whom died in their beds of very ordinary causes—not entirely surprisingly, given that two were in their eighties and the others in their seventies.

There were, of course, a few unpleasant whispers, which said (arguing *post hoc, ergo propter hoc*, as rumors often do) that my taking the tissue samples had somehow weakened or over-excited the people who died, but Gideon had done some sterling work in persuading the victims of the look that it was in their interests to co-operate with me, and none of the others shut me out.

I had no one left whose appearance was as remarkable as Gideon's. Most of the survivors in my experimental sample showed only partial stigmata of an underdeveloped kind—but they all reported suffering from the dreams now and again, and they all found the dreams sufficiently horrific to want to be rid of them if they could. They kept asking me about the possibility of a cure, but I could only evade the question, as I always had.

While I was traveling back and forth from Innsmouth on a regular basis I naturally saw a lot of Ann, and was happy to do so. We were both too shy to be overly intrusive in questioning one another, but as time went by I began to understand how lonely and isolated she felt in Innsmouth, and how rosy her memories of university in England now seemed. I saw why she had taken the trouble to write to me when she learned that I had joined the faculty at Manchester, and, in time, I came to believe that she wanted to put our relationship on a more formal and permanent basis—but when I eventually plucked up enough courage to ask her to marry me, she turned me down.

She must have known how hurt I was, and what a blow to my fragile pride I had suffered, because she tried to let me down very gently—but it didn't help much.

"I'm really very sorry, David," she told me, "but I can't do it. In a way, I'd like to, very much—I feel so lonely sometimes. But I can't leave Innsmouth now. I can't even go to Manchester, let alone back to England, and I know you won't stay in the States forever."

"That's just an excuse," I contended, in martyred fashion. "I know you own a great deal of real estate here, but you admit that it's mostly worthless, and you could still collect the rents—the world is full of absentee landlords."

"It's not that," she said. "It's...something I can't explain."

"It's because you're an Eliot, isn't it?" I asked, resentfully. "You feel that you can't marry for the same reasons that Gideon Sargent felt that *he* couldn't. You don't have a trace of the Innsmouth look about you, but you have the dreams, don't you? You nearly admitted as much to Gideon, that night when he came to the hotel."

"Yes," she said, faintly. "I have the dreams. But I'm not like those poor old mad people who locked themselves away until you came. I *know* that you won't find a cure for them, even if you can find an explanation. I understand well enough what can come of your research and what can't."

"I'm not sure that you do," I told her. "In fact, I'm not sure that you understand your own condition. Given that you don't have a trace of the look, and given that you're not directly descended from any of the Eliots of Innsmouth, what makes you think that your nightmares are anything more than just that: nightmares? As you said to Gideon when he raised the issue, everyone has dreams. Even I have dreams." In the circumstances, I nearly said *had*, but that would have been too obvious a whine.

"You're a biochemist," she said. "You think that the physical malformation is the real issue, and that the dreams are peripheral. Innsmouthers don't see it that way—for them, the dreams are the most important thing, and they've always seen the look as an effect rather than a cause. I'm an Innsmouther too."

"But you're a educated woman! You may be a historian, but you know enough science to know what the Innsmouth look *really* is. It's a genetic disorder."

"I know that the Esoteric Order of Dagon's beliefs and Obed Marsh's adventures in the South Seas are just myths," she agreed. "They're stories concocted, as you said to Gideon, to explain and excuse an inexplicable affliction caused by defective genes. But it might as easily have been the Eliots who imported those genes as anyone else, and they might easily have been in the family for many generations—England used to have its inbred populations too, you know. I know that you only took tissue-samples from me for what you called purposes of comparison, but I've been expecting all along that you would come to me and tell me that you'd found the rogue gene responsible for the Innsmouth look, and that I have it too."

"It doesn't matter," I said, plaintively. "It really doesn't matter. We could still get married."

"It matters to me," she said. "And we can't."

* * * * * * *

I suppose that incident with Ann should have redoubled my determination to trace the DNA-complex that was responsible for the Innsmouth syndrome, in order to enable me to prove to her that she wasn't afflicted, and that her dreams were only dreams. In fact, it didn't; I was hurt by her rejection, and depressed. I continued to work as hard as I ever had, but I found it increasingly difficult to go to Innsmouth, to stay in the hotel where she lived, and to walk through the streets which she owned.

I began to look for someone else to soothe my emotional bruises, while Ann and I drifted steadily apart. We were no longer good friends in any real sense, though we kept up some kind of a pretense whenever we met.

In the meantime, the members of my experimental sample continued to die. I lost three more in the second year, and it became even more obvious that whatever I discovered wasn't going to be of any practical import to the people whose DNA I was looking at. In a way, it didn't matter that much to the program—the DNA that Gideon and all the rest had provided still existed, carefully frozen and stored away. The project was still healthy, still making headway.

In the third year, I finally found what I was looking for: an inversion on the seventh chromosome, which had trapped seven genes, including three oddballs. In homozygotes like Gideon, the genes paired up and were expressed in the normal way; in heterozygotes, like most of my sample—including all of the survivors—the chromosomes could only pair up if one of them became looped around, stopping several of the genes from functioning. I didn't know what all of the genes did, or how—but my biochemical analyses had given me a partial answer.

I drove to Innsmouth the next day, in order to tell Ann the news. Although our relationship had soured and fallen apart, I still owed her as much of an explanation as I could now give.

"Do you know what Haeckel's law is?" I asked her, while we walked beside the Manuxet, past the place where the Marsh refinery had once been located.

"Sure," she said. "I read up on the whole thing, you know, after we got involved. Haeckel's law says that ontogeny recapitulates phylogeny—that the embryo, in developing, goes through a series of stages which preserve a kind of memory of the evolutionary history of an organism. It's been discredited, except as a very loose metaphor. I always thought that the Innsmouth look might turn out to have something to do with the fact that the human embryo goes through a stage where it develops gills."

"Only the ghosts of gills," I told her. "You see, the same embryonic structures that produce gills in fish produce different structures in other organisms; it's called homology. Conventional thinking, muddied by the fact that we don't really understand the business of blueprinting for physical structure, supposes that when natural selection works to alter a structure into its homologue—as when the fins of certain fish were modified by degrees into the legs of amphibians, for instance, or the forelimbs of certain lizards became the wings of birds—the blueprint genes for the new structure replace the blueprint genes for the old. But that's not the only way it could happen. It may be that the new genes arise at different loci from the old ones, and that the old ones are simply switched off. Because they aren't expressed any more in mature organisms they're no longer subject to eliminative natural selection, so they aren't lost, and even though they're bound to be corrupted by the accumulation of random mutations—which similarly aren't subject to elimination by natural selection—they remain within the bodies of descendant species for millions of years. If so, they *may* sometimes be expressed, if there's a genetic accident of some kind that prevents their being switched off in a particular organism."

She thought about it for a few moments, and then she said: "What you're saying is that human beings—and, for that matter, all mammals, reptiles and amphibians—may be carrying around some of the blueprint genes for making fish. These are normally dormant—untroublesome passengers in the body—but under certain circumstances, the switching mechanism fails and they begin to make the body they're in *fishy*."

"That's right," I said. "And that's what I shall propose as the cause of the Innsmouth syndrome. Sometimes, as with Gideon, it can happen very early in life, even before birth. In other instances it's delayed until maturity, perhaps because the incipient mutations are suppressed by the immune system, until the time when ageing sets in and the system begins to weaken."

I had to wait a little while for her next question, though I knew what it would be.

"Where do the dreams fit in?" she asked.

"They don't," I told her. "Not into the biology. I never really thought they did. They're a psychological thing. There's no psychotropic protein involved here. What we're talking about is a slight failure of the switching mechanism that determines physical structure. Ann, the nightmares come from the same place as the Esoteric Order of Dagon and Zadok Allen's fantasies—they're a response to fear, anxiety and shame. They're infectious in exactly the same way that rumors are infectious—people hear them, and reproduce them. People who have the look *know* that the dreams come with it, and knowing it is sufficient to make sure that they do. That's why they can't describe them properly. Even people who don't have the look, but fear that they might develop it, or feel that for some eccentric reason they *ought* to have it, can give themselves nightmares."

She read the criticism in my words, which said that I had always been right and she had always been wrong, and that she had had no good cause for rejecting my proposal. "You're saying that my dreams are purely imaginary?" she said, resentfully. People always are resentful about such things, even when the news is good, and despite the fact that it isn't their fault at all.

"You don't have the inversion, Ann. That's quite certain now that I've found the genes and checked out all the sample traces. You're not even heterozygous. There's no possibility of your ever developing the look, and there's no reason at all why you have to avoid getting married."

She looked me in the eye, as disconcertingly as Gideon Sargent ever had, though her eyes were perfectly normal, and as grey as the sea.

"You've never seen a *shoggoth*," she said, in a tone profound with despair. "I have—even though I don't have the words to describe it."

She didn't ask me whether I was renewing my proposal— maybe because she already knew the answer, or maybe because she hadn't changed her own mind at all. We walked on for a bit, beside that dull and sluggish river, looking at the derelict landscape. It was like the set for some schlocky horror movie.

"Ann," I said, eventually, "you do believe me, don't you? There really isn't a psychotropic element in the Innsmouth syndrome."

"Yes," she said. "I believe you."

"Because," I went on, "I don't like to see you wasting your life away in a place like this. I don't like to think of you, lonely in self-imposed exile, like those poor lookers who shut themselves away because they couldn't face the world—or who were locked up by mothers and fathers or brothers and sisters or sons and daughters who couldn't understand what was wrong, and whose heads were filled with stories of Obed Marsh's dealings with the devil and the mysteries of Dagon.

"That's the *real* nightmare, don't you see—not the horrid dreams and the daft rites conducted in the old Masonic Hall, but all the lives that have been ruined by superstition and terror and shame. Don't be part of that nightmare, Ann; whatever you do, don't give in to that. Gideon Sargent didn't give in—and he told me once, although I didn't quite understand what he meant at the time, that it was up to me to make sure that you wouldn't, either."

"But they got him in the end, didn't they?" she said. "The Deep Ones got him in the end."

"He was killed in an accident at sea," I told her, sternly. "You *know* that. Please don't melodramatize, when you know you don't believe it. You must understand, Ann—*the real horrors aren't in your dreams, they're in what you might let your dreams do to you.*"

"I know," she said, softly. "I do understand."

I understood too, after a fashion. Her original letter to me had been a cry for help, although neither of us knew it at the time—but in the end, she'd been unable to accept the help that was offered, or trust the scientific interpretation that had been found. At the cognitive level, she understood—but the dreams, self-inflicted or not, were simply too powerful to be dismissed by knowledge.

And that, I thought, was yet another *real* horror: that the truth, even when discovered and revealed, might not be enough to save us from our vilest superstitions.

* * * * * *

I didn't have any occasion to go back to Innsmouth for some time, and several months slipped past before I had a reason sufficient to make me phone. The desk-clerk at the hotel was surprised that I hadn't heard—as if what was known to Innsmouthers ought automatically to be known to everyone else on earth.

Ann was dead.

She had drowned in the deep water off Devil Reef. Her body had never been recovered.

THE INNSMOUTH HERITAGE, BY BRIAN STABLEFORD

I didn't get any sort of prize for the Innsmouth project; in spite of its interesting theoretical implications, it wasn't quite the reputation-maker I'd hoped it would be. As things turned out, it was only worth a paper after all.

THE PICTURE

The last chapter of Oscar Wilde's narrative is, of course, a mere catalogue of lies. Dorian Gray did not stab me in a fit of rage and remorse. How could he? I was the custodian of his will as well as his soul—and, for that matter, of his voice.

By the time I had achieved that state described in that final chapter, Dorian was no more than a carved dummy. He was a consummate work of art, to be sure, but he was a mere doll. He had elected to become unchanging, and that which is unchanging cannot entertain real intelligence or authentic emotion. A man's identity is not an *entity*, which may or may not change; a man's identity is a product of all the processes of change ongoing within him.

When Dorian wished change upon me and changelessness upon himself, he gave me his mind and his heart. It was a bold move, and it was a wise move, but it was the end of *his* story and the beginning of mine. Oscar Wilde had not quite understood that in 1891; after two years in Reading Gaol he knew better, but he had surrendered his own mind and heart by then, and he never committed his discovery to paper.

Some might think that Dorian Gray was the miracle that Basil Hallward wrought, while I was a mere by-product. Dorian was, after all, a handsome man blessed with eternal youth, immune to aging and the scars of disease. Alone among young men of his era, Dorian could sleep with syphilitic whores and remain untainted, because all his infections were inherited by me. Oscar Wilde, carrying the curse of syphilis within his own body, presumably thought that Dorian had the best of our bargain—but he was wrong. I was—and am—the true miracle, and Dorian Gray the by-product.

Paintings have nothing to fear from disease. We do not die, nor do we suffer; we have nothing to fear from change. Had Dorian borne the burden which he passed on to me, it would have ravaged him with pain and misery, and ultimately with death—but there is no pain or misery in *my* world, and art never dies. The march of time, which would have been nothing to him but the measure of his decay and destruction, was and is to me the glory of my evolution, my progress, my transcendence.

I began life as an item of representative art, with no greater virtue than accuracy, but, as soon as Dorian had made his bargain, I began to mature into a modernist masterpiece. I became surreal and futuristic, awesome and sublime. I became the very embodiment of genius, of magic, of power.

When Basil Hallward first painted me, those who saw me had no available response, save to compliment him because he had captured the pleasing appearance of a lovely boy—but no one who saw me now would mistake me for a mere reflection. There never was, nor ever could be, a living man who looked like me.

I have gone far beyond mere reflection, into the hinterlands of the imagination. I am now the kind of creature that can only be glimpsed in dreams. I am no longer man but overman, heir to all disease and all decay but never to defeat. I alone, in all the world, am capable of wearing such corruptions proudly, as manifestations of my absolute triumph over death and damnation.

I have already lived more lives than any man, and I am immortal; I am still in the process of *becoming*. I am no mere *work* of art; I am Art itself.

If you stare into my painted eyes—which will follow you through life, not merely into every corner of the room—you may see what human identity really is, freed from the delicate prison of the flesh.

I ought not to be here in this attic, covered and kept secret. I ought to be on display, in the National Gallery or the Louvre or the Escorial—but I could not be content with that. In an age of print and photography I ought to be reproduced in millions, so that my simulacrum might hang in every home in the world. I ought to be the property of every man of discrimination, every secular idolater, every connoisseur of the finest arts.

It is not immodesty that makes me say all this, but altruism. I could achieve so much more than I have already done, if only I had the opportunity.

I am no longer recognizable, you see, as poor Dorian Gray—nor, for that matter, as any particular individual. As a result of my evolution, I have become a potential Everyman—and Everywoman too. I could take on a far greater burden than I have so far been required to bear. Given the chance, I could take on the responsibility of moral and physical corruption for every single person in the

31

world. It is foolish of the world to let me languish here, when there is so much to be done.

It would need another miracle, but miracles are much easier to achieve than you may think; all that it would require is the passionate desire, the sincere wish, the fervent hope.

I could be *your* redeemer, if you would only let me.

I am equipped to accept into myself *all* the sins of humankind. They would not diminish me in the least, for I AM ART!

You only have to bring me down from my hiding-place and nail me to the wall, where any and all may come to see me. You only have to reproduce my image on posters and postcards, for anyone to see. Only do these little things and the world's Great Age might begin at last.

If you are hesitant, you have only to pause for consideration. It will not take you long to perceive that there is one thing, and one thing only, that matters. *Release me, and you need never age a single day, nor spend a single moment in regret.* No line will ever mar your face; no reckless act will ever weigh upon your conscience.

How can you possibly resist a temptation like that?

THE TEMPTATION OF SAINT ANTHONY

There was no moon on the night when Anthony was bitten by a vampire as he slept within the walls of the abandoned fort at Pispir; the star-shadows were so deep that he got no ore than the merest glimpse of the creature. His only abiding memories were tactile, of skeletal thinness and rags so fragmentary and dust-encrusted that they seemed more like the tatters of an ancient shroud than clothing.

The bite was ragged too, being perhaps more tear than bite, having apparently been inflicted by blunt and decaying teeth. It never entirely healed, although it did not become infected. Although little trace of spilled blood remained, Anthony was sure that he had lost a good deal—perhaps enough to kill him. For three full days he expected to die; even when he stopped expecting it, he was not at all sure that his condition could still be reckoned as life, rather than a strange kind of undeath.

When the next travelers stopped at the fort to draw water from the well that had determined its site, they found its resident hermit awake and active, but somewhat delirious. They were reassured, however, when he consented to accept a little food from them, and showed no inclination to savage them like a rabid dog. They even offered to escort him to Alexandria, if he decided that it would be best to leave his refuge, but he declined the offer.

"I have sworn to remain here for twenty years," he told them. "There will be time for preaching when my own education is complete."

"There are schools in Alexandria," the caravan's leader told him, "and the greatest library in the world, in spite of the accidents it has suffered."

"That is not the kind of learning I seek," he replied. "I want to know what is within myself—what the Lord might communicate to me if only I may hear him."

The travelers were not Christians, but they understood his notion of the Lord better than a Roman would have done. "This is the

33

desert," the leader of the band told him. "Here, the voices of the djinn are louder than the voice of God. Solitude leads to madness."

"The Devil will undoubtedly tempt me," Anthony admitted. "I am ready for that." He did not tell them that the thirst was already building within him for something richer by far than water or wine, nor what effort it required to resist the urge to cut his visitors' throats and suck the wounds till he could such no more.

He had always thought that solitude was the best thing for a man of his sort. The fact that the company of living human beings would henceforth be an endless torment of unacknowledgeable desire only served to confirm his judgment.

The travelers went on their way on the thirty-first day after Anthony had endured the vampire's bite; after that he was alone until the evening of the fortieth day, when he woke from a doze at sunset to find a simulacrum of Christ offering him a cup.

"This is my blood," said the apparent Christ. "Drink of it, and be saved."

"I have been expecting you, Satan," Anthony replied. "I knew that you would seize upon my new weakness. Why else would you have sent the demon to suck the fluid from me?"

"This is my blood," the false Christ repeated. "It is my gift, and the way to salvation."

"You are the Devil," Anthony retorted, "and you have no gift to offer but eternal damnation." He got up and went to the well, setting Satan firmly behind him. He lowered the bucket and brought it up again.

He drank—but he was still thirsty, and he knew that the darker thirst would not be assuaged by water.

Anthony did not doubt that the fluid in the Devil's cup really was blood, nor that it would answer his terrible need, but he had not come to Pispir in search of satiation—quite the reverse, in fact. He did not drink water to salve his thirst, but only because he would die without it; had he been able to drink and keep his thirst he would have done so. To be able to drink and still have thirst of a sort to test him was a privilege of sorts.

When he turned around again, determined to see things in the light of his faith, the Devil was cloven-hoofed and shaggy-legged, with horns set atop his brow. Satan did not seem comfortable in this form, for his eyes seemed pained and his gaze as roaming restlessly, but Anthony assumed that this was because honesty was a sore trial to a creature of his sort.

"You are foolish to insist on seeing me thus," the Devil complained, casting aside the cup, from which nothing spilled as it rolled over the sand-dusted flagstones bordering the well. "I am neither the Great God Pan, nor the Father of Lies, nor a prideful angel cast out of Heaven. I will admit to being a temptation personified, but mine is the temptation of knowledge and progress. I am one who can and will reveal secrets, if you will only consent to listen."

"I will not," Anthony told his adversary. "I am deaf to all but the word of the Lord, and knowledge of the Lord is the only wisdom I seek."

"I did not send the vampire to bite you," the Devil insisted, his agonized eyes looking upwards as if to welcome the deeper blue that was consuming the sky from the east. "That is not my way of working—but if I were of a mind to create such creatures, I would shape them as seductive women, whose bite would be a glorious indulgence and a pleasure unmatchable. The wretched parasite that attacked you was one of nature's sports. If God were responsible for such monstrosities—and I cannot believe that He is—they would be evidence of His sickness or His sense of humor."

"Have you come to debate with me, then?" Anthony asked. "I do not mind in the least, for the nights are long at this time of year, and often surprisingly cold. It will be a futile occupation, though, from your own point of view. There are many souls in the world, alas, that might be won with far less trouble than mine."

"This is not a contest," the Devil said, seeming a little more at ease now that the evening star was shining brightly and the atmospheric dust in the west had taken on the color of blood. "There was no war in Heaven, and there is no war on Earth for the souls of humankind. You conceive of yourself as a battleground in which a higher self of faith of virtue, aided by a guardian angel, is ceaselessly at war with a lower self of insatiable appetite and uncontrollable passion, provoked by mischievous imps, but all of that is mere illusion. If solitude really allowed you to look into yourself more clearly, you would know that you are less divided than you imagine, and that the world is not as you imagine it to be."

"Excellent," said Anthony. "Nothing can warm a man more, in the absence of tangible heat, than the labor of cutting through sophistry. Sit down, my enemy, I beg you. Let's make ourselves as comfortable as we can, given the hardness of the ground and the aching within."

"Oh no," the Devil said, seeming to grow larger as the night advanced, and now unfurling wings like those of a gigantic eagle. "I can do better than that, my friend, by way of distracting us from our mutual plight."

Anthony had observed that the Devil, in what he took to be the dark angel's natural form, was not well-adapted for sitting. His goatish limbs were not articulated like a humans; even squatting must be awkward for him. Anthony had not expected compliance when he made his teasing offer—but neither had he expected to be carried away.

The Devil did not grow claws to match his wings; indeed, the wings themselves refused to coalesce into avian feathers, but continued to grow and to change, as if they were intent on attaining the pure insubstantiality of shadow. By night, it seemed, the Ape of God and the Adversary of Humankind had more freedom to formulate himself as he wished—and what he wished to be, it seemed, was a vast cloud of negation.

Anthony felt himself caught up by that cloud, but he was not grabbed or clutched, merely elevated towards the sky. The cloud was beneath him and all around him, but it was perfectly transparent—more perfectly transparent, in fact, than a pool of pure water or the unstirred desert air.

Anthony tried to resist the sensation that he could see more clearly through the cloud of absence than he had ever been able to see before, but his eyes were unusually reluctant to take aboard his conviction and he had to fight to secure the dictatorship of his faith.

He saw the walls of the fort shrink beneath him, until the ruin was a mere blur on the desert's face. Then he saw the coastline of North Africa, where the ocean was separated from the arid wilderness by a mere ribbon of fertile ground. Then he watched the curve of the horizon extend into the arc of a circle, and he saw the sun that had set a little while before rise again in the west, as the edge of the world could no longer hide it.

"You cannot trouble me with that," he told the Devil. "I know that the world is round."

The Devil no longer had eyes to reflect his anguish, nor a leathery tongue with which to form his lies, but he was not voiceless. He spoke within Anthony's head, like an echo of a thought.

"Fear not, my friend," the voice said, softer now than before. "I have brought air enough to sustain us for the whole night long—and if, by chance, you would like to slake your thirsts, I have water and blood enough to bring you to the very brink of satisfaction."

"I have drunk my fill of the Lord's good water," Anthony told him, "and human blood I will never drink, no matter how my Devilled thirst might increase. I can suffer any affliction, knowing that my Lord loves me and that my immortal soul is safe for all eternity."

While he spoke, Anthony observed that the world as spinning on its axis, and moving through space as if to describe a circle of its own around the sun. The moon and the world were engaged in a curious dance, but the sun—whose disk seemed no bigger than the moon's, when seen from the land of Egypt—seemed to have become far more massive as the cloud moved towards it.

"Were you expecting a sequence of crystal spheres?" the Devil whispered from his hidden corner of Anthony's consciousness. "Were you unmoved by my promise of air because you never believed in the possibility of a void? Did you think that you could breathe the quintessential ether as you moved through the hierarchy of the planets towards the ultimate realm of the fixed stars?"

"There is but one Lord," Anthony replied, "and I am content to breathe in accordance with His providence."

"Alas, you'll have to breathe in accordance with my providence, for a little while," said the Adversary of Humankind. "There is neither air nor ether outside this nimbus. Can you see that the world is but one of the planetary family, toiling around the central sun? Do you see how small a world it is, by comparison with mighty Jupiter? Can you see that Jupiter and Saturn have major satellites as big as worlds themselves, and hosts of minor ones? Do you see how the space between Mars and Jupiter is strewn with planetoids? Can you see the halo from which comets come, beyond the orbits of worlds unseen from Earth, unnamed as yet by curious astronomers?"

Anthony, who was familiar with the story of Er, as told in Plato's *Republic*, looked for the Spindle of Necessity and listened for the siren song of the music of the spheres, but he was not disappointed by their absence.

"I am riding in a cloud formed by the Master of Illusion," he said, not speaking aloud but confident that the Devil, cornered within him, could hear him perfectly well. "You cannot frighten me with empty space and lonely worlds. If the Earth is indeed a solitary wanderer in an infinite void, I shall feel my kinship with its rocks and deserts more keenly than before."

"The Master of Illusion is sight constrained by faith," the Devil told him. "I am an Iconoclast, committed to breaking the idols that filter the evidence of your Earthbound eyes. I do not seek to frighten you but to awaken you. Do you see the stars, now that we are moving through their realm? Can you see that they are not fixed at all, but moving in their own paces about the chaos at the heart of the

Milky Way? Do you see the nebulae that lie without the sidereal system? Can you discern the stars that comprise them—systems like the Milky Way, more numerous by far than the stars they each contain?"

"It is a pretty conceit," Anthony admitted. "Evidence, I trust, of your sense of humor rather than your sickness of mind."

"It is the truth," said the voice within him.

"If it were real," Anthony retorted, "it would not be equal to the millionth part of the greater truth, which is faith in the Lord and His covenant with humankind." He knew, however, that while the Devil was lurking inside him, borrowing the voice of his own thoughts, he had no means of concealing the force of his realization that perhaps this was the truth, and that the world really might be no more than a mediocre rock dutifully circling a mediocre star in a mediocre galaxy in a universe so vast that no power of sight could plumb its depths nor any power of mind calculate its destiny.

Curiously enough, however, the Devil did not appear to be privy to that unvoiced thought, formulated more by dread than doubt. "It was not always thus," the Devil said. "In the beginning, it was very tiny—but that was fourteen thousand million years ago; it is expanding still, and has a far greater span before it, until the last fugitive stars expend the last of their waning light, and darkness falls upon lifelessness forever."

"The Lord said 'Let there be light'," Anthony reminded the Adversary. "He did not say 'Let there be light forever'—but what does it matter, since our souls are safe in his care?"

"*Our* souls?" countered the Devil.

"Human souls," Anthony corrected himself. "Those human souls, at least, which contrive to stay out of your dark clutches."

The cloud seemed to come to a halt then, in an abyss of space that suddenly seem vertiginous in every direction, where whole systems of stars were reduced to mere points of tentative light. "This is not so awesome," whispered the Devil, "compared with the emptiness inside an atom, where matter dissolves into animate mathematical entity and uncertainty refuses the definition of solidity. I wish I could show you that, but a human mind's eye is incapable of such imagination. Trust me when I tell you that there is void within as well as without, and that substance is rarer than you could ever comprehend."

"There is no void where the Lord is," Anthony replied, "and the Lord is everywhere—except, I must suppose, in the depths of your rebellious heart, from which He has been rudely cast out."

As he spoke, though, the hermit became more sharply aware of his thirst for blood: the curse that the Devil had inflicted upon him in order to increase his vulnerability to unreason.

Anthony struggled to keep his next thought unvoiced, but in the end he decided that he had no need to hide from the Devil, while he was still committed to the Lord. "I am a vampire now," he said, without waiting for any reply to his previous observation, "but I am no more a sinner than I was before. I thirst, but I trust in the Lord to deliver me from evil. I will not drink of human blood, no matter how intense my thirst becomes. If my life is to be a trial by ordeal, then I shall be vindicated."

"And if you should live forever, unable to die?" the Devil murmured. "What then, my friend? What if your thirst should become as infinite as the abysm of space, never ceasing to increase?"

"Eventually," Anthony reminded him, "the last star will expend the last of its light, and darkness will fall forever. I shall be safe in the bosom of the Lord."

The cloud condensed around him then, and moved through him, as if it were turning him inside out or drawing him into a fourth dimension undiscernible by human eyes—but then the dark abyss of intergalactic space was replaced by the familiar gloom of night on Earth. Anthony found himself on the edge of a cliff not far from his fort, kneeling on the bare rock and looking out over the desert dunes.

Anthony bowed his head, and was about to thank the Lord for his deliverance, when he caught sight of a moon-shadow from the corner of his eye. It appeared to be the shadow of a human being, but Anthony knew better than to trust the appearance.

He turned to look at the Devil, who now wore the appearance of an Alexandrian philosopher—an Epicurean, Anthony supposed, rather than a neo-Platonist.

"What now?" the hermit said, glad to be able to speak the words aloud, although his tongue felt thick and the inside of his mouth was parched. "Have you no one else to tempt and torment? I have seen your emptiness, and yet am full. I will no more drink of horror and despair than of human blood. I must suppose that I am a vampire now, but I still have my faith. I shall never be a minion of the Prince of Demons."

"This is not a contest," the Devil said, again. "I have nothing to gain or lose by tempting you. I do not need and do not want your soul, your heart or your affection."

"And yet, you seem to have a thirst of some sort," Anthony observed. "Perhaps you are a vampire too, avid for human blood in spite of your best intentions."

"There is a thirst," the Devil admitted, "and it might be mine. Have you ever met the Sphinx, my friend, in your lonely fort? Has she ever asked you her riddle? Her true riddle, I mean; not the one contrived by Sophocles."

"I have never met a Sphinx," Anthony said, rising to his feet and brushing the dust from the hem of his ragged coat, "but if I ever did, I would know you in that guise, and I would answer you then as I answer you now: I trust in the Lord, and Jesus Christ is my savior. I fear no possible consequence of that declaration."

"And yet there are heretics already within the Christian company," the Devil said. "There is division, disharmony and distrust even among those who worship the One God and accept the same savior. If you could see the future...but I dare say that you would see it as selectively as you see the present, filtered by the lens of faith. They will call you saint if you preach in Alexandria and write letters to the Emperor Constantine when you are done here. You will be the stuff of legend, and I shall not be entirely blameless in that, should I fail in my endeavor—but the vampire's bite is your secret and mine, and will remain so. History always has its secrets, and a world like yours has more than its share, since it uses writing so sparingly."

Anthony could look into the Devil's eyes again now, and could see that they were as restless as they had been before, although their pain seemed to have been dulled. He saw the Devil lick his lips, as if to moisten them against the dry and bitter wind that blew from the dunes.

"The scriptures are a gift from the Lord," Anthony said, although he knew that no defense was necessary. "The commandments are preserved there, as they need to be now that the Ark of the Covenant is lost."

"Writing is an awkward instrument," the Devil remarked. "Without measurement and calculation, linear reasoning and syntactical complexity, science is impossible—but the learning of letters and numbers requires specialist teachers, and the custodians of culture inevitably become jealous of the privilege the control, establishing themselves as arbiters of faith. Their empire is fragile, though; once a man is taught to read, he is better equipped to think...and to doubt."

Anthony's eyes were scanning the eastern horizon, searching for the twilight that would precede the dawn, but there was no sign of it. There must still be several hours of night remaining. He licked his own lips, thirsty now for more than blood.

"I want to show you the answer to the Sphinx's riddle," the Devil said, softly. "The riddle of life and death, of growth and ageing, of competition and selection. I cannot force you to read its significance, but I shall write it in your eyes regardless."

"I am weary," Anthony admitted, "but you cannot defeat me. My thirst may be a torment, but it keeps me alert to your wiles."

"Look," said the Father of Lies, pointing out into the shadowed desert, where the dunes had begun to stir and shift.

Anthony knew that moonlight could play tricks in the desert night. The haze that blurred the air by day seemed to disappear by night, but the fugitive light was deceptive nevertheless.

It seemed to him that the fine sand eddied into life, and that its motes, at first dissociated, began to cleave together into imitations of complex organic forms: leaves and tubers, worms and mites, slugs and crabs, trees and snakes. He saw all these creatures growing from tiny seeds and eggs into complex forms that produced more seeds and eggs, each generation dying off as the next emerged. He saw that, in order to grow, the creatures fed upon one another, not randomly but in measured and defined ways. Even the sedentary plants, whose only necessary nourishment was wind and sunlight, accepted the substance of the decaying dead into their own flesh, so that nothing that might be incorporate in flesh was lost or wasted, but always recycled and transfigured. He saw that the feeding was always competitive, and that there was also competition to delay the moment when the living became food, so that no succeeding generation was exactly the same as the one that had gone before.

Everything was changing, and would continue to change. Creation was continuous, and would never be complete.

Anthony saw, then, that the human species was a product of this process of ceaseless change, and deduced that the human species was no more immune to further change than any other. He understood that human beings were merely a part of a much larger pattern: a temporary artifact of the irresistible organic flux; a momentary fancy of the interminable restlessness of the molecules of life, which were forever in the process of consumption and excretion, hurrying from form to form with only the merest pauses for sleep, death, thought and faith. The answer to the Sphinx's riddle, the hermit determined, was that life had its own energy, its own circulation and its own busy complexity. It did not need a sculptor—and he sensed that any sculptor who ever tried to tame its innate exuberance would surely fail.

"What is this to me?" Anthony said to the Devil. "I came to the desert to escape tumult, not to conjure it up in my dreams. It is in loneliness that one finds the Lord, and becomes close to the Lord. Life's transactions are not uninteresting to me, nor are they irrelevant, but my first concern is the immortal soul, which rests immune to all of this confusion."

"And yet, my friend," the Devil said, "you thirst for water and you thirst for blood. Your flesh has no immunity to need, and your mind can have no immunity to the thirst induced by that need."

The disguised Father of Lies took a dagger from the folds of his clothing, rolled up his sleeve, and cut his forearm from the crook of the elbow to the junction of his palm. "Come and drink," he said, as the blood welled out and began to rain down on the rocky escarpment. "Drink of my blood, and be content."

"I will not," Anthony replied. "Not now, or ever. You cannot terrify me, demon that you are, for I am armored by my faith in the Lord, and in Jesus Christ my savior. You cannot tempt me, demon that you are, for I am armored by the certainty of my salvation, and the inviolability of my immortal soul. Water I shall drink as the need arises, but blood I never shall; I shall bear my thirst to the grave, no matter how long it might take to arrive there."

The Devil lifted his arm, and licked his own blood, seeming to take considerable comfort therefrom. Then he turned, and looked behind him.

Anthony had not seen the four human figures that were creeping through the night until the Devil looked directly at them, but that did not mean that they had not been there all along, moving forward surreptitiously, as men who are abroad at night are wont to do.

"Ah!" the Devil said, as if he were not surprised to find them there, even though he had not suspected their presence until some tiny sound caused him to turn around. "Here are some who won't refuse a drop of blood, though I dare say they haven't thirsted quite as long as you, my friend." He held out his arm, inviting the four to approach.

They did so, warily. They, at least, were surprised. They were not used to such offerings—or, indeed, to any offerings at all.

Anthony stared at the shadowed figures as they came closer, illuminated by a moon that was less than half full but whose light served nevertheless to augment the feeble glimmer of the distant stars. The newcomers were so thin as to seem like walking skeletons, their clothing reduced to mere ribbons—but their eyes were large and bright and greedy, and their thin lips were pursed in anticipation.

The Devil offered his arm freely. The cut was long enough to allow them all to drink simultaneously, two on each side; if the Devil had as much blood in him as a common man, they might have taken a stomach-full apiece and still left a residue behind—but that was not what happened.

The four vampires leapt upon their prey like a pack of jackals, clawing and snapping at him and at one another. Maddened by the combination of their thirst and their proximity to the means of slaking it, they lashed out in every direction, each of them seemingly more intent on keeping his companions away from the prize than to claim it for himself.

They bit and sucked, lapped and swallowed—but for every drop they claimed a dozen were spilled on the rocky ledge. The Devil went down beneath their assault, bitten on both his legs as well as his arms, and about his face and throat as well. He sustained a dozen new wounds within a minute, a hundred within five. All of them bled with what seemed to Anthony to be unnatural copiousness—as if the vampires' saliva had some agent within it that prevented the blood from clotting.

In his home town of Coma, and in Alexandria too—within the shadow of the library wall—Anthony had seen starving dogs fighting over a bone, but this was different. Even starving dogs retained some vestige of respect for one another, snarling and howling at the expense of inflicting deadly bites. The four vampires knew no such restraint. They did not howl and they did not snarl, but they clawed and they bit. They gouged at one another's eyes and aimed deadly blows at one another's throats. Their intentions were rarely fulfilled, in the immediate sense, but, as time went by and the Devil's blood leaked away unharvested, the destruction they sought to wreak could hardly be avoided.

They were close to the edge of the cliff. One went sprawling over the edge, and then another. That left two—at which point the conflict became far less chaotic, more sharply focused.

The two vampires fought with all their might, and the Devil's precious blood continued to ebb away.

Anthony watched, dumbfounded.

Eventually, one vampire went down for the last time—not dead, but broken in his limbs and stunned into unconsciousness. The survivor, who was by no means uninjured, immediately set about trying to lick the last few rivulets of blood from the Devil's wounds, and to lap up the few fugitive pools that the rock had cupped. It seemed to Anthony to be a rather meager meal.

When the vampire had finished he sat back warily, supporting himself with his scarred and twisted hands, and he looked up at Anthony. His eyes were bright and wild, but not devoid of intelligence.

"You can't allow yourself to be paralyzed by fear, my friend," the vampire said. "You're one of us now."

"Are you the one who bit me?" Anthony asked.

"What does that matter?" the vampire retorted, licking his lips avidly in search of one last drop of sustenance. "It's done. You should come with us—we're heading for Alexandria."

"Us?" Anthony echoed. "I think you will be alone from now on—and deservedly so, given that you treat your friends so vilely."

"They'll recover," the vampire said. "They'll be thirsty, but their bones will knit and their scratches will heal. They'll bear me no ill will. They know that there's strength in numbers, even if the contest that results when we find a lone victim can have only one winner. In Alexandria, it will be different. Cities were made for our kind. If you stay out here, though, alone, they'll catch you eventually. Then they'll behead you, and burn your body. There's no way back from that. You'd best come with us—you have a great deal to learn."

"You have the Devil's blood in you now," Anthony told the creature. "It might make you stronger, I suppose, but it's poison nevertheless."

"If that were true," the vampire replied, "it would make little enough difference to me, who was damned a long time ago—but I know the blood of a philosopher when I taste it. An Epicurean, I believe—the least intoxicating of all."

"He wore the guise of an Epicurean," Anthony admitted, "but he was the Devil. He had been a cloud of transparent darkness only an hour or so before."

"The desert's full of djinn," the vampire told him. "There's no blood in them, but they can play tricks with your head. Thirst makes it easier. If he gets up again, he'll be one of us—but they don't always get up. I was lucky; so were you. Him too, although he won't feel it when he wakes up." The creature inclined his head briefly in the direction of his erstwhile companion and adversary, who was still unconscious.

"You cannot hurt me, monster," Anthony said.

"I certainly could," the monster replied, "but I've nothing to gain by it, and the thirst will punish you enough, if you insist in your stubbornness. You're welcome to come with us if you wish. If not, do as you will."

"I shall pray to the Lord for my salvation," Anthony said, defiantly. "I shall bear my thirst proudly, grateful to be tried and not found wanting. I shall guard my immortal soul until I die, and then confide it to the loving care of my savior and my Lord. The Devil could not tempt me, and nor shall you."

The vampire came to his feet, wincing at the pain in his limbs and spine. He leaned over the Devil's body, then knelt down beside it. "He might come back, I suppose," was the monster's off-hand judgment, "but I doubt it. Too much damage done. They say that nothing short of beheading and burning will make certain, but that's just superstitious dread. Don't worry about inviting me back to the fort—I'll camp out down there, in the shadow of the cliff, till nightfall comes again. Are you sure you won't come with us to Alexandria? They'll start hunting for us eventually, of course, and we'll have to move on, but there's plenty of blood to be had in the meantime. The city is our natural environment."

Anthony gathered himself together and came to stand opposite the vampire, looking down at the body of the man who had consented to be murdered. Anthony had to agree that it was impossible to believe that the corpse would ever be reanimated—but the Devil was a master of deception. He turned round abruptly, and walked away, in the direction of the fort. He suspected that the vampire was staring at the back of his head, but he did not look back.

"The flesh is a distraction," the hermit said to himself, formulating the words clearly although he did not pronounce them aloud. "Its mortification is an irrelevance. The spirit is capable of rising above such trivial matters. Prayer will sustain me, no matter how long I am forced to endure this torment. As God wills, I shall do, even if I live to be a hundred."

According to history, he lived to be a hundred and five, but he knew what a liar history can be when legend-mongers get involved in it, and he had lost count long before he died. Once he was officially declared a saint, Anthony was able to ascend to Heaven and look back upon the Earth, so he was able to watch with interest when his old Adversary, the Devil, tried his luck again in Heidelberg thirteen hundred years later, with a slightly different result.

After that, the cities of the world began to grow in earnest, and vampires to multiply. Anthony estimated that it might soon be time to call a halt to the whole sorry mess, perhaps to try again somewhere else in the vast and various universe, but he was not privy to the Lord's intentions.

"Personally," Saint Leocadia said to him one day, as they watched the outbreak and rapid progress of World War Three, "I'm glad to be out of it. I don't miss a single thing—except, I suppose...." She trailed off, as the saints always tended to do at that point in the conversation

Anthony was too polite to finish the sentence for her, although he knew perfectly well what she meant. He certainly didn't miss the terrible thirst for blood that the Devil's minion had cruelly inflicted upon him, nor any of the thousand other shocks that flesh was heir to, pleasant or unpleasant—but every so often, he missed the little intellectual shocks that had stimulated his mind while his faith was yet to find its final justification.

The saint knew now that he had been right all along to trust in his savior and the grace of God, and that he would be right in everything he believed for all eternity. There was a certain undeniable satisfaction in the irresistibility of that confirmation—but he also understood, now, what the Devil had meant when he had insisted that it *wasn't a contest*. The Devil really hadn't had the slightest interest in winning his soul, and really had been trying to explain the answer to the Sphinx's riddle.

By virtue of that realization, every now and again—if only a little—Saint Anthony couldn't help missing temptation.

THE UGLY CYGNET

BY HANS REALIST ANDERSEN

It was glorious out in the country. All around the fields and the meadows were great forests, and in the midst of these forests were calm and glittering lakes. On the shore of one of these lakes a swan wife sat upon her nest, warming her eggs.

One by one, the eggs cracked and the cygnets came out to look around, wonderingly, at the blue water and the green trees. "How wide the world is!" they exclaimed, one after another.

"It's much wider than it seems," their mother told them. "When you've learned to fly, you'll understand how wide it really is."

When there was only one egg left unhatched, the swan husband came to take his turn at sitting on the nest. "It hardly seems worth it," he said. "That last egg is much smaller than the rest."

"If a job's worth doing," the swan wife said, "it's worth doing well. Let's give it a few more days."

The small egg broke at last, and its occupant reluctantly emerged.

"I told you so," said the swan husband. "Did you ever see such a scrawny cygnet? And it's a boy, too."

"Well, no," admitted his wife, "but we must treat him as generously as our other children."

The next day was spent teaching the cygnets to swim. They took to it readily enough, even the smallest one. The mother swan was greatly relieved to see that the late arrival was able to cope with the water, and she dared to hope that he might be able to grow fast enough to catch up with his brothers and sisters.

Alas, the smallest cygnet did not have half as much appetite as his older siblings, and he remained small. When the swans paraded their offspring around the shore of the lake politeness compelled the other birds to compliment them on their brood, but they all took a less-than-secret delight in adding their commiserations regarding the weakling of the family. "Pity about the little one," they would say. "Quite lets the side down, doesn't he?"

The smallest cygnet longed to ask how wide the world was, but feared the answer he might receive.

"Ugly little devil can't keep up," the swan husband observed. "He's slowing us all down. The rats will have him if we're not careful."

"We're not in any hurry," the swan wife replied, "and it's up to us to make sure that the rats don't get to him."

Unfortunately, the small cygnet overheard everything that was said of him, and realized that he was an embarrassment to his family. He would have run away had he not been so terribly afraid of the rats. Fortunately, the swan husband was a fearsome deterrent, not merely to rats and magpies but foxes and humans, so the smallest cygnet was able to do as much growing up as he was capable of doing—which was, alas, not nearly as much as his handsome brothers and sisters. With every week that passed the ignominy of the smallest cygnet's existence was further increased, and so was his shame.

Autumn came, and it was time for the swans to migrate.

"The rest are ready," said the swan wife, "but I don't think the little one's up to it. Perhaps we should give the Mediterranean a miss this year. How bad can winter be?"

"Ask the frogs and the squirrels," the swan husband replied. "It's so bad they try to sleep through the whole thing. I'm too old to learn to hibernate—and what kind of swans would we be if we didn't fly south for the winter? The runt will have to keep up as best he can."

"We really ought to stay," said the swan wife, dutifully—but it was obvious to everyone, including the smallest cygnet, that she didn't really mean it. This time, the smallest cygnet figured, it really was time to run away, for the sake of the family. It was bad enough that he was holding them back on the shore of the remote lake; how could they possibly hold up their heads on the Mediterranean with something as small and ugly as him in tow?

So the ugly cygnet went into the forest and hid, until all the swans had flown away.

Had it not been for global warming, the ugly cygnet would not have made it through the long winter, but the winter was exceptionally mild. The lake never froze, and the competition for food was so relaxed that the ugly cygnet managed to find enough food to stay alive and to provide for such meager growth as he was capable of making. He knew that he would never catch up with his siblings in terms of their size, but he did hope that he might one day match them for whiteness. Alas, every time he looked at his reflection in the water he saw that he was getting more and more colorful with every week that passed. By the time spring arrived, he was a vivid patchwork. He knew that his parents and siblings would laugh at him, but he looked forward to their return nevertheless. They were, after all, the only family he had.

But when the swan wife and the swan husband returned to their nesting-site to raise a new brood, they did not recognize the little creature that emerged squawking from the weeds, joyfully addressing them as "Mum" and "Dad".

"Don't be ridiculous," the swan husband said. "You're not a swan at all—you're a duck."

"Technically," the swan wife pointed out, "he's a drake. But the effect is the same. He's definitely not one of ours."

"But I am!" the smallest cygnet protested. "My egg might have got into your nest by accident, but you sat on me, and protected me from the rats and the magpies, and the foxes and the humans. You're my real father and my real mother, no matter what appearances may say."

"No way," said the swan husband.

"We couldn't have made a mistake like that," said the swan wife.

The ugly cygnet realized then that he was not and never had been a real cygnet, and that he would never, under any imaginable circumstances, be accepted as a swan.

"But I can fly," he said. "Not as fast or as far as you, perhaps, but I *can* fly. I can find out for myself how wide the world is."

"Good idea," said the swan husband.

"The sooner the better," said the swan wife. Being a swan, she had the grace to wait until the drake had flown away before she added, in a tone of deep disgust: "Me, raise a *duck*! As if!"

"Nasty little paint-pot with delusions of grandeur," said the swan husband, nodding his handsome head in agreement. "Still—it all goes to prove what they say. Once a loser, always a loser. It's the way of the world. He can fly all the way around it if he wants to, but he won't find anywhere different."

ART IN THE BLOOD

"Art in the blood is liable to take the strangest forms."
(A. Conan Doyle, "The Adventure of the Greek Interpreter")

It was not yet five o'clock; Mycroft had barely sunk into his nook and taken up the *Morning Post* when the Secretary appeared at the door of the reading room and gestured brusquely with his right hand. It was a summons to the Strangers' Room, supplemented by a particular curl of the little finger, which told him that this was no casual visitation but a matter in which the Diogenes Club had an interest of its own.

Mycroft sighed, and hauled his overabundant flesh out of his armchair. The rules of the club forbade him to ask the Secretary what the import of the summons was, so he was mildly surprised to see his brother Sherlock waiting by the window in the Strangers' Room, looking out over Pall Mall. Sherlock had brought him petty puzzles to solve on several occasions, but never yet a matter of significance to any of the Club's hidden agendas. It was obvious from the rigidity of Sherlock's stance that this was no trivial matter, and that it had gone badly thus far.

There was another man in the room, already seated. He seemed tired; his grey eyes—which were not dissimilar in hue to those of the Holmes brothers—were restless and haunted, but he was making every effort to maintain his composure. He was obviously a merchant seaman, perhaps a second mate. The unevenness of the faded tan that still marked his face—the lower part of which had long been protected by a beard—testified that he had returned England from the tropics less than a month ago. The odors clinging to his clothing revealed that he had recently visited Limehouse, where he had partaken of a generous pipe of opium. The bulge in his left-hand coat pocket was suggestive of a medicine bottle, but Mycroft was too scrupulous a man to leap to the conclusion that it must be laudanum. Mycroft judged that the seaman's attitude was one of reluctant resignation: that of a man determined to conserve his dignity even though he had lost hope.

Mycroft greeted his brother with an appropriate appearance of warmth, and waited for an introduction.

"May I present John Chevaucheux, Mycroft," Sherlock said, immediately abandoning his position by the window. "He was referred to me by Doctor Watson, who saw that his predicament was too desperate to be salvageable by medical treatment."

"I'm pleased to meet you, sir," the sailor said, coming briefly to his feet before sinking back into his chair. The stranger's hand was cold, but its grip was firm.

"Doctor Watson is not here," Mycroft observed. It was not his habit to state the obvious, but the doctor's absence seemed to require explanation; Watson clung to Sherlock like a shadow nowadays, avid to leech yet another marketable tale from his reckless dabbling in the mercurial affairs of distressed individuals.

"The good doctor had a prior engagement," Sherlock reported. His tone was neutral but Mycroft deduced that Sherlock had taken advantage of his friend's enforced absence to carry this particular enquiry to its end. Apparently, this was one "adventure" Sherlock did not want to re-read in *The Strand*, no matter how much admiring literary embellishment might be added to it.

Given that Chevaucheux's accent identified him as a Dorset man, and that his name suggested descent from Huguenot refugees, Mycroft thought it more likely that the seaman's employers were based in Southampton than in London. If the man had come to consult Watson as a medical practitioner, rather than as Sherlock's accomplice, he must have encountered him some time ago, probably in India—and must have known him well enough to be able to track him down in London despite his retirement. These inferences, though far less than certain, became more probable in combination with the ominous news—which *was* ominous news, although it had not been reported in the *Post*—of the sudden death, some seven days ago, of Captain Pye of the *S.S. Goshen*. The *Goshen* had dropped anchor in Southampton Water on the twelfth of June, having set out from Batavia six weeks before. Captain Pye was by no means clubbable, but he was known to more than one member of the Diogenes as a trustworthy agent.

"Do you know how Dan Pye died, Mr. Chevaucheux?" Mycroft asked, cutting right to the heart of the matter. Unlike Sherlock, he did not like to delay matters with unnecessary chitchat.

"He was cursed to death, sir," Chevaucheux told him, bluntly. He had obviously been keeping company with Sherlock long enough to expect that Holmesian processes of deduction would sometimes run ahead of his own.

"Cursed, you say?" Mycroft raised an eyebrow, though not in jest. "Some misadventure in the Andamans, perhaps?" If Pye had been about the Club's business—although he would not necessarily have known whose business he was about—the Andamans were the most likely spot for him to run into trouble.

"No, sir," Chevaucheux said, gravely. "He was cursed to death right here in the British Isles, though the mad hatred that activated the curse was seething for weeks at sea."

"If you know the man responsible," Mycroft said, amiably, "where's the mystery? Why did Watson refer you to my brother?" The real puzzle, of course, was why Sherlock had brought the sea-man here, having failed to render any effective assistance—but Mycroft was wary of spelling that out. This could be no common matter of finding proofs to satisfy a court of law; the Secretary's little finger had told him that. This mystery went beyond mere matters of motive and mechanism; it touched on matters of blood.

Sherlock had reached into his pocket while Mycroft was speaking, and produced a small object the size of a snuffbox. His expression, as he held it out to Mycroft, was a study in grimness and frustration. Mycroft took it from him, and inspected it carefully.

It was a figurine carved in stone: a chimerical figure, part-human—if only approximately—and part-fish. It was not a mermaid such as a lonely sailor might whittle from tropic wood or walrus ivory, however; although the head was vaguely humanoid the torso was most certainly not, and the piscine body bore embellishments that seemed more akin to tentacles than fins. There was something of the lamprey about it—even about the mouth that might have been mistaken for human—and something of the uncanny. Mycroft felt no revelatory thrill as he handled it, but he knew that the mere sight of it was enough to feed an atavistic dream. Opium was not the best medicine for the kind of headaches that Chevaucheux must have suffered of late, but neither he nor Watson was in a position to know that.

"Let me have your lens, Sherlock," Mycroft said.

Sherlock passed him the magnifying-glass, without bothering to point out that the lamplight in the Strangers' Room was poor, or that the workmanship of the sculpture was so delicate that a fine-pointed needle and the services of a light microscope would be required to investigate the record of its narrow coverts. Mycroft knew that Sherlock would take some meager delight in amplifying whatever conclusions he could reach with the aid of the woefully inadequate means to hand.

Two minutes' silence elapsed while Mycroft completed his superficial examination. "Purbeck stone," he said. "Much more friable than Portland stone—easy enough to work with simple tools, but liable to crumble if force is misapplied. Easily eroded too, but if this piece is as old as it seems, it's been protected from everyday wear. It could have been locked away in some cabinet of curiosities, but it's more likely to have been buried. You've doubtless examined the scars left by the knives that carved it and the dirt accumulated in the finer grooves. Iron or bronze? Sand, silt or soil?" He set the object down on a side-table as he framed these questions, but positioned it carefully, to signify that he was not done with it yet.

"A bronze knife," Sherlock told him, without undue procrastination, "but a clever alloy, no earlier than the sixteenth century. The soil is from a fallow field, from which hay had been cut with considerable regularity—but there was salt too. The burial-place was near enough to the sea to catch spray in stormy weather."

"And the representation?" Mycroft took a certain shameful delight in the expression of irritation that flitted across Sherlock's finely-chiseled features: the frustration of ignorance.

"I took it to the Museum in the end," the great detective admitted. "Pearsall suggested that it might be an image of Oannes, the Babylonian god of wisdom. Fotherington disagreed."

"Fotherington is undoubtedly correct," Mycroft declared. "He sent you to me, of course—without offering any hypothesis of his own."

"He did," Sherlock admitted. "And he told me, rather impolitely, to leave Watson out of it."

"He was right to do so," Mycroft said. *And to notify the Secretary in advance*, he added, although he did not say the words aloud.

"Excuse me, sir," said the sailor, "but I'm rather out of my depth here. Perhaps you might explain what that thing is, if you know, and why it was sent to Captain Pye...and whether it will finish me the way it finished him. I have to admit, sir, that Rockaby seemed to have near as much hatred of me as he had of the captain towards the end, even though we were friends once and always near neighbors. I don't mind admitting, sir, that I'm frightened." That was obvious, although John Chevaucheux was plainly a man who did not easily give in to fear, especially of the superstitious kind.

"Alas, I cannot give you any guarantee of future safety, Mr. Chevaucheux," Mycroft said, already fearing that the only guarantees to be found were of the opposite kind, "but you will lose nothing by surrendering this object to me, and it might be of some small service to the Diogenes Club if you were to tell me your story, as you've doubtless already told it to Doctor Watson and my brother."

Sherlock shifted uneasily. Mycroft knew that his brother had hoped for more, even if he had not expected it—but Sherlock and he were two of a kind, and knew what duty they owed to the accumulation of knowledge.

The seaman nodded. "Telling it has done me good, sir," he said, "so I don't mind telling it again. It's much clearer in my head than it was—and I'm less hesitant now that I know there are men in the world prepared to take it seriously. I'll understand if you can't help me, but I'm grateful to Mr. Sherlock for having tried."

Anticipating a long story, Mycroft settled back into his chair—but he could not make himself comfortable.

* * * * * * *

"You'll doubtless have judged from my name that I'm of French descent," said Chevaucheux, "although my family has been in England for a century and a half. We've always been seafarers. My father sailed with Dan Pye in the old clippers, and my grandfather was a middy in Nelson's navy. Captain Pye used to tell me that he and I were kin, by virtue of the fact that the Normans who came to England with William the Conqueror were so-called because they were descended from Norsemen, like the Vikings who colonized the north of England hundreds of years earlier. I tell you this because Sam Rockaby was a man of a very different stripe from either of us, although his family live no more than a day's ride from mine, and mine no more than an hour on the railway from Dan Pye's.

"Captain Pye's wife and children are lodged in Poole, my own on Durlston Head in Swanage, near the Tilly Whim caves. Rockaby's folk hail from a hamlet south of Worth Matravers, near the western cliffs of Saint Aldhelm's Head. To folk like his, everyone's a foreigner whose people weren't clinging to that shore before the Romans came, and no one's a true seaman whose people didn't learn to navigate the channel in coracles or hollowed-out canoes. Doctor Watson tells me that every man has something of the sea in his blood, because that's where all land-based life came from, but I don't know about that. All I know is that the likes of Rockaby laugh

54

into their cupped hands when they hear men like Dan Pye and Jack Chevaucheux say that the sea is in our blood.

"Mr. Sherlock tells me that you don't get about much, sir, so I'll guess you've never been to Swanage, let alone to Worth Matravers or the sea-cliffs on the Saint's Head. You're dead right—and then some—about the way the local people work the stone. They used Portland stone to make the frontage of the Museum Mr. Sherlock took me to yesterday, but no one has much use for Purbeck stone because it crumbles too easily. These days, even the houses on the isle are mostly made of brick—but in the old days, stone was what they had in plenty, and it was easily quarried, especially where the coastal cliffs are battered by the sea, so stone was what they used. They carved it too, though never as small and neat as that *thing*, and you'll not see an old stone house within ten miles of Worth Ma-travers that hasn't got some ugly face or deformed figure worked into its walls. Nowadays it's just tradition, but Sam Rockaby's folk have their own lore regarding such things. When Sam and I were boys he used to tell me that the only real faces were those that kept watch on the sea.

"'Some'll tell ye they're devils, Jacky boy,' Sam told me once, 'an' some'll tell ye they're a-meant for the scarin' away of devils—but they ain't. The devils in hell are jest fairy tales. Mebbe these are the Elder Gods, and mebbe they're the *Others*, but either way, they're older by far than any Christian devil.' He would never tell me exactly what he meant, though, so I always figured that he was teasing me. It was the same with the chapels. All along that coast there are little chapels on the cliff, where whole villages would go to pray when their menfolk were caught at sea by a storm. Even in Swanage the rumor was that it wasn't just for the safe return of fish-ermen that Rockaby's folk prayed, for they were wreckers even be-fore they were smugglers, but Sam sneered at that kind of calumny.

"'They rearranged the stones to build the chapels,' he told me, 'An' threw away the ones that scared 'em—but the stone knows what it was before your Christ was born, an' fer what its eyes were set to watch. The Elders were first, but their watchin' did no good. The Others came anyway, an' printed their own faces in the stone.' He was always a little bit crazy—but harmless, I thought, until the fire got him.

"Rockaby's father and mine sailed together once or twice. So far as I know they got on well enough with Dan Pye and one an-other. When I first signed on the *Goshen* Sam's dad was still on the sailing ships, and I reckon Sam would have followed him if the age of sail wasn't so obviously done. Sam never like steam, but you can't hold back the tide, and if you want to work, you have to go where the work is. He was a seaman through and through, and if going under steam was the price of going to sea, he'd pay it. I don't think he was resentful of my having got my mate's papers by the time he joined the *Goshen*, even though he was older by a year or two, because he didn't have an ounce of ambition. He was a good seaman—and the most powerful swimmer I ever saw—but he wasn't in the least interested in command. I always wanted to be master of my own ship, but he never wanted to be master of anything, not even his own soul.

"I can't put my finger on any one incident that first set Rockaby and Captain Pye at odds. It's in the nature of seamen to grumble, and they always find a scapegoat on the bridge. I wasn't aware that anything new had crept into the scuttlebutt when the *Goshen* set out, although the talk grew dark soon enough when the weather wouldn't let up. Landlubbers think that steam's made seafaring easy, but they don't know what the ocean's like. A steamship may not need the wind for power, but she's just as vulnerable to its whims. Sometimes, I could swear that the wind tries twice as hard to send a steamship down, purely out of pique. We had a rough ride out, I can tell you. I never saw the Mediterranean so angry, and no sooner were we through the canal and into the Red Sea than the storms picked us up again. Rockaby was the only man in the crew who wasn't as sick as a pig—and that, I suppose, might be why things between him and Dan Pye began to get worse. Rockaby said he was being picked on, given more than his fair share of work—and so he was, because he was sometimes the only man capable of carrying out the orders. The captain did more than his own share too, and I tried, but there were times when we were all laid low.

"There's nothing to be ashamed of in being sick at sea. They say Nelson took days to find his sea-legs. But the ordinary kind of sea-sickness was only the beginning—laudanum got us through the fevers and the aches, until we were far enough east to buy hashish and raw opium. You might disapprove of that, Mr. Mycroft, but it's the way things work out east, at least among seafaring men. You have bad dreams, but at least you can bear to be awake—or so it usually goes. But this time was different; the ocean seemed to have it in for us. We were carrying mail for the Company, so we had to make a dozen stops on the Indian mainland and the islands, and somewhere along the way we picked up the fire. Saint Anthony's fire, that is.

"Doctor Watson told that he'd encountered similar cases while he was in India—I first met him in Goa thirteen years ago, while I was an able seaman on the *Serendip*—and that the cause was bad bread, contaminated with ergot. Maybe he's right, but that's not what seamen believe. To them, the fire is something out of Hell. The men who took it worse said they felt as if crabs and snakes were crawling under their skin, and they had blinding visions of devils and monsters. This time, Rockaby was affected just as badly as anyone else, and he took it very bad indeed. He began blaming Dan Pye, saying that the captain had ridden him too hard, and brought the affliction on the ship by the insult to his blood.

"We lost two more men before we made port in Padang and laid in fresh supplies. That was when Rockaby disappeared—overboard, we thought, although he was too strong a swimmer to drown so close to shore, raving or not. We nearly shipped out without him, but he got back to the ship just in time, unfortunately. He was over the Fire, didn't seem any worse for wear than the rest of us, physically speaking—quite the reverse, in fact—but we soon found out that his mind hadn't made the same recovery as his body. No sooner were we under way that he began twitching and jabbering away, sometimes mumbling away as if in a foreign language, stranger than any I'd ever heard. He did his work, mind—there was no lack of strength in him—but he was a changed man, and not for the better. Captain Pye said that his mumbling was nonsense, but it really did sound to me like a language, though maybe one designed for other tongues than human. There were names that kept cropping up: Nyarlathotep, Cthulhu, Azathoth. When he did speak English, Rockaby told anyone who would listen that we didn't understand and couldn't understand what the world was really like, and what it will become when the *Others* return to claim it.

"Captain Pye could see that Sam was ill, and didn't want to come down hard on him, but ships' crew are direly superstitious. That kind of ill-wishing can make any trouble that comes along a thousand times worse. No one likes to be part of a jittery company, even at the best of times, and when a ship's already taken a battering, and there are typhoons to be faced and fought...well, a captain has no alternative but to try to shut a Jonah up. Dan tried, but it only made things worse. I tried to talk some sense into Sam myself, but nothing anyone could say had any effect but to make him crazier. Perhaps we should have dropped him off in Madras or Aden, but he was a Purbeck man, when all's said and done, and it was our responsibility to see him safely home. And we did, though I surely wish we hadn't.

"By the time we came back into Southampton Water, Rockaby seemed a good deal better, although we'd dosed him with opium enough to keep an elephant quiet and maybe taken any unhealthy amount ourselves. I thought he might make a full recovery once he was back home, and I travelled with him on the train to Swanage to make sure that he got back safely. He was calm enough, but he wasn't making much sense. 'Ye're a fool, Jacky,' he said to me, before we parted. 'Y'think you can make it right but y'can't. The price has to be paid, the sacrifice made. The Others never went away, y'know, when they'd seen off the Elder Gods. They may be sleeping, but they're dreaming too, and the steam filters into their dreams the way sails never did, stirrin' an' simmerin' an' seethin'. Ain't no good hopin' that they'll let us all alone while there's tides in the sea an' the *crawlin' chaos* in our blood. Y'can throw away the faces but y'can't blind the eyes or keep the ears from hearin'. I know where the curses are, Jacky. I know how Dan Pye'll die, an' how it has to be done. Cleave to him an' ye're doomed, Jacky. List to me. I know. I've the *old blood* in me.'

"I left him at Swanage station, waiting for a cart to take him home, or at least as far as Worth Matravers. He was still mumbling to himself. I heard no more from or about him—but less than two weeks later I got a letter from Dan Pye's wife begging me to come to their house in Poole. I caught the first train I could.

"The captain was confined to his bed, and fading fast. His doctor was with him, but didn't have the faintest idea what was wrong with him, and had nothing to offer by way of treatment save for laudanum and more laudanum. I could see right way that it wouldn't be enough. All laudanum can do is dull the pain while your body makes its own repairs, and I could tell that the captain's body was no longer in the business of making repairs. It seemed to me that his flesh had turned traitor, and had had enough of being human. It was changing. I've seen men with the scaly disease, that makes them seem as if they're turning into fish, and I've seen men with gangrene rotting alive, but I never saw anything like the kind of transformation that was working in Dan Pye. Whatever kind of flesh it was that he was trying to become, it was nothing that was ever ancestor to humankind, and no mere decay.

"He had breath enough left in him to tell me to get rid of the doctor and to send his wife away, but when we were alone he talked fast, like a man who didn't expect to be able to talk for long. 'I've been cursed,' he told me. 'I know who did it, though he isn't entirely to blame. Sam Rockaby never had the least vestige of any power to command, though he's a good follower if you can get mastery over him, and a powerful swimmer in seas stranger than you or I have ever sailed. Take this back to him, and tell him that I understand. I don't forgive, but I understand. I've felt the crawling chaos and seen the madness of darkness. Tell him that it's over now, and that it's time to throw it off the Saint's Head, and let it go forever. Tell him to do the same with all the rest, for his own sake and that of his children's children.' The thing he gave me to give back to Rockaby was that thing your brother just gave you.

"He said more, of course, but the only thing relevant to the story was about the dreams. Now, Dan Pye was a seaman for forty years, and no stranger to rum, opium and hashish. He knew his dreams, Dan did. But these, he said, were different. These were real visions: visions of long-dead cities, and creatures like none that Mother Earth could ever have spawned, whether she's been four thousand or four thousand million years in the making. And there were words, too: words that weren't just nonsense, but parts of a language human tongues were never meant to speak. 'The Elder Gods couldn't save us, Jack,' he said. 'The Others were too powerful. But we don't have to give ourselves up—not our souls, not our will. We have to do what we can. Tell Rockaby that, and tell him to throw the lot into the sea.'

"I tried to do what Dan asked me to, but when I went to Worth Matravers I found that Rockaby had never arrived home after I left him at Swanage station. I didn't throw the stone off the cliff because I found out that the curse that killed Dan had already started in me, and I thought it best to show it to whomever might be able to help me. I knew Doctor Watson from before, as I said, and I knew he'd been in India. I wasn't certain that he'd be able to help, but I was sure that there wasn't a doctor in Dorset who could, and I knew that any man who's been long in India has seen things just as queer and just as bad as whatever has its claws in me. So I found Doctor Watson through the Seamen's Association in London, and he sent me to see Mr. Sherlock Holmes—who has promised to find Sam Rockaby for me. But he wanted to come here first, to ask your advice about the cursing-stone, because of what this chap Fotherington told him at the museum. And that's the whole of it—apart from this."

While he completed this last sentence John Chevaucheux had unbuttoned his coat and the shirt he wore beneath it. Now he drew back the shirt to display his breast and abdomen to Mycroft's gaze.

The seaman's eyes were full of horror as he beheld himself, and the spoliation that had claimed him.

The creeping malaise appeared to have commenced its spread from a point above Chevaucheux's heart, but the disfiguration now extended as far as his navel and his collarbone, and sideways from one armpit to the other. The epidermal deformation was not like the scaly patina of icthyosis; it seemed more akin to the rubbery flesh of a cephalopod, and its shape was slightly reminiscent of an octopus with tentacles asprawl. It was discolored by a multiplicity of bruises and widening ulcers, although there seemed to be no sign yet of any quasi-gangrenous decay.

Mycroft had never seen anything like it before, although he had heard of similar deformations. He knew that he ought to make a closer investigation of the symptoms, but he felt a profound reluctance to touch the diseased flesh.

"Watson has no idea how to treat it," Sherlock said, unnecessarily. "Is there any member of the Diogenes Club who can help?"

Mycroft pondered this question for some moments before shaking his head. "I doubt that anyone in England has a ready cure for this kind of disease," he said. "But I will give you the address of one of our research laboratories in Sussex. They will certainly be interested to study the development of the disease, and may well be able to palliate the symptoms. If you are strong, Mr. Chevaucheux, you might survive this, but I can make no promises." He turned to Sherlock. "Can you honor your promise to find this man Rockaby?"

"Of course," Sherlock said, stiffly.

"Then you must do so, without delay—and you must persuade him to lead you to the store of artifacts from which he obtained this stone. I shall keep this one, if Mr. Chevaucheux will permit, but you must take the rest to the laboratory in Sussex. I will ask the Secretary to send two of the functionaries with you, because there might be hard labor involved and this is not the kind of case in which Watson ought to be allowed to interest himself. When the artifacts are safe—or as safe as they can be, in human hands—you must return here, to tell me exactly what happened in Dorset."

Sherlock nodded his head. "Expect me within the week," he said, with his customary self-confidence.

"I will," Mycroft assured him, in spite of the fact that he could not echo that confidence.

* * * * * * *

Sherlock was as good as his word, at least in the matter of timing. He arrived in the Strangers' Room seven days later, at four-thirty in the afternoon. He was more than a little haggard, but he had summoned all his pride and self-discipline to the task of maintaining his image as a master of reason. Even so, he did not rise from his seat when Mycroft entered the room.

"I received a telegram from Lewes this morning," Mycroft told him. "I have the bare facts—but not the detail. You have done well. You may not think so, but you have."

"If you are about to tell me that there are more things in heaven and earth than are dreamt of in my philosophy...." Sherlock said, in a fractured tone whose annoyance was directed more at himself than his brother.

"I would not presume to insult you," Mycroft said, a trifle dishonestly. Tell me the story, please—in your own words."

"The first steps were elementary," Sherlock said, morosely. "Had Rockaby been in London, the Irregulars would have found him in a matter of hours; as things were, I had to put the word out through my contacts in Limehouse. Wherever Rockaby was, I knew that he had to be dosing himself against the terrors of his condition, and that was bound to leave a trail. I located him in Portsmouth. He had gone there in search of a ship to carry him back to the Indian Ocean, but no one would take him on because he was so plainly mad, and he had given up some time before, in favor of drinking himself into oblivion. Chevaucheux and I went down there *post haste*, and found him in a wretched condition.

"There were no signs of Captain Pye's disease on Rockaby's body—which gave me some confidence that the stone was not carrying any common-or-garden contagion—but his mind was utterly deranged. My questions got scant response, but Chevaucheux had slightly better luck. Rockaby recognized him, in spite of his madness, and seemed to feel some residual obligation to him, left over from a time when they were on better terms. 'I shouldn't of done it, Jacky,' he said to Chevaucheux. 'It warn't my fault, really, but I shouldn't of. I shouldn't of let the blood have its way—an' I'm damned now, blood or no blood. Won't die but can't live. Stay away, lad. Go away and stay away.'

"Chevaucheux asked him where the remainder of the stones could be found. I doubt that he would have told us, had he been well, but his condition worked to our advantage in that matter. Chevaucheux had to work hard, constantly reminding Rockaby of the ties that had bound them as children and shipmates, and in the end he wormed the location out of him. The place-names meant nothing to me, and probably meant nothing to anyone who had not roamed back and forth across the isle with the child that Rockaby once was, but Chevaucheux knew the exact spot near the sea-cliffs that Rockaby meant. 'Leave 'em be, Jacky,' the madman pleaded. 'Don't disturb the ground. Leave 'em be. Let 'em come in their own time. Don't hurry them, no matter how you burn.' We did not take the advice, of course."

Mycroft observed that Sherlock seemed to regret that, now. "You went to Saint Aldhelm's Head," he prompted. "To the sea-cliffs."

"We went by day," Sherlock said, his eyes glazing slightly as he slipped back into narrative mode. "The weather was poor—grey and drizzling—but it was daylight. Alas, daylight does not last. Chevaucheux led us to the spot readily enough, but the old mine where the stone-workers had tunneled into the cliff-face was difficult to reach, because the waves had long since carried away the old path. The mine-entrance was half-blocked, because the flat layers of stone had weathered unevenly, cracking and crumbling—but Rockaby had contrived a passage of sorts, and we squeezed through without disturbing the roof.

"When your clubmen set to work with a will, one plying a pick-axe and the other a miner's shovel, I was afraid the whole cliff might come down on us, but we were forty yards deep from the cliff-face, and the surrounding rock had never been assailed by the waves. I never heard such a sound, though, as the wind got up and the sea became violent. The crash of the waves seemed to surge through the stone, to emerge from the walls like the moaning of a sick giant—and that was before your men began pulling the images out and heaping them up.

"You studied the one that Chevaucheux gave you by lamplight, and magnified its image as you did so, but you can't have the least notion of how that crowd of faces appeared by the light of *our* lamps, in that Godforsaken hole. More than a few were considerably larger than the one Rockaby sent to Captain Pye, but it wasn't just their size that made them seem magnified: it was their malevolence. They weren't carrying a disease in the same way that a dead man's rags might harbor microbes, but there was a contagion in them regardless, which radiated from their features.

"Chevaucheux had shown me the stone faces built into the houses in Worth Matravers, but they'd been exposed for decades or centuries to the sun and the wind and the salt in the air. They had turned back into mere ugly faces, as devoid of virtue as of vice. These were different—and if they had stared at me the way they stared at poor Chevaucheux...."

Mycroft knew better than to challenge this remarkable observation. "Go on," he prompted.

"Reason tells me that they could not really have stared at Chevaucheux—that he must have imagined it, in much the same way that one imagines a portrait's gaze following one around a room—but I tell you, Mycroft, *I imagined it too*. I did not perceive the eyes of those monsters as if they were looking at me, but as if they were *looking at him*...as if they were accusing him of their betrayal. Not Rockaby, although he had told Chevaucheux where to find them, and not you or I, although we were the ones who asked him to locate them on behalf of your blessed club, but *him* and him alone. Justice, like logic, simply did not enter into the equation.

"'Do you see it, Mr. Holmes?' he asked me—and I had to confess that I did. 'It *is* in my blood,' he said. 'Sam was wrong to think himself any more a seaman than Dan Pye or Jacky Chevaucheux. There are stranger seas, you see, than the seven on which we sail. There are greater oceans than the five we have named. There are seas of infinity and oceans of eternity, and their salt is the bitterest brine that creation can contain. The dreams you know are but phantoms...ghosts with no more substance than rhyme or reason...but there are dreams *of the flesh*, Mr. Holmes. I have done nothing of which I need to be ashamed, and yet...*I cannot help but dream.*'

"All the while that he was speaking, he was moving away, towards the narrow shaft by which we had gained entry to the heart of the mine. He was moving into the shadows, and I assumed that he was trying to escape the light because he was trying to escape the hostile gaze of those horrid effigies—but that was not the reason. You saw what was happening to his torso when he was here, but his face was then untouched. The poison had leached into his liver and lights, but not his eyes or brain...but the bleak eyes of those stone heads were staring at him, no matter how absurd that sounds, and... do you have any idea what I am talking about, Mycroft? Do you understand what was happening in that cave?"

"I wish I did," Mycroft said. "You, my dear brother, are perhaps the only man in England who can comprehend the profundity of my desire. Like you, I am a master of observation and deduction, and I have every reason to wish that my gifts were entirely adequate to an understanding of the world in which we find ourselves. There is nothing that men like us hate and fear more than the *inexplicable*. I do not hold with fools who say that there are things that man was not meant to know, but I am forced to admit that there are things that men are not yet in a position to know. We have hardly begun to come to terms with the ordinary afflictions of the flesh that we call diseases, let alone those which are extraordinary. If there are such things as curses—and you will doubtless agree with me that it would be infinitely preferable if there were not—then we are impotent, as yet, to counter them. Did Chevaucheux say anything more about these *dreams of the flesh?*"

"He had already told me that Dan Pye had been right," Sherlock went on. "They were more than dreams, even when they were phantoms. Opium does not feed them, he said, but cannot suppress them. He had told me, very calmly, that he had already seen the deserts of infinity, the depths within darkness, the horrors that lurk on reason's edge...and that he had heard the mutterings, the discordance that underlies every pretence of music and meaningful speech...but when he moved into the shadows of the cave...."

Sherlock made an evident effort to gather himself together. "He never stopped talking," the great detective went on. "He wanted me to know, to understand. He wanted you to know. He wanted to help us—and, through us, to help others. 'The worst of it all,' he said, 'is what I have *felt*. I have felt the *crawling chaos*, and I know what it is that has me now. Saint Anthony's fire is a mere caress by comparison. I have felt the hand of revelation upon my forehead, and I feel it now, gripping me like a vice. I know that the ruling force of creation is blind, and worse than blind. I know that it is devoid of the least intelligence, the least compassion, the least *artistry*. You may be surprised to find me so calm under such conditions as this, Mr. Holmes, and to tell you the truth I am surprised myself—all the more so for having seen Dan Pye upon his deathbed, and Sam Rockaby on a rack of his own making—but I have learned from you that facts must be accepted as facts and treated as facts, and that madness is a treason of the will. You might think that you and your brother have not helped me, but you have...in spite of everything. Take these monstrous things away, and study them...learn what they have to teach you, no matter what the cost. That's better by far than Sam Rockaby's way, or mine....'" Sherlock trailed off again

"Mr. Chevaucheux was a brave man," Mycroft said, after a moment's pause.

Sherlock met his eyes then, with a gaze full of fear and fire. Am I damned, Mycroft?" he demanded, harshly. "Is the disease incubating in me, as it was in him? Are my own dreams worse than dreams?"

Mycroft had no firm guarantees to offer, but he shook his head. "There was something in Chevaucheux, as there was in Pye, which responded to the curse. You and I are a different breed; the art in our blood is a different kind. I cannot swear to you that we are immune, or will remain so, but I am convinced that we are better placed to fight. Those effigies you took to Lewes may have the power to make some men see a terrible truth, and to make some human flesh turn traitor to the soul, but they are not omnipotent, else the human race would have succumbed to their effect long ago. At any rate, there is no safety in hiding them, or in hiding from them. Whatever the risk, they must be studied. Such studies are dangerous, but that does not excuse us from our scholarly duty. We must try to understand what they are—what *we* are—no matter how hateful the answer might be."

"You believe that we are safe from this contagion, then—you and I?"

Mycroft had never seen Sherlock so desperate for reassurance. "I dare to hope so," He said, judiciously. "The Diogenes Club has some experience in matters of this sort, and we have survived thus far. The entities that men like Rockaby term the *Others* have proved more powerful in the past than those he calls the Elder Gods, but the blood of Nodens is not extinct; it flows in us still and it has its expression. The gift that was handed down to men like us is not to be despised. You sometimes suspect that I think less of you because you have become famous instead of laboring behind the scenes of society, as I do, but I am glad that you have become a hero of the age, because the age is direly in need of your kind of hero. Our art is in its infancy, and many more confrontations such as this one will expose our incapacity in years—perhaps centuries—to come, but we must nurture it regardless, and store its rewards. What else can we do, if we are to be worthy of the name of humankind?"

Sherlock nodded, seemingly satisfied.

"Tell me, then," Mycroft said, "what happened in the cave. I know that you and my faithful servants succeeded in taking the artifacts to Lewes, but I know that Chevaucheux was not with you. Rockaby has been committed to a lunatic asylum, where an agent of ours will be able to interrogate his madness, but I gather from the tone of your account that Chevaucheux will not be available for further study. Do you feel able now to tell me what became of him?"

"What became of him?" Sherlock echoed, fear flooding his eyes again. "What *became*...? Ah...." As he paused, he put his hand into his pocket and took out a bottle. Mycroft had no way to be sure, but it seemed to him to be an exact match to the outline he had observed in John Chevaucheux's clothing a weeks before. The label on this bottle, scrawled in a doctor's unkempt hand, confirmed that it was laudanum.

Sherlock put his hand to the cork, but then he stopped himself, and put the unopened bottle down on the side-table. "It does no good," he said. "But they are only dreams, are they not? Mere phantoms? There is no necessity that will turn them into dreams of *my* flesh. That is what Chevaucheux told me, at any rate, when he reached forward to give me the bottle, before he ran away. I think that he was trying to be kind—but he might have been kinder to remain in the shadows. He had faith in me, you see. He thought that I would want to *see* what had *become*...and he was right. He ought to have been right, and he was. Before he ran to the end of that makeshift corridor of stone, and hurled himself into the thankless sea, where I hope to God that he died....

"That brave man wanted me to see what the crawling chaos had done to him, as it turned his flesh into a dream beneath the evil eyes of those *creatures* we had excavated from their hiding place....

"And I did see it, Mycroft."

"I know," Mycroft answered. "But you must tell me what it was you saw, if we are ever to come to terms with it." And he saw his brother respond to this appeal, seeing its sense as well as its necessity. All his life, Sherlock Holmes had believed that when one had eliminated the impossible, whatever remained—however improbable—must be the truth. Now he understood that, when the impossible was too intractable to be eliminated, one had to revise one's opinion of the limits of the possible; but he was a brave man, in whom the blood of Nodens still flowed, after a fashion, still carrying forward its long and ceaseless war against the tainted blood of the *Others*.

"I saw the flesh of his face," Sherlock went on, stubbornly ringing his tale to its inevitable end, "whose texture was like some frightful, pulpy cephalopod, and whose shape was dissolving into a mass of writhing, agonized worms, every one of them suppurating and liquefying as if it had been a month decaying...and I met his eyes...his glowing eyes that were blind to ordinary light...which were staring, not at me, but into the infinite and the eternal...*where they beheld some horror so unspeakable that it required every last vestige of his strength to pause an instant more before he hurled himself, body and soul, into the illimitable abyss."*

MR. BRIMSTONE AND DR. TREACLE

As soon as he had read Utterson's manuscript, as reproduced in Stevenson's account of the strange case of Dr. Jekyll and Mr. Hyde, the one thought in Hector Treacle's mind was to re-create the Jekyll formula.

Whereas other men seemingly regarded Utterson's revelations as a cautionary tale warning scientists against unwary tampering with the mysteries of Nature, Dr. Treacle saw the true potential of the elixir. The fact that a prototype had malfunctioned was, in Treacle's opinion, no reason to give up on the project; all new technologies had their teething-troubles, which could be worked out by those who persevered. Like Stevenson—but unlike Jekyll or Utterson—Hector Treacle was a Scotsman; unlike Stevenson, however, he was the kind of Scotsman who was much given to perseverance. He was a sterner man by far than Henry Jekyll.

With time and effort, Treacle felt sure, he could deliver a product that would not only separate the good in men from the evil, but would empower the good to strangle and obliterate the evil. He immediately gave up all other work in order to concentrate on this great mission, instructing his servants to turn all would-be patients away from his door no matter how desperate their condition might be.

After several years of hard labor, and many experiments, Hector Treacle finally succeeded in his endeavor. He produced a serum that would tear his personality in two as violently and as precisely as Henry Jekyll's had been riven, but would also place the higher self firmly in the driving seat of the soul.

Gladly, he drank it down.

At first, as was only to be expected, Treacle suffered a few problems. He had always been a man of very precise habits—perfectly regular in his attendance at the kirk, unable to tolerate the slightest laxity on the part of his wife or his domestic staff, utterly scrupulous in the management of his inheritance—but the darker side of his personality, temporarily liberated in order that it might be conclusively crushed, disrupted his routines severely.

Treacle had expected his *alter ego*—which immediately adopted the appropriately diabolical pseudonym Lucifer Brimstone—to be a creature of pure but all-inclusive malignity, as Jekyll's Hyde had seemingly been, but he was not. Brimstone appeared to be an individual motivated entirely by the deadly sin of wrath, but his was a sly kind of wrath that was by no means all-consuming.

Naturally enough, Brimstone hated everything that Treacle's nobler self loved, and did his best to wreak havoc therewith, but he did so with low cunning rather than frank brutality.

Brimstone loathed the church for the sternness of its morality and its abomination of sin; he had the temerity to interrupt the pastor's sermons with all manner of serpentine sophistries. Worse still, Brimstone took a positive delight in all the most vulgar trappings of sexual intercourse—even with Mrs. Treacle, on one or two occasions when he happened to take control of Treacle's flesh by night. To add insult to injury, Brimstone took advantage of another brief interval of tenure to give a firm promise that he would not dismiss a pregnant kitchen girl, which poor Treacle had of course to honor. Worst of all, however, the demonic Brimstone began to give away significant amounts of money to the most unsuitable causes imaginable: hospitals for the poor; mechanics' institutes; hostels for battered wives and abused children; societies for the promotion of racial equality, and even the Labor Party!

To add further insult to these further injuries, it seemed that for some utterly unaccountable reason, everyone liked the man! Even Mrs. Treacle, who had long since ceased to exhibit any conspicuous affection for her husband, visibly warmed to the appalling presence of Lucifer Brimstone!

Fortunately, Hector Treacle had done his work far better than poor Henry Jekyll. Lucifer Brimstone's influence upon the world was mercifully short-lived. Treacle's higher self ground him gradually but inexorably into dust.

Within a matter of months, the good doctor had purified himself, body and soul. It only remained to give his invention to the world, thus to institute Utopia.

This he did, in a spirit of humility and generosity.

The way ahead was not smooth. For some incomprehensible reason, large numbers of people objected to the serum and refused to take it. In order to overcome their obduracy, the drug eventually had to be force-fed to them by their wiser and better-disciplined fellows. In the end, however, the triumph of Treacle's elixir was assured.

Outrage, moral laxity and vulgar pleasure were banished from the world of men, never to return.

The entire Earth—even including England—became the kind of paradise of which every Scottish Presbyterian had always dreamed.

* * * * * * *

[Author's note: When I first dreamed this story it had a different and far more nightmarish conclusion. Fortunately, in exactly the same way that Fanny Stevenson pointed out to Robert that he had missed the opportunity to pen a telling moral fable, and forced him to burn the original, my dear wife Chastity intervened to persuade me to consign the uncensored version to perdition. She insisted that I owed it to the world to provide a happy and uplifting ending, so I did.]

JEHAN THUN'S QUEST

The day had been clear when Jehan Thun set off from the inn on the outskirts of the city of Geneva, but the weather in the lake's environs was far more capricious than the weather in Paris. He had hoped that the sky might remain blue all day, but it was not long after noon when grey cloud began spilling through the gaps in the mountains, swallowing up the peaks and promising a downpour that would soak him to the skin and render his path treacherous.

There were villages scattered along the shore of the lake but he had no thought of asking for shelter there. The time seemed to be long past when one could be confident of receiving hospitality from any neighbor, and the people in Geneva who had recognized his surname had looked at him strangely and suspiciously, although none had actually challenged him. It would have been better, in retrospect to avoid Geneva altogether, since the Château of Andernatt was on the French side of the lake and he could have followed the course of Rhone, but he had hoped to find the city of his ancestors more welcoming by far than any other he had passed through on his flight from Paris. At least the many repetitions of his grandmother's story had drummed the stages of the route that she and Aubert had followed into Jehan's mind: Bessange, Ermance, ford the Dranse; Chesset, Colombay, Monthey, the hermitage of Notre-Dame-du-Sex.

When Jehan's grandparents had made that journey the churches of Geneva had still been affiliated to Rome; now, fifty years after Calvin's advent, they preached a very different faith. Notre-Dame-du-Sex was on the French shore, but Jehan was not at all certain that the hermitage would still be occupied. The apparatus of charity that had supported the hermit who gave temporary refuge to Aubert Thun and the daughter of Master Zacharius had been transformed for several leagues around the city, just as the environs of Paris had been transformed before St. Bartholomew's Day.

THE INNSMOUTH HERITAGE, BY BRIAN STABLEFORD

The rain began before Jehan had reached the Dranse, but it was no deluge at first and the torrent had not become impassable. The downfall became steadier as he left the shore, though, and the further he went up the slopes the greater its volume became. He dared not stop now, or even relent in his pace. It had taken his grandparents more than twenty hours to reach the base of the Dent-du-Midi, but they had been slowed down by Old Scholastique; he reckoned on covering the same ground in fourteen hours at the most—as he would have to do if he were to avoid spending the night on the bare mountain.

He had hoped that fifty years of footfalls might have smoothed the paths a little since his grandparents' day, but it seemed that hardly anyone came this way any more; parts of the path had all but disappeared. On a better day, the Dent-du-Midi would have served as a fine beacon, but with its top lost in the clouds he was unable to sight it.

Jehan Thun was a man well used to walking, but the gradients in and around Paris were gentle, and he was glad now that he had had to cross the forbidding slopes of the Jura in order to reach Geneva, for his legs had been hardened in the last few weeks. His cape and broad-brimmed hat protected him from the worst effects of the driving rain, but that would not have been enough to sustain him had he not been capable of such a metronomic stride. He had walked like an automaton since St. Bartholomew's Day, but even an automaton needs strength in its limbs and power in its spring.

It was a close-run thing, in the end; had he been a quarter of an hour later, he would not have been able to catch a glimpse of the hermitage before darkness fell. Had he not seen it in the fast-fading twilight he could not have found it, for no light burned in its window, and it had obviously been abandoned for decades, but the roof had not yet caved in. It leaked in a dozen places, but there was enough dry space within to set down his pack. He lit a candle—not without difficulty, for all that he had kept his tinder dry.

There was no point in trying to gather wood to build a fire that would burn all night, so Jehan made a rapid meal of what little bread he had left before wrapping himself more tightly in his cloak and lying down in a corner to sleep. Even as he reached out to snuff out his candle, though, he was interrupted. A voice cried in the distance, in German-accented French, asking what light it was that was showing in the darkness. For a moment he was tempted to extinguish the candle anyway, in the hope that the other traveler would not be able to find him once the guide was gone—but that would have been a terrible thing to do, even if the other turned out to be a bandit or a heresy-hunter. Instead, he shouted out that he was a traveler who had lost his way, and had taken refuge in an abandoned hermitage.

A few minutes later, a man staggered through the doorway, mingling curses against the weather with profuse thanks for guidance to the meager shelter. He took off a vast colporteur's pack, letting it fall to the floor with a grateful sigh. He was approximately the same age and build as Jehan Thun; even by candlelight Jehan could see the anxiety in the way the newcomer measured him, and knew that it must be reflected in his own eyes. He imagined that the other must be just as glad as he was to see that they were so evenly matched, not merely in size and apparent health but in the manner of their dress.

"I did not see you on the path ahead of me," the newcomer said, "so I presume that you must be coming away from Geneva while I am going towards it. I don't know which of us is the wiser, for they say that Geneva is like a city under siege nowadays. My name is Nicholas Alther. I was born in Bern, although my course takes me far and wide in the Confederation, France and Savoy."

Jehan knew that the complications of Geneva's political situation extended far beyond matters of religious controversy; although the city was allied with Bern it was not a member of the Swiss confederation, and its position as a three-way juncture between Switzerland, Savoy and France created tensions over and above the residue of Calvin's reforms.

"My name is Jehan Thun," he admitted, a trifle warily. "I'm stateless now, although I've recently been in France." Jehan watched Nicholas Alther carefully as he spoke his name; there was a manifest reaction, but it was not the same one that the name had usually evoked in Geneva, and Nicholas Alther did not make the same attempt to conceal it. "Thun?" the colporteur echoed. "There was once a clockmaker in these parts named Thun."

"That was a long time ago," Jehan said, very carefully.

"Yes," Alther agreed. "He was a fine mechanician, though, and his work has lasted. I have one of his watches in my pack—my own, not for trading." So saying, the colporteur rummaged in one of the side-pockets of his capacious luggage and brought out a forty-year-old timepiece. Jehan Thun observed that its single hand was making slow progress between the numbers ten and eleven. "You doubtless have a better one," Alther prompted, as he put the device away again and brought out a cheese instead.

"No," Jehan confessed. "I have no watch at all."

73

"No watch!" Alther seemed genuinely astonished. He offered Jehan Thun the first slice of cheese he cut off, but Jehan shook his head and the other continued, punctuating his speech with the motions of his meal. "Perhaps you are not related to the old clockmaker—but your French has a hint of Geneva in it, and I doubt there was another family hereabouts with that name. Aubert Thun must have been one of the first men ever to use a spring to drive a clock, or at least a fusée regulator in place of a stackfreed—and the escapements he made for weight-driven clocks will preserve his reputation for at least a century more, for they're still in use in half the churches between here and Bern. He was a greater man than many whose names will be better preserved by history, although I don't recall hearing of anything he did after he quit Geneva."

Jehan Thun looked at the colporteur sharply when he said that, wondering whether Alther might have the name of Calvin in mind, but all he said, reluctantly, was: "Aubert Thun was my grandfather."

"Did he abandon his trade when he went away?" the colporteur asked.

"No," Jehan admitted, "but there are locksmiths and clockmakers by the hundred in Paris, which means that there are escapements by the thousand and far more watch-springs than anyone could count. He had the reputation there of a skilled man, but there was no reason why rumor of his skill should carry far. It has surprised me that his name is still remembered here; he told me that he was only an apprentice to the man who first used springs in Genevan watches and first put verge escapements into the region's church clocks."

"Is that true?" Alther replied, his features expressing surprise. He had wine as well as cheese, and offered the flask to Jehan Thun, but Jehan shook his head again. Alther took a deep draught before continuing: "I heard the same, but always thought Master Zacharius a legend. Even before Calvin, Genevans were reluctant to think that anything new could be produced by the imagination of a man; everything had to be a gift from God or an instrument of the Devil. The tale they tell of Thun's supposed master is a dark and fanciful one, but nothing a reasonable man could believe."

Jehan knew that the conversation had strayed on to unsafe ground, but he felt compelled to say: "I agree, and I'm sorry to have found people in Geneva who still look sideways at the mention of my grandfather's name. Master Zacharius did go mad, I fear, but the stories they tell of him are wildly exaggerated."

"And yet," Alther observed, "you're coming away from Geneva. Are you, by any chance, heading in the direction of Evionnaz...and the Château of Andernatt?"

Jehan suppressed a shiver when Alther said that. Colporteurs were notorious as collectors and tellers of tales, for it oiled the wheels of their trade; Alther's stock was obviously broad and deep. He said nothing.

"I've seen the château on the horizon," the colporteur went on, eventually, "And that's more than most can say. No one goes there, and it seems to have fallen into ruins. Whatever you're looking for, I doubt that you'll find it."

"My destination might lie further in the same direction," Jehan pointed out.

"There is nothing further in that direction," Alther retorted. "Evionnaz is the road's end. I've traveled it often enough to know."

"The world is a sphere," Jehan said, knowing as he said it that it was not an uncontroversial opinion, and hence not entirely safe. "There is always further to go, in every direction, no matter how hard the road might be—and the Dents-du-Midi are not impassable at this time of year."

"That's what I thought before the rain set in," Alther grumbled, following his cheese with some kind of sweetmeat—which, this time, he did not bother to offer to his companion, "but the people of Evionnaz think the world has an edge, no more than a league from the bounds of their fields. They never go to Andernatt."

"I have not said that I am going that way," Jehan said, rudely. "But if I were, it would be no one's business but my own." He felt that he had said too much, even though he had said very little, and he indicated by the way in which he gathered his cloak about himself that he did not want to waste any more time before going to sleep, now that the colporteur had finished his meal.

"That's true," Alther agreed, shrugging his shoulders to indicate that it was of scant importance to him whether the conversation was cut short. "I'll venture to say, though, that you'd be unlikely to meet the Devil if you did go that way, whether or not there's anything more than a ruin at Andernatt. There are half a hundred peaks on this side of the lake alone where Satan's reported to have squatted at one time or another—and that's not counting dwellings like this one, whose former inhabitant was reckoned his minion by the Calvinists down in Geneva."

"I'll be glad of that, too," Jehan assured him, and said no more.

* * * * * * *

Jehan Thun and Nicholas Alther parted the next morning on good terms, as two honest men thrown briefly together by chance ought to do. They wished one anther well as they set off in near-opposite directions. Whether Alther gave another thought to him thereafter, Jehan did not know or care, but he certainly gave a good deal of thought to what Alther had said as he made his way towards Evionnaz. It was a difficult journey, but when he finally reached the village, huddled in a narrow vale between two crags, he was able to buy food and fill his flask. He passed through with minimal delay into territory where the paths that once had been were now hardly discernible. No one in the village asked him where he was bound, but a dozen pairs of eyes watched him as he went, and he felt those eyes boring into his back until he had put the first of many ridges between himself and the village.

Jehan no longer had precise directions as to the path he must take; he had not dared to mention the château in Geneva. All he had to guide him now was vague advice handed on by his grandmother, which told him no more than to steer to the left. Inevitably, Jehan soon became desperately unsure of his way. While the sun de-scended into the west he wandered, searching the narrow horizons for a glimpse of the ruins that Nicholas Alther claimed to have seen. At least the sun was visible, so he was able to conserve a good no-tion of the direction in which Evionnaz lay, but by the time he de-cided that he would have to turn back he knew that it would be diffi-cult to reach the village before nightfall.

Then, finally, he caught sight of a strange hump outlined on a slanting ridge. He was not certain at first, given the distance and the fact that he was looking at it from below, that it really was the rem-nant of an edifice, and it seemed in a far worse state than he had hoped, even after hearing Alther's judgment.

Because it lay in a direction diametrically opposite to the route that would take him towards Evionnaz, Jehan Thun knew that he would be in difficulty if there were nothing on the site but broken stones, but he had to make the choice and he was not at all confident that he could find his way back to his present location if he did not press on now. He decided that he must trust to luck and do his ut-most to carry his quest forward to its destination.

Again he reached his objective just as night was falling, and again he saw no light as he toiled uphill towards the crumbled stonework, until he lit his own candle—but this time, there seemed at first glance to be no roof at all to offer him shelter, merely a tangle of tumbled walls, cracked arches and heaps of debris.

He did not realize for some little while that he had only found an outer part of the ancient edifice. He might easily have lain down to sleep without making any such discovery, but, as chance would have it, he was fortunate enough to see a flock of bats emerging from a crevice behind a pile of rubble. When he climbed up to see if he could insinuate himself into the gap, he did not expect to find anything more than a corner of a room, but he was able to make a descent into a much broader and deeper space that had two doorways. These gave access to further corridors, each of which contained a stairway leading into what had seemed from beneath to be the solid rock of the ridge. He quickly came to the conclusion that the château must have been much larger than it now seemed, built into a groove in the ridge rather than perched atop level ground. The lower parts of its walls had been so completely overgrown that the casual eye could not distinguish them from the native rock that jutted up to either side.

One stairway turned out to be useless, the wooden-beamed storage-cellar to which it led having caved in, but the other led to further rooms and further portals, some with ceilings and doors still intact. The route was awkward, not least because of the stink—the bats had been depositing their excreta for generations—but he managed to open three of the closed doors to expose further spaces beyond, two no bigger than closets but one of a more appreciable size. This one had a slit-like window, through which the stars were clearly visible, although no such aperture had not been discernible from the side of the hill he had climbed on his first approach.

That first room was uninhabitable, but when he went on again he found one that the bats had not yet turned it into a dormitory, because the shutter on its window was still intact. The bare wooden floorboards seemed more hospitable than stone, and they seemed remarkably free of dirt, so Jehan set his pack down. He was so exhausted that he stretched himself out and blew out his candle without making a meal.

His thoughts immediately returned to what Nicholas Alther had said about Master Zacharius, and he began to regret not asking exactly what story it was that Alther had heard. According to his grandmother—who believed far more of the tale than her husband—her father had put his soul into the spring of a clock commissioned by the Devil, thus conceding the Adversary power to transmogrify and finally obliterate his work. Aubert Thun's son, Jehan's father, had been as skeptical as the old man, and Jehan had the same attitude; he would never have come here had it not become impossible for him to stay in Paris—but once the capital of France had become as unsafe for Protestants as Geneva had once been for Catholics, the only choice remaining to him was the direction in which to flee. Since he had had to go somewhere, and had no other destination in mind, it had seemed to Jehan that he might as well do what his grandmother—who had died of natural causes thank God, long before the massacre—had always wanted his father to do. Now that he was here, though, he could not help reflecting lugubriously on the fact that he had come in order to have a destination at which to point his automation limbs, not because he believed that there would be any treasure to find or any curse to lift.

He decided before he fell asleep that he would explore the ruins as thoroughly as was humanly possible on the following day, and then make further plans. The food he had bought in Evionnaz would be enough to sustain him for more than a day, although it should not be difficult to find pools of rainwater to drink. He would have to decide soon enough whether to retrace his steps in the direction of inhospitable Geneva, or to make his way back to the Rhone and follow the path that Nicholas Alther had presumably been walking, or make his way eastwards along the north shore of the lake—or go on into the Dents-du-Midi, into a bleak and empty region that the people of Evionnaz took to be the limit of the world.

* * * * * * *

In the morning, Jehan Thun was awakened by a hand placed on his shoulder. The room was still gloomy but the shutter had been partially opened; the beam of sunlight streaming through the narrow window brightened the plastered walls, reflecting enough light to show him that the person who had woken him was very short and stout: a dwarf.

That was a terrible shock—not because it was unexpected, but for the precisely the opposite reason. His grandmother had told him that the Devil had come to her father, Master Zacharius, in the form of a dwarf named Pittonaccio.

"Who are you?" Jehan stammered, quite ready to believe that he was face to face with the Devil. The moment of awakening is a vulnerable one, in which deep impressions can be made that are sometimes difficult of amendment.

The little man paused momentarily, as if he had not expected to be addressed in French, but he answered fluently enough in the same language. "I am the Master of Andernatt," he said, proudly. "The question should rather be: Who are you? You are the invader here—are you a bandit come to rob me of my heritage?" His Germanic accent was not as pronounced as Nicholas Alther's, but was evident nevertheless.

"I'm no bandit," Jehan said.

"Are you not? Are you a guest, then? Did you knock on any of the doors you passed through last night? Did you call out to ask for shelter?"

"I saw no light," Jehan protested.

"You would have seen a light had you taken more care to look around," the dwarf replied. "My chamber has a broader window than this one, and I lit my lamp before sunset. I suppose you did not see my goats on the ledges either, or my garden in the vale."

"No," said Jehan, becoming increasingly desperate as the challenges kept coming. "I saw no goats—but if I had, I'd have taken them for wild creatures. Nor did I see a garden, but it was dusk when I approached and I was fearful that I might not reach the shelter of the ruins before night plunged me into darkness."

"The stars were shining," the dwarf observed, "and there's near half a moon. Your eyes must be poor—but I suppose you came from the direction of Evionnaz, from which my window would have been hidden. You still have not told me who you are, or what business you have here."

Jehan Thun hesitated fearfully; he felt a strong temptation to declare that his name was Nicholas Alther, and that he was a colporteur who had lost his way—but he had no pack of goods and trinkets, and no good reason to lie. In the end, he plucked up his courage and said: "My name is Jehan Thun. My grandfather was Aubert Thun, apprentice to Master Zacharius of Geneva."

The dwarf recognized the names, but he did not look sideways in suspicion, let alone recoil in horror. Instead, he smiled beatifically, and the expression caused his unhandsome face to become quite pleasant. "Ah!" he said. "The answer to my prayer! There have been others here before you, searching for the clock, but none named Thun. Zacharius must have been your great-grandfather, Master Jehan, for Aubert Thun married the clockmaker's daughter, Gérande."

Jehan was terrified already, so the fact that the dwarf knew all this gave him little further distress. "And you?" he said, in a quavering voice. "Are you...?" He could not say the word. His grandmother had been twice devout, once as a Catholic and once as a Protestant, and had prayed incessantly for her father in either mode, but Jehan had never been able to put quite as much trust as that in the attentiveness of Heaven or the menace of Hell. Even so, for the moment, he could not say either "the Devil" or "Pittonaccio."

"Not even his great-grandson, Master Jehan," the dwarf said. "My name is Friedrich—very ordinary, as I'm sure you'll agree; but I'm Master of Andernatt nevertheless, at least for now, and I do have the clock. I have nearly completed its reconstruction, but have faltered lately for lack of proper tools and a skilful hand. Have you brought your own tools?"

"I've brought my grandfather's," Jehan confessed.

"Then you're a wiser man than those who came before you. Did you also bring his skill?"

The truth seemed to have taken firm hold of Jehan Thun's tongue; he could not seem to twist it. "I'm not a watchmaker," he confessed. "I'm a printer—or was. The mob was as anxious to smash up my press as it was to break my neighbors' heads. I can cast and trim type, and work in wood, and I have some skill as an engraver, but I haven't curled a spring or wrought a fusée since I helped my father in his shop as a boy. Times have changed, and it's the printing-press that has changed them. There are hundreds of clockmakers in Paris, but only a dozen printers as yet—at least one less, now."

The dwarf looked at him long and hard then, as if he were following some train of thought to an unexpected terminus. "I have a printed book," he admitted, finally. "It's a Bible."

"I printed a great many of those myself," Jehan told him. "Too many, perhaps."

"Well," said the dwarf, "whether you called out or not, Master Jehan, you're a guest now, and the most welcome one I've ever had. Come to breakfast—and then I'll show you the clock."

* * * * * * *

The corridors that Jehan Thun had thought rather labyrinthine the previous evening were even more extensive and complex than he had imagined. They were, however, far better ventilated than the initial barrier of bat droppings had suggested and many of them were dimly illuminated by daylight creeping through window-slits and cracks in the masonry. One such slit overlooked the "garden" to which the master of the ruins had referred—which was actually a vegetable-plot and orchard. Jehan Thun saw immediately why he had not caught sight of it before; the dell in which it was situated was itself a covert, hidden by a massive buttress of rock. There was evidently another way into the cavernous part of the edifice from that side, which allowed the dwarf to avoid the difficulties of the way by which Jehan had gained entry.

The dwarf took him to a room more brightly lit than the rest, which also looked out over the garden. It had a fire burning in the grate, but the chimney let out into the same covert, so its smoke would not have been easily visible as Jehan Thun had approached on the previous evening. There was a cooking pot simmering beside the fire, and various items of game hung from a rack on the chimney-breast. The furniture was sparse but there was a sturdy table and two good chairs. Jehan sat down gladly, and ate a good meal.

The printed Bible that the dwarf had mentioned was laid flat on a shelf; the dust on its binding implied that it had not been opened for some while. Jehan lifted the cover to inspect the quality of the printing, but the type was florid Gothic and the text was not in Latin.

"Come, Master Jehan, my godsend," said the dwarf. "I will show you what you came to see."

According to Jehan's grandmother, the iron clock of Andernatt had been fastened to the wall of a great hall. It had been shaped by Master Zacharius to resemble the facade of a church, with wrought-iron buttresses and a bell-tower, with a rose-window over the door in which the clock's two hands were mounted. The same witness had testified that the clock had exploded and its internal spring had burst out like a striking snake to secure the damnation of its maker.

The clock was not in a great hall now but in a small room that had no window. The buttresses and the bell-tower must have been transported in several pieces, but they had been reassembled so carefully that they seemed whole again. The window had been pieced together, and all of its glass replaced, although the cobwebbing cracks made it obvious that the stained-glass had once been shattered. The doors of the church had been replaced, with newer wood, and they stood open to display the inner works of the clock—but the giant spring that Master Zacharius had set in place was not there now, nor was the verge-escapement that had regulated it. There was, instead, a more complex mechanism, whose most prominent feature was a mysterious brass rod, mounted vertically on a spindle, pivoted so that it might swing from side to side, whose lower extremity was shielded by a polished silver disc.

This remarkable object caught and held Jehan's gaze for several seconds, delaying his search for the clock's most unusual feature: the copper plate between the door and the dial, in which words appeared as each hour struck.

His grandmother had described this plate as a magic mirror, on which words appeared and disappeared by diabolical command, but his grandfather had assured him that there was nothing magical about it. There was actually a series of twelve plaques mounted on the rim of a hidden wheel, which rotated as the clock's spring unwound and the hands made their own rotation. Each plaque was itself held back by a tiny spring, which would release as the hour struck, displaying the motto inscribed on the plaque with startling suddenness in a space that had been occupied only a second before by a blank face of copper.

The original set of plaques furnished by Master Zacharius, Aubert Thun had assured his grandson, had been inscribed with conventional pieties, many of them take from the Sermon on the Mount—but once the clock had been installed at Andernatt, its owner had replaced the plaques with a new set offering different maxims.

"Your grandmother is convinced that the replacement was the work of the Devil," Aubert Thun had told him, "but it was not even a task that would have required a locksmith's metal-working skills, once the wheel's casing had been removed. Her father was already mad, but the discovery that his work of art had been altered was the ultimate insult. That is why he tried to stop the clock—but the spring broke because its iron was too poor to sustain its stress. No spring could power a clock like that for very long, for the alloy is not yet discovered that can bear the strain of continual winding in a strip so vast. Now that the necessity is obvious, better materials will doubtless be devised, but Zacharius could only work with what he had, and it was not adequate to his ambition.

"It was Zacharius's vanity, not his soul, that was embodied in the mechanism—and it was his vanity, not some diabolical bargain, that struck him dead. My wife would never believe it, though, and she will swear to her dying day that she saw the dwarf Pittonaccio disappear into the bowels of the earth with the spring in his grasp, bound for the Inferno. She believes that she and I were cursed on the day he died, and that all the force of her constant prayers—and mine—has only served to keep the curse at bay. Your father is an exceedingly devout man, and I do not criticize him for that, but you must make up your own mind what to believe, and there are better fates than to live in fear."

Jehan had taken his grandfather's word over his grandmother's, far more determinedly his father had, and had tried very hard not to live in fear. Aubert Thun had not lived to see the death of his son on Saint Bartholomew's Day in 1572, and Jehan driven into exile—but Jehan knew that Aubert would have been adamant that it was the way of the world that had brought that evil day about, and that Jehan's printing-press was no more to blame for his father's death than the residue of any curse that had one attached to the Clock of Andernatt. Jehan Thun's grandmother had, however, carried the conviction to her grave that she and her son were cursed—and now that Jehan had seen the cellars and inner rooms of the Château of Andernatt, he understood far better how she might have witnessed the broken spring being borne into the hollows of the mountain, whether or not it was bound for Hell.

Jehan asked the dwarf about Zacharius's broken spring, but the present Master of Andernatt told him that it was long discarded, replaced by a far better mechanism.

As the dwarf had said, the clock was not quite finished, but very nearly so. The parts scattered on the floor of the room were all tiny, and they all required to be fitted into the narrow space above the rose-window, behind the part of the facade that resembled a bell-tower—an awkward task, hampered by the casing of the wheel bearing and concealing the motto-engraved plaques.

"The face of the tower can still be removed," the dwarf told Jehan, "and I can compensate for my lack of stature by standing on a stool, but I don't have your slender fingers or your delicate touch. Even if you have not dabbled in clockwork since you were a child, your own work must have maintained your dexterity, and my escapement is a not as delicate as a fusée. You could complete the work in a matter of days."

"I don't understand the mechanism," Jehan Thun objected. "I've never seen its like."

"It's simple enough, once explained," the dwarf assured him.

Jehan Thun's gaze redirected itself then to the blank copper plate that would presumably be eclipsed by a plaque if the mechanism were actually to prove capable of moving the hands and activating the chimes.

"You need have no fear on that score," the dwarf said. "I've replaced the maxims that caused your grandmother such distress."

"With the original set?" Jehan Thun asked.

"Those were discarded long ago. I made my own replacements. They're all in place, but now that the casing is sealed they can't be seen until the clock is completed and started. I trust that you didn't come here without any bolder hope than to melt down the remains of the mechanism and separate out the precious metals therefrom. You did say, did you not, that you are no bandit?"

"I expected to find the clock in ruins, like the château," Jehan Thun said, hesitantly. "My grandmother told me that the place was considered accursed, and that no one would be living here."

"Calvin redoubled the fear of the Devil that the good people of Geneva already had," the dwarf told him, "but there are always men who are careless of curses. Had I not been here to hide and stand guard over the pieces of the clock they'd have been looted long ago. Even I could not resist a whole robber band—but it's a clock, after all, not a gold mine. You wouldn't have come so far just for a little metal, I'm sure—but I'm equally sure that you haven't come in the hope of reclaiming the spring that might or might not have been the soul of Master Zacharius."

Jehan considered the possibility of telling the dwarf about his grandmother's sorrows and delusions, and how she had begged his father to make the journey in order to destroy the last remnants of the clock and lift the family curse with prayer, but he did not want to do that. "I came to examine the fusée," he said, eventually, although he was not *entirely* certain that it was true. "One of the few things on which my grandparents agreed, save for the fact that they loved one another very dearly, was that it was a new type, better than any previously used in a spring-driven clock. Aubert thought that he could reproduce it, but he never contrived to do it, and came to believe in the end that he had misremembered some small but essential detail. Alas, he was in Paris by then."

"You came to study the fusée?" the dwarf repeated, in a tone that had a strange satisfaction in it as well as a certain skepticism. "But you say that you're not a watchmaker, Master Thun—merely a printer."

"There's nothing mere about printing," Jehan retorted. "Had printers not put the word of God directly into the hands of every man who can read there would have been no Lutheran armies, no Calvinist legions. Printing is changing the way that men think, believe and act—but I'm a printer without a press, and there are hundreds of clockmakers in every city in Europe eager to discover a better escapement for watches. Is that escapement the one my great-grandfather built to regulate the missing spring?"

"No—but your grandparents were mistaken about the originality of the first escapement. There was only one thing new about the fusée I discarded, and that was its material. It was brass, not iron; it did not rust, but, if it worked any better as a regulator than any other, it was by virtue of the quality of its workmanship, not the detail of its design. The one I have made is better adapted to its own mechanism; it could not regulate a watch spring any more than a pendulum could drive the hand of a watch. On the other hand, what you say is perfectly true: there are a hundred clockmakers in every city in Europe who would be eager to know what might be done with *my* mechanism, and you shall share in the profits that will accrue from the dissemination of the secret if you will help me finish my work. Once we have completed the clock, you will be better equipped than you could have hoped to spread new knowledge throughout the continent—and beyond, if you care to. The world is, as you doubtless know, a sphere, and there is always further to go in every direction than the cities we already know. There's a new world now, beyond the Atlantic Ocean, and a vast number of undiscovered islands in the far Pacific."

It did not seem remarkable to Jehan that the dwarf's comment about the world being a sphere was echoing a statement he had made the day before, in another place. "Very well, then," he said. "I shall fetch my grandfather's tools. If you will explain what needs to be done, I shall do my very best to carry out your instructions."

* * * * * * *

Jehan Thun was as good as his word, and so was the dwarf. Working to instruction, Jehan's nimble hands pieced together the last parts of the mechanism, although it was no mere matter of assembly. There was a good deal of drilling to be done, a great many threads to be worked, and an abundance of accurate filing, as well as a certain amount of casting. Fortunately, the dwarf possessed a crucible and a vice, and a good stock of charcoal with which to charge his furnace. The dwarf's own fingers were thick and gnarled, and he could never have done the delicate work that Jehan did, but he was a clever man with plans and his strong arms could certainly work a bellows hard.

Once Jehan had set to work the hours seemed to melt away. Because there was no natural light in the room where the clock was kept Jehan did the greater part of his work in a different one much higher in the château's hidden structure, but he soon became used to shuttling back and forth between the two. He worked long into the evening, conserving that fraction of his labor that did not need good light, but the dwarf was conscientious about interrupting him, not only to make meals but to explain the new mechanism he had built for the clock.

"It's a secret that no one else has discovered," the little man bragged, "although it's obvious enough. How long have there been slingshots and other devices in which solid objects swing freely at the ends of cords? At least since David slew Goliath. Children play with such devices—and yet no one has observed, as I have, the isochronism of the freely-swinging weight—or, if anyone has, he could not go on to the naturally consequent thought, which is that a pendulum might do as well as a system of weights or a mere spring to regulate the motions of a clock. Just as the descent of weights require refinement by escapements, so does the swing of a pendulum, so I devised one appropriate to it.

"I have tried out my pendulum in humbler boxes with elementary faces, but never in a clock with two hands, let alone a masterpiece like the Zacharius Machine. I could have got it working, after a fashion, but a masterpiece is a masterpiece, and it sets its own standard of perfection. I might have gone to Geneva in search of a skilled clockmaker, but how could I dare, given my appearance? Even before Calvin came, Master Zacharius was remembered by many as a sorcerer, and those who hold such opinions are always among the first converts to any new fad—including Calvin's philosophy. Of all the cities in the world, why did Andernatt have to be placed so close to Geneva? No one actually casts stones at me in Evionnaz, or any other village within hiking range, but they way they look at me informs me that it would not do to linger too long in any such place, let alone make any attempt to settle there. I was a wanderer before I came here, although I did not want to be. I am a recluse now, although that would not have been my choice before I realized how fearful people are of anything out of the ordinary. Dwarfs are not rare, you know, and they cannot all be the Devil in disguise, but men who do not travel far do not realize how many kinds of men there are."

"Noblemen employ dwarfs as clowns and jesters in France, Italy and the Germanic states," Jehan observed. "They like automata too, to strike the hours on church clocks or merely to perform mechanical acrobatics for credulous eyes."

"I am not a clown, Master Jehan," the dwarf said. "Nor am I a jester. I am the man who discovered the isochronicity of the pendulum, although I would wager that history will give the credit to a taller man—perhaps to you."

"History often makes mistakes," Jehan assured him. "Master Zacharius never received credit for the fusée, because there was a man named Jacob the Czech who worked in Prague, and Prague is a far better source of fame than poor Geneva. I do not charge this Jacob with theft, mind, for the device is obvious enough once a man's mind turns in that direction, just as your pendulum-clock might be. There may well be another man who has already made the discovery—in Florence, say, or Vienna—whose discovery has not yet been noised around. I think that luck has more to do with matters of reputation than height."

"Yet Pittonaccio was reckoned an imp," the dwarf reminded him. "Had he been as handsome as you, he might have been reckoned an artificer himself, and your great-grandfather might never have gone mad. But Pittonaccio's long dead, for men of my kind rarely live as long as men of yours."

"My father might have lived a while longer," Jehan said, somberly, "had he not been a Protestant in Paris at an unfortunate hour. Hatred is not reserved for those of strange appearance; it thrives like a weed wherever faith puts forth new flowers."

The dwarf allowed Jehan to have the last word on that occasion, perhaps because he did not want to offend his guest in advance of the clock becoming workable. On that score, he did not have much longer to wait, for Jehan still felt that he was more automaton than man, and the work that he did allowed him to conserve that placid state of mind, absorbing him completely into matters of technical detail. The hours sped by, and the days too—six in all—until he arrived at the time when the last piece of the puzzle was correctly-shaped, and ready to be fitted.

When he had set it in place, Jehan Thun stepped back, and looked at what he had done.

It did not seem, now that he had finished, that it was his work. He was a printer, after all, not a locksmith or a clockmaker. He had *played* at being a locksmith and a clockmaker when he was a child, using the very same tools that had served him so well now, but it had always been play rather than work. Clock-making had never been his vocation, even though circumstance seemed to have turned him into something more like clockwork than flesh, at least for a while.

He watched the dwarf set the hands of the clock.

He watched the pendulum swing back and forth, with a regularity that was quite astonishing, in spite of its utter obviousness.

"If only the world were like that," he murmured.

"It shall be," the dwarf assured him. "We have the example now, far better than any commandments from on high."

As he spoke, the clock's faster moving hand reached the vertical, and the clock began to chime.

Even though he had watched the dwarf set the clock's hands, Jehan had not bothered to wonder whether the time that was being set was correct, or take any particular notice of what it was.

The clock chimed seven times, and with a barely-perceptible click the blank face of the copper plate was replaced by a plaque bearing words. They were not inscribed in red but in black, the letters having been engraved with loving care by a patient short-fingered hand.

TIME, said the legend, IS THE GREAT HEALER.

Jehan let out his breath, having been unaware of the fact that he was holding it. His grandmother could hardly have objected to such an innocent adage. There was little enough piety about it, but there was certainly no diabolism.

Jehan became aware then that the clock was ticking as the pendulum swung back and forth, almost as if the machine had a beating heart. He was not afraid, however, that he had surrendered his soul to the mechanism while he worked to complete it. If he had lost that, he had left it somewhere in Paris, smeared on the bloodstained cobbles.

"It's a masterpiece all right," the dwarf stated, his tone indicating that he was only half-satisfied, as yet. "All that remains is to see how well it keeps time. I can compare it against my watch, for now, but in order to prove that it can do far better I'll need to calibrate it against the movements of the zodiac stars."

"A pity, then, that you rebuilt the facade in a room that has no window," Jehan observed.

"I can measure brief intervals accurately enough," the dwarf assured him. The question is how well the clock will measure days and weeks. Even so, the more rapidly information can be conveyed between the clock and the observation-window, the better my estimates will be. You may help me with this too, if you wish. I hope you will—but if you would like to leave, to carry the secret of the pendulum to the cities of the world, you may go with my blessing."

"I'm in no hurry," Jehan assured him, "and I'm as interested as you are to see how accurately your clock keeps time."

* * * * * * *

What he had said was true; Jehan Thun was momentarily glad to have the prospect of further work to do—even work that could not possibly absorb his mind as the intricate labor of delicate construction. Any hope that it might permit him to extend the quasi-mechanical phase of his own existence was quickly dashed, however. Indeed, the work of attempting to calibrate the clock against the movements of the stars was worse than having nothing to do at all, for it involved a great deal of patient waiting, which made the time weigh heavily upon his mind. Waiting called forth daydreams, memories and questions, as well as the horrors of Saint Bartholomew's Eve and its hideous aftermath.

For weeks before his arrival in Andernatt Jehan had been walking, not with any rhythmic regularity but at least with grim determination, never laying himself down to sleep until exhaustion had robbed him of any prospect of remembering his nightmares. For days after his arrival at the château he had been able to focus his attention on demanding tasks, which had likewise been devoid of any kind of rhythmic regularity, but had nevertheless supplied him more than adequately with opportunities for grim determination. Now that the clock was finished, though, he could not use the time it mapped in any such vampiric fashion. Its demands were different now, not suppressing thought but nourishing and demanding it, forcing him to fill the darkness of his own consciousness with something more than blind effort.

At first, there was a certain fascination in scurrying back and forth between the dwarf's observatory and the room where the clock was entombed, to check the position of the hands against the position of the stars. Perhaps—just perhaps—there might have been enough activity in that to keep dark meditation at bay, if only the sky had remained clear. But this was a mountainous region where the air was turbulent, and the sky was often full of cloud. It was not always possible for the dwarf to make the observations he needed to make, and although the dwarf was philosophical about such difficulties, they preyed on Jehan Thun's mind, teasing and taunting him.

There was also a certain interest, for a while, in discovering what was inscribed on the other plaques, which had been hidden from Jehan while he worked on the completion of the clock by their housing. He did not see them all within the first twelve hours of the clock's operation, nor even the second, but it only required two days for him to see each of them at least once, and thus to reconstruct their order in his mind.

One o'clock brought forth the legend CARPE DIEM.

Two o'clock supplied TIME TEACHES ALL THINGS.

Three o'clock suggested that TIME OVERTAKES ALL THINGS.

Four o'clock claimed that THERE IS TIME ENOUGH FOR EVERYTHING.

Five o'clock observed that TEMPUS FUGIT.

Six o'clock warned that OUR COSTLIEST EXPENDITURE IS TIME.

Eight o'clock advised that THERE IS A TIME FOR EVERY PURPOSE.

Nine o'clock pointed out that FUTURE TIME IS ALL THERE IS.

Ten o'clock stated that EVERYTHING CHANGES WITH TIME.

Eleven o'clock was marked by TIME MUST BE SPENT.

Midnight and noon alike, perhaps reflecting increasing desperation in the expansion of the homiletic theme insisted that TIME NEVER WAITS.

All in all, Jehan Thun concluded, while there was nothing among the legends to which a good man could object, there was also nothing as adventurous or imaginative as the blasphemies that his grandmother had seen...or imagined that she had seen.

He had not thought before to question the dwarf as to what he had read before discarding the allegedly-blasphemous ones, but now he did. "Was there really one that said: *Whoever shall try to make himself the equal of God shall be damned for all eternity?*" Jehan asked his host, while they were gathering apples in the orchard one day.

"I can't remember the exact wording," the dwarf told him, "but I think not. The sayings were pithier than that, and more enigmatic. Do you not approve of mine? I'm a clockmaker after all—or would be, if I had not been cursed with the body and hands of a clumsy clown. A clock ought to symbolize time, do you not agree? Common time, that is, not the grand and immeasurable reach of eternity."

"Even common time reflects the time of the heavens," Jehan observed. "The movements of Creation spell out the day and the year, with all their strange eccentricities."

"The stars are mere backcloth," the dwarf informed him, as he moved off up the slope with his basket half-full. "The earth's rotation on its own axis specifies the day, and its rotation about the sun defines the year. The eccentricity of the seasons is a matter of the inclination of its axis."

"So says Copernicus," Jehan agreed, "but how shall we ever be sure?"

"We shall be sure," the dwarf told him, "When we have better clocks, more cleverly employed. Calculation will tell us which of the two systems makes better sense of all that we see. Better mechanisms will give us more accurate calculations, and more accurate calculations will enable us to make even better mechanisms."

"And so *ad infinitum*?" Jehan suggested.

"I doubt that perfection is quite so far away," said the dwarf, smiling as he set his basket down by the door. "And I doubt that mere humans will ever attain to perfection, even in calculation—but there's scope yet for further improvement. The milking-goat is tethered on the far side, where the grazing is better. Will you come with me to soothe her?"

Jehan agreed readily enough, and they went around the ruins together, to the side which looked out towards Evionnaz. They saw the platoon of soldiers as soon as they turned the corner, for the approaching men were no more than a thousand paces away. The men—a dozen in all—were heading directly for the château.

"That's Genevan livery," the dwarf said bleakly. "Not that a party of men carrying half-pikes would be a more reassuring sight if their colors were Savoyard or Bernese."

"Their presence may have nothing at all to do with the château, let alone the clock," Jehan said, although he could not believe it. He knew, as he watched the armed men coming on, that he had spoken his name too often during his brief sojourn in the city, He had stirred up old rumors and old memories that had been too shallowly buried, even after all this time. Someone had begun asking questions, and exercising an overheated imagination. The dwarf's presence here might not be widely known, but the little man had been to Evionnaz and other villages in the vicinity; the suspicion that he had been joined at Andernatt by Aubert Thun's grandson had been the kind of seed that could grow into strange anxieties.

"They're soldiers," the dwarf said, "not churchmen. They have lived with clocks all their lives. They cannot be so very fearful." But he too sounded like a man who could not believe what he was saying. He had been a wanderer before settling here; he knew what fears were abroad in a world torn apart by wars of religion. He knew, probably better than any man of common stature ever could, how often people spoke of witchcraft and the devil's work, and what fear there was in their voices when they did so. He knew that Geneva was a city under permanent siege, where all kinds of anxiety seethed and bubbled, ever-ready to overflow.

"We should run and hide," Jehan said. "They will not stay long, whatever they do while they are here."

"No," said the dwarf. "I shall receive them as a polite host, and speak to them calmly. I shall persuade them, if I can, that there is nothing here to be feared. What manner of man, do you think, is the one who bears no arms and who seems to be guiding them?"

Jehan shaded his eyes against the sunlight and squinted. The dwarf was presumably afraid that the man walking with the captain at the head of the column might be a churchman, but he was not. "I know him," Jehan said. "He's a colporteur by the name of Nicholas Alther. Our paths crossed on the far side of Evionnaz, and he guessed where I was bound. He told me he'd seen the ruins of the château on the horizon. That may be why they brought him as a guide—but he didn't seem to me to be a fearful or a hateful man."

This judgment proved not unsound, for as the party came closer Jehan was able to read in Nicholas Alther's face that he was certainly not the leader of the expedition, and that he would far rather be somewhere else, about his own business.

"I know him too," murmured the dwarf. "I've seen him in Evionnaz, and bargained with him for needles and thread—and metal-working tools, alas." Raising his voice, the little man added: "Ho, Master Alther! Welcome to my home. Where's your pack?"

Alther did not reply, but thumped his chest to imply that he was out of breath in order to excuse his rudeness. It was the captain who spoke, saying: "This is not your home; the land belongs to the city of Geneva, and the ruins too. You have no right here."

"I am doing no harm, captain," the dwarf replied. "I make no claim upon the land or the house; I merely took shelter here when I was in need."

"Is your name Pittonaccio?" the captain demanded.

"No," said the dwarf. "It's Friedrich Spurzheim—and Spurzheim is a good Swiss family name, worn by many a man in Geneva and even more in Bern. I'm a Christian, as you are, and I have my own Bible."

It was the first time that Jehan had ever heard the dwarf's surname—and he realized, as he heard the little man's forename spoken for the second time, that he had never addressed him by it, or even thought of doing so, since he had first heard it pronounced. He had always thought of his host as "the dwarf."

The captain did not repeat the name either. "Where is the Devil's clock?" he demanded.

"I doubt that the Devil possesses a clock, or needs one," Friedrich retorted, boldly. "If he does, he certainly does not keep it here. The only clock here is mine."

Jehan was not in the least displeased to be offered no credit for he restored Clock of Andernatt. He had seen the expression on the captain's face before. There had been soldiers abroad on Saint Bartholomew's Eve and the day that followed; there were always soldiers abroad when there was killing to be done, for that was their trade.

Jehan felt fingers plucking at his sleeve, and allowed himself to be drawn aside by Nicholas Alther.

"It was not I who betrayed you," the colporteur whispered, fearfully. "They do not know that I met you on the road. For the love of God, don't tell them. I could not refuse to lead them here, for they knew that I knew the way, but I mean you no harm. Say nothing, and they'll let you alone—but you must say nothing, else we'll both be damned." He stopped when he saw that the captain was looking at him, and raised his voice to say: "This man only took shelter in the château—he has nothing to do with the clock."

The captain immediately fixed his stare on Jehan's face. "Are you Jehan Thun?" he demanded.

"I am," Jehan replied, knowing that it would do no good to lie.

"What business have you here?"

"I was a Protestant in Paris, until it became impossible to be a Protestant in Paris," Jehan said, flatly. "My father was born in Geneva, which is a Protestant city, so that was where I came—but everywhere I went in the city, people who heard my name looked strangely at me, and I was afraid all over again. My grandmother had spoken of a village named Evionnaz as a remote and peaceful place, so I decided to go there, but when I arrived I found the same dark stares, so I continued on my way. Friedrich Spurzheim is the first man I have met hereabouts who did not look at me that way, and he made me welcome as a guest."

"Are you a clockmaker?" the captain asked.

"No," Jehan said. "I'm a printer. I made Bibles in Paris. My father was murdered, my press smashed and my home burned."

"Have you seen the Devil's clock?"

For the first time, Jehan hesitated. Then he said; "There is only one clock in the château. It is shaped to resemble a church. There is nothing devilish about it."

"Lead us to it," the captain instructed.

Jehan exchanged a glance with Friedrich; the little man risked a brief nod of consent. Jehan led the way around the château, through the garden ad in through the door on whose step the basket of apples still lay. Then he led the captain and his men to the Clock of Andernatt.

It was an hour after noon; while the soldier was studying the clock, the hour struck and the words CARPE DIEM appeared, as if by magic, in the space beneath the rose window.

"What does that say?" demanded the captain of Nicholas Alther, his voice screeching horribly.

"I don't know!" the colporteur replied.

"It says *Carpe Diem*," Friedrich told them. "It's Latin. It means *Seize the Day*. The other mottoes...."

But it did not matter what the other mottoes were, any more than it mattered what *carpe diem* actually signified. It would have made no difference had the motto been in French or German rather than Latin, or whether it had been a quotation from the Sermon on the Mount.

Much later, Jehan guessed, the captain and all of his men would be willing to swear, and perhaps also to believe, that the mysterious legend that had appeared as if by magic had said HAIL TO THEE, LORD SATAN or DAMNATION TO ALL CALVINISTS or CURSED BE THE NAME OF GENEVA, or anything else that their fearful brains might conjure up. They would also be willing to swear, and perhaps also to believe, that when they attacked the clock with half-pikes and maces, sulfurous fumes belched out of its mysterious bowels, and that the screams of the damned could be heard, echoing all the way from the inferno. They would probably remember, too, that the château itself had been buried underground, extending its corridors deep into the rock like shafts of some strange mine, connected to the very centre of the spherical earth.

When they had finished smashing the clock the soldiers smashed everything else Friedrich Spurzheim had owned, and cast everything combustible—including his printed Bible—into the flames of his fire. They killed his milking-goat, and as many of the others as they could catch. They ripped up all the vegetables in his garden and stripped the remaining apples from his trees. Then they smashed the shutters that remained on some few of the château's windows, and the doors that remained in some few of its rooms. But they did not kill the dwarf, nor did they kill Jehan Thun. They worked out all their ire and fear on inanimate objects, and contented themselves with issuing dire warnings as to what would happen if Friedrich Spurzheim or Jehan Thun were ever seen again within twenty leagues of Geneva.

Afterwards, when the captain and his men were preoccupied with the items they had kept as plunder-which included, of course, the silver disc that had served as a pendulum bob—Nicholas Alther took Jehan aside again, and offered him something wrapped in silk. Jehan did not need to unwrap it to guess that it was the colporteur's watch.

"Your grandfather made it," the colporteur said. "You should have it, since you do not have one of your own. It keeps good time."

"Thank you," Jehan said, "but it isn't necessary. You owe me no debt."

"I didn't betray you," Nicholas Alther insisted. "I didn't want this to happen."

"I know that," Jehan assured him, although there was no way that he could.

"I won't repeat the tale," the colporteur went on, in the same bitter tone. "If this becomes the stuff of legend, it shall not be my doing. There will come a day when all this is forgotten—when time will pass unmolested, measured out with patience by machines that no man will have cause to fear."

"I know that, too," Jehan assured him, although there was no way that he could.

When the soldiers had gone, Jehan went back to the clock's tomb. Friedrich was waiting for him there.

"One day," Jehan said, "you will build another. In another city, far from here, we shall start again, you and I. You will build another clock, and I shall be your apprentice. We shall spread the secret throughout the world—all the world. If they will not entertain us in Europe, we'll go to the New World, and if they are madly fearful of the devil there, we'll go to the undiscovered islands of the Pacific. The world is a spinning sphere, and time is everywhere. Wherever men go, clocks are the key to the measurement of longitude, and hence to accurate navigation. What a greeting we'll have in the far-flung islands of the ocean vast!"

The little man had been picking through the wreckage for some time, and his clumsy hands had been busy with such work as they could do. He had detached half a dozen of the plaques from the wheel that was no longer sealed in its housing. Now he laid them out, and separated them into two groups of three. TIME OVERTAKES ALL THINGS, TEMPUS FUGIT and TIME NEVER WAITS he kept for himself; THERE IS TIME ENOUGH FOR EVERYTHING, THERE IS A TIME FOR EVERY PURPOSE and FUTURE TIME IS ALL THERE IS he offered to Jehan. "I'd give you the pendulum itself," Friedrich said, "but they stole it for the metal, and the escapement too. It doesn't matter. You know how it works. You can build another."

"So can you," Jehan pointed out.

"I could," Friedrich agreed, "if I could find another home, another workplace. The world is vast, but there's no such place in any city I know, and wherever there are men there's fear of the extraordinary. It's yours now; you're heir to Master Zacharius, and to me. You have the stature and the strength, as well as the delicate hands. The secret is yours, to do with as you will. The world will change regardless, so you might as well play your part."

"Wherever we go, we'll go together, Friedrich," Jehan told him. "Whatever we do, we'll do together, even if we're damned to Hell or oblivion."

And he was as good as his word—but whether they were damned to Hell or oblivion we cannot tell, for theirs is a different world than ours, unimprisoned by our history; all things are possible there that were possible here, and many more.

AUTHOR'S NOTE

Jules Verne is rather vague about the exact time-period in which the events of "Master Zacharius" take place and exactly what kind of escapement mechanism the Genevan clockmaker is supposed to have invented. So far as history is concerned, though, small spring-driven clocks and watches were reputedly invented by Peter Henlein *circa* 1500; given that "Master Zacharius" takes place before Calvin's reformation of Geneva, that implies a date somewhere in the first two decades of the sixteenth century. Verge escapements, consisting of crossbars with regulating weights mounted on vertical spindles, had been in use in weight-driven clocks for some time by then, so the escapement credited by Verne to Zacharius must have been either a stackfreed (a kind of auxiliary spring) or a fusée—a conical grooved pulley connected to a barrel round the mainspring.

The latter invention is usually credited to Jacob the Czech *circa* 1515; I have assumed that to be the device Verne might have had in mind, but I have also credited Zacharius with manufacturing a fusée in brass, although history has no record of that being done before 1580. The discovery of the isochronicity of the pendulum is, of course, credited by our records to Galileo in the early seventeenth century; pendulum clocks first appeared in our world *circa* 1650 and were first equipped with recoil escapements ten years thereafter, some eighty-seven years later than the device credited to Friedrich Spurzheim in the story.

"Master Zacharius" was one of the earliest stories Verne wrote, and embodies ideas that he subsequently set firmly aside; this sequel is, I think, far more Vernian in the best sense of the word.

THE IMMORTALS OF ATLANTIS

Sheila never answered the door when the bell rang because there was never anyone there that she wanted to see, and often someone there that she was desperate to avoid. The latter category ranged from debt collectors and the police to Darren's friends, who were all apprentice drug-dealers, and Tracy's friends, who were mostly veteran statutory rapists. Not everyone took no for an answer, of course; the fact that debt-collectors and policemen weren't really entitled to kick the door in didn't seem to be much of a disincentive. It was, however, very unusual for anyone to use subtler means of entry, so Sheila was really quite surprised when the white-haired man appeared in her sitting-room without being preceded by the slightest sound of splintering wood.

"I did ring," he said, laboring the obvious, "but you didn't answer."

"Perhaps," she said, not getting up from her armchair or reaching for the remote, "that was because I didn't want to let you in."

Even though she hadn't even reached for the remote, the TV switched itself off. It wasn't a matter of spontaneously flipping into stand-by mode, as it sometimes did, but of switching itself *off*. It was eleven o'clock in the morning, so she hadn't so much been watching it as using it to keep her company in the absence of anything better, but the interruption seemed a trifle rude all the same.

"Did you do that?" she asked.

"Yes," he said. "We need to talk."

The phrase made her wonder if he might be one of her ex-boyfriends, most of whom she could hardly remember because their acquaintance has been so brief, but he certainly didn't look like one. He was wearing a suit and tie. The suit looked sufficiently old-fashioned and worn to have come from the bargain end of an Oxfam rail, but it was still a suit. He was also way too old—sixty if he was a day—and way too thin, with hardly an ounce of spare flesh on him. The fact that he was so tall made him look almost skeletal.

Sheila would have found it easier to believe in him if he'd been wearing a hooded cloak and carrying a scythe. He was carrying a huge briefcase—so huge that it as a miracle he'd been able to cross the estate without being mugged.

"What do you want?" Sheila asked, bluntly.

"You aren't who you think you are, Sheila," was his reply to that—which immediately made her think "religious nut." The Mormons and Jehovah's Witnesses had stopped coming to the estate years ago, because there were far easier places in the world to do missionary work—Somalia, for instance, or the parts of Afghanistan where the Taliban still ruled supreme—but it wasn't inconceivable that there were people in the world who could still believe that God's protection even extended to places like this.

"Everybody around here is who they think they are," she told him. "Nobody has any illusions about being anybody. This is the end of the world, and I'm not talking Rapture."

"I knew this wasn't going to be easy," the tall man said. "There's no point wasting time. I'm truly sorry to have to do this, but it really is for the best." He put his suitcase down, pounced on her, dragged her to her feet and bound her hands behind her back with a piece of slender but incredibly strong cord.

She screamed as loudly as she could, but she knew that no one was going to take any notice. He must have known that too, because he didn't try to stop her immediately. He selected the sturdiest of her three dining-chairs, set it in the middle of the room and started tying her ankles to the legs of the chair.

"My boyfriend will be home any minute," Sheila said. "He's a bouncer. He'll break you into little pieces."

"You don't have a boyfriend, Shelia," the white-haired man informed her. "You've never had a relationship that lasted longer than a fortnight. You've always claimed that it's because all men are bastards, but you've always suspected that it might be you—and you're right. You really do put them off and drive them away, no matter how hard you try not to."

Sheila was trussed up tightly by now, with more cord passed around her body, holding her tight to the back of the chair. The way she was positioned made it extremely unlikely that he intended to rape her, but that wasn't at all reassuring. Rape she understood; rape she could cope with, and survive.

"I do have a son," she told him. "He may not be as big as you but he's in a gang, and he's vicious. He carries a knife. He might even have graduated to a gun by now—and if he hasn't, some of his mates certainly have."

"All true," the white-haired man conceded, readily enough, "but it leaves out of account the fact that Darren hardly ever comes home any more, because he finds you as uncomfortable to be with as all the other men who've briefly passed through your wretched life. To put it brutally, you disgust him."

"Tracy loves me," Sheila retorted, feeling far greater pressure to make that point than to ask the man with the briefcase how he knew Darren's name.

The briefcase was open now, and the tall man was pulling things out at a rate of knots: weird things, like the apparatus of a chemistry set. There were bottles and jars, flasks and tripods, even a mortar and pestle. There was also something that looked like a glorified butane cigarette lighter, whose flame ignited at a touch, and became more intense in response to another.

"That's true too," her remorseless tormentor went on. "There's a lot of love in Tracy, just as there was always a lot of love in you, always yearning for more and better outlets. She can't hang on to relationships either, can she? She hasn't give up hope yet, though. Darren wouldn't be any use, because the mitochondrial supplement atrophies in males long before they reach puberty, but I could have gone to Tracy instead of you, and would probably have found her more cooperative. It wouldn't have been sporting, though. She's still a child, and you're entitled to your chance. It wouldn't be fair simply to pass you over. Her life will change irrevocably too, once you're fully awake. So will Darren's, although he probably won't be quite as grateful."

That was too much. "What the fuck are you talking about, you stupid fuck?" Sheila demanded, although she knew that he would see that she was cracking up, that he had succeeded in freaking her out with his psychopathic performance.

"My name—my true name, not the one on my driving license— is Sarmerodach," the tall man said. "This body used to belong to an oceanographer named Arthur Bayliss, Ph.D., but I was able to rescue him from an unbelievably dull life wallowing in clathrate-laden ooze. The predatory DNA crystallized in my viral avatar dispossessed his native DNA, little by little, in every single cell in his body, and then set about resculpting the neuronal connections in his brain. The headaches were terrible. I wish I could say that you won't have to suffer anything similar, but you will—not for nearly as long, but even more intensely. I wish it were as simple as feeding you a dose of virus-impregnated ooze, but it isn't. Your predatory DNA is already latent in your cells, secreted in mitochondrial supplements, awaiting activation. The activation process is complex, but not very difficult if you have the right raw materials. I have—although it wasn't easy to locate them all. It will take an hour to trigger the process, and six months thereafter to complete the transition."

Sheila had hardly understood a word of the detail, but she thought she had got the gist of the plan. "Transition to what?" she asked, thinking of the Incredible Hulk and Mr. Hyde.

"Oh, don't worry," he said. "You'll still look human. Your hair will turn white overnight, but you'll be able to watch the flab and the cellulite melt away. You won't look like a supermodel, but you will live for thousands of years. In a sense, given that the *real* you is locked away in your mitochondrial supplements, you already have. Your other self is one of the Immortals of Atlantis."

Sheila had always felt that she was fully capable of dealing with psychopaths—she knew so many—but she knew from bitter experience that negotiating with delusional schizophrenics was a different kettle of fish. She started screaming again, just as loudly and even more desperately than before.

In all probability, she thought, there would be at least a dozen people in the neighboring flats who could hear her. The chances of one of them responding, in any way whatsoever, were pretty remote—screaming passed for normal behavior in these parts—but it might be her last hope.

Arthur Bayliss, Ph.D., alias Sarmerodach, obviously thought so too, because he crammed a handkerchief into her open mouth and then used more of his ubiquitous cord to make a gag holding it in place.

Then he got busy with his chemistry set.

* * * * * * *

Sheila had no idea what the ingredients were that her captor was mixing up in his flasks, but she wouldn't have been at all surprised if she'd been told that they included virgin's blood, adder's venom and the hallucinogenic slime that American cane toads were rumored to secrete. There were certainly toadstool caps, aromatic roots and perfumed flowers among the things he was grinding up in the mortar, and Sheila was prepared to assume that every one of them was as poisonous as deadly nightshade and as dangerous to mental health as the most magical magic mushrooms in the world.

The tall man talked while he worked. "I'd far rather observe the principle of informed consent," he said, "even though I'm not really a PhD any more, let alone a physician, but it's not really practical in the circumstances. Your false self would be bound to refuse to realize your true self, no matter how worthless a person you presently are or how wretched a life you presently lead, because selves are, by definition, selfish."

He paused to deploy a spatula, measuring out a dose of red powder. He tipped it into the flask whose contents were presently seething away over the burner. He didn't use scales, but the measurement was obviously delicate.

"If caterpillars had the choice," he continued, "they'd never consent to turn into butterflies. Some kinds of larvae don't have to, you know—it's called paedogenesis. Instead of pupating and re-emerging as adults they can grow sex organs and breed as juveniles, sometimes for several generations. They still transmit the genes their descendants will eventually need to effect metamorphosis, though, in response to the appropriate environmental trigger, so that those descendants, however remote, can eventually recover their true nature, their true glory and their true destiny."

He paused again, this time to dribble a few drops of liquid out of the mortar, where he'd crushed a mixture of plant tissues, into a second flask that had not yet been heated at all.

"That's what the Immortals of Atlantis did," he went on, "when they realized that they were about to lose all their cultural wealth when their homeland disappeared beneath the sea. They knew that the next generation, and many generations thereafter, would have to revert to the cultural level of Stone Age barbarians and take thousands to years to achieve a tolerable level of civilization, but they wanted to give them the chance to become something better, when circumstances became ripe again. So the Immortals hid themselves away, the best way they could. The Atlantean elite were great bio-technologists, you see; they considered our kind of heavy-metal technology to be inexpressibly vulgar, fit only for the toilsome use of slaves."

This time he stopped to make a careful inspection of some kind of paste he'd been blending, lifting a spoonful to within a couple of inches of his pale grey eyes. He didn't have a microscope either.

"What would our elite do, do you think," he resumed, "if the Antarctic ice melted and the sea swamped their cities, and the methane gushing out of the suboceanic clathrates mopped up all the oxygen and rendered the air unbreathable? I think they'd retreat underground, burrowing deep down and going into cultural hibernation for a thousand or a hundred thousand years, until the ever-loyal plants had restored the breathability of the atmosphere again. But that's not going to happen, because you and I—and the other Immortals, when we've located and restored a sufficient number—are going to see that it doesn't. We'll have the knowledge, once you're fully awake, and we'll have the authority. The only way the world can be saved is for everyone to work together and do what's necessary, and that isn't going to happen unless someone takes control and reinstitutes a sensible system of slavery. The Immortals will be able to do that, one we've resurrected enough of them. This is just the beginning."

He took one flask off the burner and replaced it with another; the pause in his monologue was hardly perceptible.

"As you might be able to see," he said, gesturing expansively to take in all the different compounds he was making up, "the process of revitalization has five stages—that's five different drugs, all of them freshly-prepared to very specific recipes, administered in swift sequence. Don't worry—it doesn't involve any injections, or even swallowing anything with a nasty taste. All you have to do is breathe them in. It's even simpler than smoking crack. I know it looks complicated, and it could all go wrong if I made the slightest mistake in the preparation or administration, but you have to trust me. Dr. Bayliss has never done anything like this before, but Sarmerodach has. He hasn't lost the knack, even though he's spent the last few thousand years lying dormant in the suboceanic ooze encoded as a crystalline supervirus. Everything's just about ready. You mustn't be afraid, Sheila, you really...."

He stopped abruptly as the doorbell rang. For a second or two he seemed seriously disconcerted—but then he relaxed again, He knew her children's names, and more about her than anyone had any right to know, He knew that she never answered the doorbell.

For the first time in her life, Shelia yearned to hear the sound of someone kicking the door in, splintering the wood around the lock and the bolts.

Instead, she heard several sets of shuffling footsteps moving away from the flat. If she'd screamed *then* it might just have made a difference, but she couldn't.

"Good," said the man with the Ph.D. "We can get on with the job in peace."

* * * * * * *

The first drug, which the tall man administered simply by holding a loaded spoon beneath her nostrils, made Sheila feel nauseous. It wasn't that it stank—its odor was delicately sweet, like the scent of sugared porridge heating up in the microwave—but that it disturbed her internal equilibrium in a fashion she'd never experienced before.

The second, which he administered by pouring warm liquid on to cotton wool and holding it in the same position, disturbed her even more profoundly. At first, it just tickled—except that she'd never been tickled *inside* before, in her lungs and liver and intestines instead of her skin. Then the tickling turned into prickling, and it felt as if a thorn-bush were growing inside her, jabbing its spines into every last corner of her soft red flesh. She hadn't known that it was possible to endure such agony without being rendered unconscious by shock and terror.

"Just be patient," he said, infuriatingly. "It will pass. Your cells are coming back to life, Sheila. They've been half-dead for so long—much longer than your own meager lifetime. A metazoan body is just a single cell's way of making more single cells, you see; sex and death are just means of shuffling the genetic deck, so that cells are capable of evolution. All metazoan cells are partly shut down—they have to be, to specialize them for specific physiological functions—but they can all be reawakened, wholly or partially, by the right stimulus."

The pain abated, but not because her captor's voice had soothed it away. It abated because the second drug had now completed its work, having been scrupulously ferried to every hinterland of her being by her dutiful bloodstream. It had taken time, but that phase was finished.

Sheila felt better, and not just in the way she usually felt better after feeling ill or depressed, which was only a kind of dull relief, like that obtainable by such proverbial means as ceasing to bang one's head against a brick wall. She actually felt *better*, in a positive sense. It was a very strange sensation, by virtue of its unfamiliarity—but there were still three drugs to go.

The ex-Ph.D. had been measuring her condition with his uncannily skilful eyes. He had to get the timing right, but he was as adept at that as he had been at the mixing and the cooking. He had the third compound ready, and he lifted the whole flask up and swirling its contents around to make the vapor rise up from its neck.

This time, the effect was narcotic, or at least anesthetic. Sheila felt that she was falling asleep, but she didn't lose consciousness, and she didn't begin to dream. It was a little like getting high, albeit more in the crystal meth vein than a heroin kick, but it was quite distinct. For one thing, it didn't seem that she was only feeling it in her head, or in her nerves. It seemed that she was feeling it in every organic fiber of her being, and then some. It made her feel much bigger than she was, and much more powerful—but not, alas, powerful enough to break the bonds that held her tight to the chair. Its anesthetic effect wasn't dulling, or straightforwardly euphoric, but something that promised to take her far beyond the reach of pain.

It was, alas, flattering only to deceive. It hadn't taken her beyond the reach of pain at all, but merely to some existential plane where pain came in different, previously-unknown forms. The fourth drug—the first one whose vapor was hot enough to scald the mucous membranes of her nasal passages and bronchi—was a *real* bastard. It gave her the migraine to end all migraines, visual distortions and all; it plunged a millions daggers into her flesh; it sent waves of agony rippling through her like sound-waves, as if she were imprisoned in a gigantic church bell smashed by a sequence of steel hammers—but the vibrations were silent, even though she hadn't gone deaf.

She could still hear Sarmerodach rambling on, and make out every word in spite of her excruciation.

"You'll begin to feel more yourself soon," he said. "You'll begin to feel Sheila slipping away, like the husk of a redundant cocoon. You'll be able to sense your true being and personality—not well enough for a while to put a name to yourself, but well enough to know that you exist. You'll be able to catch glimpses of the possibilities inherent within you—not just the power but the aesthetic sensibility, the awareness of the physiological transactions of hormones and enzymes, the ecstasy of the mitochondria and the triumph of the phagocytes. The agony is just a kind of birth-trauma, a necessary shock. As it fades, you'll begin to sense what you truly are, and what you might eventually...."

The last word of the sentence died on his thin lips as the doorbell sounded again. This time, the repeated ring was swiftly followed by the sound of fists pounding on the door. No one shouted "Police!" though—what they shouted instead was: "Darren! We know you're in there!"

The boys at the door didn't have Sarmerodach's uncanny powers of intuition. What they thought they "knew" was utterly false. Wherever Darren as hiding, it wasn't at home.

As the white-haired man reached for his spoon again, with a hand that had begun, ever so slightly, to tremble. The sound of thumping fists was replaced by the sound of thudding boots. The door had far too little strength left in it to resist for long. It splintered, and crashed against the hallway wall.

Sarmerodach was already holding the spoon up to Sheila's nose. Wisps of vapor were already curling up into her nostrils. She could already sense its exotic odor—which she normally wouldn't have liked at all, but which somehow seemed, at this particular moment, to be the most wonderful scent she'd ever encountered.

Time seemed to slow down. The sitting-room door burst open in slow motion, and the boys stumbled through it in a bizarrely balletic fashion, floating with impossible grace as they got in one another's way. Only one of them had a gun, but the other three had knives, and all four were ready for action.

There was something irredeemably comical about the way they stopped short as they caught sight of the scene unfolding before their eyes. Their jaws dropped; their eyes seemed actually to bulge.

Under normal circumstances, of course, they'd have threatened Sheila with their weapons. They'd have threatened to hit her, and then they would probably have slashed her face, not because she was being uncooperative in refusing to tell them where Darren was, but simply because they were pumped up and incapable of containing their violence. They might even have raped her, and told themselves afterwards that they were "teaching Darren a lesson"—but when they saw her tied up and helpless, apparently being threatened by *a man in a suit*, if only with a spoon, a different set of reflexes kicked in. Suddenly, Sheila was one of their own at the mercy of a feral bureaucrat.

Somehow, the tall man had crossed the estate with his briefcase without attracting sufficient attention to be mugged, but he wasn't inconspicuous any more.

The members of the pack hurled themselves upon the outsider. At first, they probably only intended to kick the shit out of him—but three of them were wielding knives. The one with the gun never fired it; he, at least, still had a vestige of self-restraint. The others were not so intimidated by the talismanic power of their own armaments.

The killing would probably would have qualified as manslaughter rather than murder, even if it hadn't seemed to its perpetrators to be a clear case of justifiable homicide; not one of the boys was capable of formulating an intention to kill within the very limited time at their disposal. Even so, the tall man was dead within a matter of seconds—down and out in ten, at the most, and well on his way to exsanguination after forty, by which time his heart had presumably stopped and his brain was no longer getting sufficient oxygen to function.

The spoon flew from his hand and disappeared from view, taking its cargo of aromatic pulp with it.

Sheila had been saved, in the proverbial nick of time. If the spoon had been held in place for ten seconds more....

* * * * * * *

Sheila really had been saved, and she knew it. If she had breathed in the prescribed dose of the fifth perfume, she would have ceased to be herself and would have begun an inexorable process of becoming someone else.

She never believed, even momentarily, that she would actually have become one of the Immortals of Atlantis, ready to take command of her faithful slave and restore her sisters to life, in order that they could take over the world and save humankind from self-destruction by means of benevolent dictatorship. She wasn't *that* mad...but she knew that, however crazy or deluded Sarmerodach had been, he had been dead right about one thing. She wasn't really the person she thought she was, and never had been. There really as a flab-free, cellulite-free, thinking individual lurking somewhere inside her, in the secret potentialities of her cellular make-up—a person who might have been able to get out, if only four pathetic rivals of Darren's equally-pathetic gang hadn't decided that it was his turn to be taken out in their lame and stupid drug-war.

Sheila had no idea who that latent person might have been. She certainly couldn't put a name to her. One thing she did know, though, without a shadow of lingering doubt, was that all that hideous pain would somehow have been worthwhile, if only she'd been able to complete the ritual.

It *was* a ritual, she decided, even though it really was some kind of occult science, and not mere magic at all. It was an initiation ceremony: a symbolic process of existential transition, like marriage or graduation, but a million times better and more accurate.

Whether she had turned out to be one of the Immortals of Atlantis or not, Sheila knew, she would have become *somebody*. She would have become a butterfly-person instead or a caterpillar-person—or maybe, even better, a dragonfly-person or someone equipped with a deadly sting. She had not seen anything distinctly when she had sucked those first few wisps of vapor number five avidly into her aching lungs, but she had felt such a yearning for sight as she had never conceived before, or ever thought conceivable—and still did.

But she had lost the opportunity, probably forever.

The police came, and she told them what had happened, naming no names. For once, though, when the police had rounded up the usual suspects, the boys also condescended to tell the police, proudly, exactly what had what had happened. All the stories matched—which made the police furious, because they really wanted to put the boys away for something meaty, and knew full well that even a charge of possessing illegal weapons wouldn't stick, in the circumstances. They would have liked to have put Sheila away too—for perverting the course of justice, if nothing else—but they knew that they wouldn't be able to make that stick either, even though the victim had once been a respectable oceanographer before he had flipped his lid and gone utterly gaga.

In the end, the body was taken away. Sheila was kicked out of the flat, because it was a crime scene, and because the bloodstains and all the "miscellaneous potentially-toxic contaminants" would need the careful attention of a specialist cleaning-squad before the council could "deem it fit for re-habitation". Darren couldn't be found, but social services managed to locate Tracy so that she could be "temporarily rehoused", along with her mother, in a single room in a run-down B&B.

In the twenty minutes or so before Tracy skipped out again to find somewhere less suitable to sleep, Sheila gave her a big hug.

"There's no need to worry about me, love," she said, unnecessarily. "I'm okay, really I am. But I want you to know, before you go, that I love you very much."

There was, of course, much more that she might have said. She might have said that she also wanted her daughter to know that she was the flesh of her flesh, and that it was very special flesh, and that if ever a mysterious man came into her life who'd been messing about with ooze dragged up from the remote ocean bed, and had picked up some sort of infection from it that had driven him completely round the twist, then maybe she should show a little patience, because it would probably be Sarmerodach, reincarnate again and trying heroically to fulfill his age-long mission, just like the freak in bandages from *The Mummy*, but in a smoother sort of way. She didn't, of course. It would have been ridiculous, and Tracy wouldn't have taken a blind bit of notice.

Once Tracy had gone, though, and she was alone in her filthy and claustrophobic room, with the TV on for company but not really watching it, Sheila couldn't help wondering whether there might be a glimmer of hope, not just for her and Tracy, or Darren, but for the whole ecocatastrophe-threatened world.

She decided, eventually, that she might as well believe that there was.

BETWEEN THE CHAPTERS

> Therefore the Lord God sent him forth from the Garden of Eden, to till the ground from whence he was taken.
> So He drove out the man; and He placed at the east of the garden of Eden Cherubims, and a flaming sword which turned every way, to keep the way of the tree of life.
>
> [*Genesis* 3:23-24]

* * * * * * *

There had been no wind within the garden, but there was a wind without; Adam, who had never felt a chill, shivered as it stung him. Night within the garden had always been softly starlit, but the sky without was heavy with cloud and the darkness was almost total. Adam, who had only known the fear of the Lord God, trembled as new anxieties tormented him.

In the distance, a lion roared. Within the garden, the lion had lain down with the lamb until they were sent forth into the world bearing names, but Adam—who had tasted the fruit of the tree of knowledge of good and evil—knew that the lion and the lamb stood in a very different relationship without.

Adam had been put out of the garden beside one of the four branches of the river that divided within its bounds. Adam followed the river, because it seemed the natural thing to do. The river had direction, and direction was something he needed. He did not think to wait for the woman to whom he had finally given a name. He remembered, instead, that Lilith had been expelled before him, and he wondered whether he might be able to find her. Their parting had been his first sorrow. The Lord God had refused to explain why He had expelled her, but Adam suspected now that she might have tasted forbidden fruit before him.

Adam had never felt fatigue in the garden, but he soon became weary as he walked. He was thirsty, and drank from the river, but found the water foul. In the garden, its parent's water had always been pure, but even the most perfect garden generates waste; Adam supposed that all four outflows must be equally polluted.

Dawn broke while he dozed, and the light woke him. Adam walked on. The cloud soon cleared, leaving him at the mercy of the blazing sun. He found bushes bearing fruit, and was able to appease his hunger, but the fruit was bitter. The fruit in the garden—which he had eaten purely for pleasure, never having felt hunger there— had always been sweet, but Adam was beginning to sense a pattern in the course of events.

The scar on Adam's midriff, where his rib had been removed, began to ache. That, too, was the legacy of a fault; he had been lonely when his true counterpart had been driven out of the garden, and had asked the Lord God for a new wife. The Lord God had obliged, but not without a certain resentment, reflected in the rude manner in which the replacement had been achieved. Adam decided that he should have known that the woman was essentially untrustworthy, and that the Lord God must certainly have known it. Within the garden, Adam had never had cause to doubt the Lord God's generosity, nor His forgiveness, but outside the garden, everything seemed doubtful.

As soon as Adam caught sight of the fields of corn he knew what they were. There had been no fields in the garden, but the Lord God had cursed him "to till the ground from whence he was taken" and the curse would have been impotent had he not been informed as to the nature of tillage. He was, however, surprised to find that some of the land outside the garden was already under cultivation. There had been little sense of the passage of time in the garden, where urgency and boredom were equally unknown, so Adam had no idea how many days and nights had elapsed since Lilith had been expelled. He could not imagine, though, that she had been able to sow a single cornfield unaided, let alone the dozens he could see.

It was evening by the time he reached the fields. There was no one working in them, but he could see a village of reed huts, and the flickering blaze of a cooking-fire. It was obvious that this was a considerable settlement, whose population must be counted in dozens.

Fearful as he was, Adam went directly to the village. He was only slightly reassured to discover that many of its inhabitants were similar in appearance to himself, and many of the rest similar to the woman, although some were much smaller in stature. Their sun-

111

weathered skins were darker in hue and their clothing was more neatly tailored than the coat of animal-hides that the Lord God had given him. He had not plucked up the courage to speak to them before they began to crowd around him suspiciously. "Who are you?" their spokesman asked. "What do you want here?"

"My name is Adam," Adam said. After the briefest of pauses, he added: "I'm looking for Lilith."

The hostile attitudes of the villagers immediately relented. "We were asked to watch for you," his interrogator said. "Come this way."

Adam was taken to the centre of the village, to the largest of the reed huts that comprised it. As he approached with his escort, two individuals came out of the hut to greet him. One was Lilith. The other was not unlike himself in his physical form, but Adam sensed that he was not really a man. Within the garden, appearances had never been deceptive, but he was not in the garden now.

"I thought you would come after me long ago," Lilith said to him. "At first, I assumed that you'd follow me of your own accord. Then I thought that it surely wouldn't take the Lord God long to find fault with you. Then I began to wonder...but you're here now, and I'm glad to see you."

"Who's he?" Adam asked, staring at Lilith's companion.

"This is Azazel," Lilith said. "He's a demon. He's not such a powerful creator as the Lord God, but tilling the ground isn't a solitary occupation; in order for his curse to work, the Lord God either had to make more humans himself, or give permission for someone else to do it. He gave permission—I suppose it seemed simpler in the short run, although I can already foresee complications. So you finally got around to trying the forbidden fruit?"

"It wasn't my fault," Adam was quick to say.

"It hardly matters," Lilith said. "It's not so bad out here—the fruit of the tree of life is the bitterest in Eden, but by far the most nourishing."

"It wasn't that sort of forbidden fruit I ate," Adam said. "I tasted the fruit of the tree of knowledge of good and evil. It wasn't bitter, although it did have a very odd aftertaste."

"Maybe that's for the best," Lilith said. "I've tasted one and you've tasted the other, so we'll have the benefit of both now."

"It was the woman who made me do it," Adam said, defensively. "The serpent tempted her and she tempted me."

"Who's *the woman?*"

"I was lonely without you," Adam explained. "I asked the Lord God to make me a replacement."

The only jealousy and anger within the garden had been the Lord God's. Lilith's jealousy and anger were not quite as terrifying to behold as the Lord God's, but they did not seem trivial to poor Adam.

"I didn't know where you'd gone," he protested, feebly. "The Lord God wouldn't tell me why he got rid of you. I didn't know you'd eaten forbidden fruit. You didn't try to tempt me the way the woman did."

Lilith had calmed down while he was speaking, but Adam could not imagine that it was the effect of his excuses. Azazel had put a hand on her arm, and the demon's touch appeared to have a considerable soothing effect.

"The replacement," Lilith observed, witheringly, "was evidently adequate, for a while."

Within the garden, Adam had never thought to compare the woman with Lilith, but he could hardly help doing so now. Lilith, his true counterpart, was very like him in every respect save one, but the woman had been shorter, softer and more in need of demonstrations of affection. While Lilith had been out of sight and out of mind, Adam had not spared a thought for those differences, but now that Lilith was standing in front of him he was forced to weigh them up. As soon as he focused his thoughts on the problem, he realized that Lilith and the woman were really very different. He wasn't sure which of them he preferred—but it seemed only natural, in the circumstances, that Lilith's advantages should leap more readily to the eye.

Adam looked Lilith up and down—and then he looked at Azazel. Azazel was taller than Adam, considerably more muscular, and his expression was suggestive of great intelligence, if not of wisdom. Perhaps, Adam thought, Lilith had found her true soulmate now—in which case, he might have done better to wait by the garden, to see whether she would be driven out in her turn.

"I don't know what happened to the woman," Adam said, feebly. "I would have waited outside the garden, but He posted angels there, and a flaming sword that moved in a threatening manner. It seemed wisest to come away. I see that there are some of the woman's kind here, though, who have already taken to motherhood without waiting to be cursed. Azazel seems to have mimicked the Lord God's second creation rather than his first."

Lilith was about to speak again when Azazel squeezed her arm. "You look tired and hungry, Adam," he said. "Would you like to come in to rest, and have a bite to eat? I'm sure you're thirsty too. We have a new drink here, which we prefer to water. It's a trifle bitter, but I think you might like the after-effects."

* * * * * * *

Once Adam had been sent on his way, Eve faced up to Lord God's further judgment. She suspected that there might be additional punishments yet to be visited upon her. She had eaten far more of the fruit than Adam, and its digestion had ensured that she was all too well aware of the awful extent of her fault.

"Adam won't wait for you outside the garden," the Lord God said, spitefully. "He blames you for his expulsion. He wants to get away."

"So he should," Eve lamented, painfully gripped by her new-found knowledge of good and evil. "It was all my fault. The serpent beguiled me, but it was me who beguiled Adam. Having fallen prey to temptation myself, I should have know better than to turn temptress—but I hadn't had time to digest the fruit. Even so, I deserve to bear children in sorrow and to have my husband to rule over me. I admit that."

The Lord God did not respond immediately. He was much calmer now, having already vented the greater part of his sudden wrath. While she waited, Eve wondered why the garden looked so much lovelier now than it ever had before. It had always been lovely, but it was not until now that she had realized how very lovely it was.

"I suppose it was as much my fault as yours," the Lord God said, eventually, with a sigh. "I created you, after all, and deliberately made you weaker of will than his first wife so that you wouldn't rebel of your own accord. I made the serpent too, and Adam. Mind you, I couldn't have foreseen this. Omniscience only extends as far as things that can be known, and once you've created agents with free will, the future become unknowable, at least to the extent that it depends on the exercise of that free will. Freedom has to include the freedom to rebel—not to mention the freedom to be stupid and reckless. Once you create free will, you have to expect the unexpected."

"I'm sorry," Eve said. "I wasn't really rebelling, you know."

"I know," the Lord God admitted. "You were being stupid and reckless—or perhaps just curious. Did you like the fruit?"

"It wasn't bitter," Eve said, judiciously, "but it has a strange aftertaste. I'm not sure that I do."

"Knowledge of good and evil is awkward nourishment," the Lord God observed. "The garden wouldn't have been complete without the tree, though, any more than it would have been complete without the tree of life. Creation requires coherency; everything a Creator improvises on a whim has extensive corollaries, including unexpected ones. A Creator has to compromise with the logical consequences of His intentions. He can establish the raw materials of an entire universe with a momentary outburst inspiration, but once that's done, matters of order and detail unfold of their own accord. At first I thought I could keep an entire planet under total control, but in the end I had to settle for cultivating one little garden...and it didn't take long for that to go awry."

"I'm sorry," Eve said, again, expressing sympathy rather than apologizing—but she knew that the sympathy was bound to ring false, given that she had no personal experience of the problems of creativity.

"So am I," said the Lord God, "but what's done can't be undone. Even an omnipotent God can't change the past; that's another corollary of bringing order and detail out of chaos and nebulosity. If I let you stay, it's no use asking me to make you a new husband to replace Adam; I've already tried that kind of move. Those who can't learn from their mistakes are condemned to repeat them, first as tragedy then as farce. I can tolerate my Creation taking a tragic turn, but if it turns farcical, that might be too much to bear. Now that you've digested the knowledge of good and evil, what do you think I ought to do with you?"

Eve thought about the curses that had already been imposed on her, and those that had been on the serpent and Adam. She looked around at the garden, savoring its loveliness again, but knew as she did so that the loveliness was a lie. The garden's beauty was a beguiling mask, a product of excessively careful artifice. Without the Lord God's constant attention and continual hard work, the garden couldn't sustain itself. It would return to wilderness soon enough. To live in the garden, she would have to live with the Lord God, obedient to his rules and whims alike.

"I ought to go after Adam," she said, eventually, wondering how much room she had for negotiation with regard to the term of her expulsion. "I ought to try to make it up to him, to the extent that

I can. I'd like to be able to help him, and to comfort him, if that's possible."

"It might not be," the Lord God observed. "He's bound to meet up with Lilith."

"Who's Lilith?" Eve asked. Adam had never mentioned the name to her; she had no idea that she was Adam's second wife.

"I created humankind like every other species, in male and female versions," the Lord God told her. "It seemed somehow appropriate to follow the pattern, although I really should have made an exception. The whole point of making two of every other animal was that the worldly members of the species could multiply once Adam had named their archetypes, but Adam and Lilith weren't supposed to have any worldly equivalents, in the beginning. They were supposed to provide me with company in the garden—that's why I gave them intellect as well as free will. I thought I needed more than one, so I made two—but I shouldn't have made them different sexes. It was an unnecessary complication. I had a second chance once Lilith had gone, but Adam demanded another wife, not another man, and I felt obliged to humor him. Maybe I didn't put my heart into the job. It's surprisingly easy for a creator to become a trifle resentful of his own creations. That's why I thought it might be a good idea to delegate some of the responsibility...but I'm not so sure about the way that's turning out, either."

"Are you saying that Adam's back with his first wife," Eve said, grasping the essentials of the argument although some of the detail evaded her. "Does that mean that I'll have to find some other husband to rule over me?" It wasn't a pleasant thought, and felt rather like a curse in its own right.

"Not necessarily," the Lord God said. "Lilith's been with Azazel for some time, and he's even trickier than the serpent. There's no telling what he might want or do."

"Who's Azazel?" Eve asked.

"A demon. In their native form, or rather formlessness, they're free-floating entities of pure will, but they can take on material forms if they so desire. I thought it would be useful, or at least interesting, to have creatures around who could experiment with new possibilities on my behalf, but they developed their own agendas. At present, Azazel has taken on manlike form. He'll get bored with it soon enough, but, for some time now, he's been busy creating and shaping the kind of community that Lilith and Adam—and you, for that matter—will need if humans are to survive and thrive outside the garden."

Eve understood that if she were to be driven out of the garden, she too would need a community if she were to survive, let alone thrive, but the more she heard about Lilith and Azazel the less sure she was that she wanted to go after Adam. She also understood why the Lord God was so reluctant to subject her to the same fate as Adam now that He'd calmed down, even though He'd clearly intended her to share his punishment when He'd first started strewing curses around. The Lord God still needed intellectual companionship of some sort, perhaps even intellectual challenge. He had the option of raising the consciousness of some or all of the angels, but if he did that, they would acquire the same potential for rebellion as human beings and demons, and perhaps the same penchant. Eve realized that the Lord God was hesitating, wondering whether it might not be better to stick with the adversary he knew than to start creating new ones.

Eve wasn't at all sure that she wanted to provide the Lord God with intellectual companionship and challenge, until the time came when He lost His temper again and lashed out. It might, she thought, be better to come to some other arrangement while He was calm and relatively contrite. The garden was full of exquisite scents, but she knew now that perfume was direly unreliable as a guide to virtue.

"I really do think I ought to share Adam's fate," she eventually decided, figuring that it probably was better to cleave to the adversary she knew, if she could. "It was my fault, after all. I'd like to be able to make things easier for him, if I can. I know you can't take back what you said about bearing children in sorrow and my husband ruling over me, but you could make some compensating amendments, if you were so minded."

"That's the fruit talking," the Lord God said, with a sigh. "I told you to leave it alone."

* * * * * * *

"So where do we stand?" Adam asked, when he and Lilith were finally alone in the reed hut. "It seems that you've grown tired of waiting for me, and set up home with Azazel." The hut was feebly lit by a tallow candle, and it was haunted by a humid animal stink that turned his stomach, but at least its walls sheltered his sensitive skin from the wind, and hid him from the inquisitive eyes of Azazel's creations.

"Azazel has done a great deal for us," Lilith told him. "He's a mine of information about tillage and all manner of crafts. We don't have much in the way of tools as yet, but he's set us on a progressive road and given us the means to follow it. He's not going to stick around, though. He's a demon—he can't be content to maintain human form for long, or to take an interest in human beings. He has too much potential in him. He can't even be content with one world for very long."

"Are there other worlds?" Adam asked.

"More than you can imagine. Every star in the sky is a sun, with planets of its own, and the stars that the human eye can see are only an infinitesimal fraction of their number. The Lord God's attention is focused here, at least for the time being, but there are trillions of other worlds. Azazel is learning while he teaches us, and he'll doubtless put his education to good use elsewhere when he gets the urge to move on."

"And he won't take you with him?" Adam said.

The expression on Lilith's face told Adam that he'd hit a slightly sore point. No, Lilith didn't—couldn't—believe that Azazel would take her with him when he got the urge to go, but she *wanted* to believe that he might, because she wanted to go. "He's a demon," was all that Lilith actually said.

"What nourishment did you obtain from the other forbidden fruit?" Adam asked, curiously. "When the Lord God drove me out of Eden, he said that I'd live forever if I ate it—but I'd always assumed that I'd live forever. Everything in the garden lives forever."

"Nothing stays the same forever, in the garden or out of it," Lilith told him. "The fruit of the tree of life slows down the process of change, but can't prevent it. I'll be around for a very long time—far longer than you, I dare say—but not forever. I'll die one day, and I'll change in the meantime, but very slowly. You'll grow old and die before I have a single wrinkle, and a hundred generations of your descendants will perish before I grow old, but the difference is one of degree, not of kind. I could travel with Azazel, if he'd let me, even though he can travel no faster than the speed of light...." She stopped, unwilling to give fuller expression to her faint hope. In the sickly candlelight, her beautiful face took on a sinister tint.

"I don't know what's involved in *growing old*, or *dying*," Adam said—but realized, as he spoke the words, that it was a lie. He had tasted the fruit of the tree of knowledge of good and evil, if only slightly, and he did now have an inkling of what it would mean to grow old, and to die. The awareness was vague and fugitive, but undeniable. He wondered whether Lilith, having tasted the fruit of the tree of life, could possibly know how precious life now seemed to a man of his mortal kind.

"The world is an uncomfortable place," Lilith told him, with a deliberate harshness in her voice, "no matter what duration your existence has within it—but it's not without its rewards."

"I know," Adam admitted. "There's nothing like an awareness of evil to tutor intelligence in the value of good. The aftertaste of the fruit I ate is odd, but it's not horrific. Life outside the garden is possible; I understand that. The Lord God knew that I would when he cursed me. He drove me out, but he gave me better clothes first. He had to know that I'd find you. Perhaps that's why he didn't send Eve out with me."

"Perhaps it is," said Lilith, dubiously. "Will she follow you, do you think, if she has the choice?"

"I don't know," Adam admitted. "I haven't thought too much about it, because I don't suppose she'll be given the choice. Whether she follows me or not it will be at the Lord God's command, in answer to his curse."

Outside, in the darkness, a lion roared. Another answered. Perhaps, Adam thought, the two were mates—and as he thought it, the knowledge popped into his head that male lions had more than one mate. Perhaps, he thought, humans might aspire to the condition of lions.

"But if she *did* have the choice," Lilith persisted, "would she follow you? And if she were to follow you, what would she do if she found us together?"

"I don't know," Adam said, a little more aggressively than before. "I don't even know what I would do. I don't even know what I want." He bit his tongue as soon as he'd said it, because he was anxious as well was confused. He knew that his uncertainty might be no more than an after-effect of having tasted the forbidden fruit—but it seemed to him that the bitter liquid that Azazel had given him to drink, instead of water, was having after-effects too. It was Azazel's potion that was making him garrulous and dizzy.

"That's an enviable position to be in," Lilith said. She said no more, but it was obvious to Adam that she knew exactly what she wanted—and was almost sure that she could not achieve it.

"I'm sorry," he said. "Perhaps we should have done as we were told, and left the trees in the centre of the garden alone."

"It was only a matter of time," Lilith said, with a sigh. She lowered hr head, so that her features were in shadow. "Sooner or later, it had to come to this. I should have tempted you myself, and avoided complications—but I wanted to take responsibility for my own actions, and I wanted you to take responsibility for yours. We can't always foresee what the consequences of our actions will be...but that's a good thing, isn't it? Even the Lord God couldn't tolerate a world in which everything was determined, from beginning to end."

An owl hooted in the distance, and another responded. The cries seemed plaintive and full of regret.

"I think I'd find the alternative more attractive," Adam said, "if I too had eaten the fruit of the other tree."

* * * * * * *

Eve went in search of the serpent, which had gone into hiding. She finally found it cowering beneath the branches of the hedge that marked the garden's boundary, close to one of the outflowing branches of the river. It wasn't easy to strike up a conversation comfortably, now that the serpent had to lie upon the ground, and hadn't yet got the knack of legless traction, but while it was still in the garden the serpent could still talk.

Rather than lie down herself, Eve picked up the serpent and draped it over a protruding branch at head height.

"Why did you do it?" she wanted to know. "What possible reason could you have had for bringing the Lord God's wrath down upon all three of us?"

"I was trying to do you a favor," the serpent said, coiling itself around the branch and trying unsuccessfully to move along it.

"How so?"

"It seemed to me that life might be enriched by the knowledge of good and evil—and when I tasted the fruit, I was convinced that I was right. The garden suddenly seemed so much lovelier than it had before. I wanted to share the experience. Perhaps I was hasty—I didn't expect the aftertaste."

"I can hardly complain about your desire to share the experience," Eve conceded, "given that I felt exactly the same way—but why did you have to pick me to share it with?"

"I thought you might appreciate it more than most," the serpent said. "You're the smartest creature in the garden, after all."

"Except for Adam," Eve observed, dutifully.

The serpent hissed and flickered its forked tongue incredulously.

"I suppose life *is* enriched by the knowledge of good," Eve admitted, "but the Lord God's right about corollaries, isn't he? The knowledge of good is also the knowledge of evil, which is anything but enrichment. Innocence was, at least, bliss. You lied, though, when you said that I'm not certain to die, because the knowledge of good and evil tells me that I surely shall. Why did you lie?"

"I didn't intend to," the serpent said, coiling itself more tightly around the branch as if possessed by a sudden fear of falling. "At least, I don't think I intended to. The knowledge of good and evil makes us question our own motives, doesn't it? Oh, that after-taste...."

"You're not helping," Eve said.

"No, I'm not," The serpent replied. "It's strange how everything twists around itself when you have to move as I do. I could swallow my own tail if I wanted to, and devour myself from end to beginning. As surely as we shall all die, I dare say, we all tell lies." The serpent gave up the struggle to control its motion and settled uncomfortably into stillness, with its beady eyes fixed on Eve's. "It's our nature," the creature continued, yawning and displaying its poisonous fangs. "We should be proud of the opportunity, for it numbers among our freedoms, and is the foundation of our meager creativity. We're never nearer to God than when we lie, and not so far away as we might think when we finally come to die. I think I'm getting the hang of this now. All that twisting and turning was making me dizzy. With a little more practice, you know, I might yet learn to make progress. Are you sure you should be talking to me, given that the Lord has seen fit to put enmity between us? If you're hoping that he might let you stay in the garden a while longer, you might do better to avoid me."

"I just wanted an explanation," Eve told the serpent. "You tasted the fruit yourself, and you wanted to share the experience— no matter what the risk."

"Perhaps I wanted to share the blame, too," the serpent said, in a speculative tone. "Perhaps I wanted to lighten my own inevitable punishment by spreading the burden of guilt. Perhaps, having tasted the knowledge of good and evil, and seen how good the garden was, I wanted to sample a little evil too. It's so difficult to be sure, once one starts looking inwards with one's mind's eye, isn't it?"

"I never had any difficulty," Eve said, "until...."

"Exactly," said the serpent, when she left the sentence dangling. "I couldn't have put it better myself, although I'd certainly have taken a more roundabout route. Do you think I'd poison myself, if I bit my own tongue? Do you really want to stay here, now that Adam's gone? I'd appreciate the company, of course, but I doubt

that I'll be staying long myself. The Lord God has declared us enemies, and he'll have to expel us for the curse to take effect. There's
no enmity in the garden."

"If you were to bite me," Eve asked, "would I die?"

"Not now," the serpent said, "but if we were on the other side of
the hedge, you might. Do you think I should, while it's still safe, just
to see what happens?"

"No, I don't," said Eve. "I might store the poison, and drop
dead the moment I stepped outside. Did you want to bite me?"

"Not really," the serpent said. "Perhaps I've had my fill of evil
for a while." It paused to flex its coils again, under the spur of a new
inspiration, "I suppose I ought to explore the other side of the coin,
for the sake of balance. Is there anything I can do to make it up to
you?"

"I doubt it," Eve replied.

"It wasn't *entirely* my fault," the serpent told her, defensively.
"Lilith started it. If I hadn't seen her eat the fruit of the tree of life, I
might not have been tempted myself. I didn't have to follow her example, though, any more than Adam had to follow yours."

"Have you eaten the fruit of both trees, then?" Eve said.

"Yes, I have. When the Lord God condemned me to eat dust for
all the days of my life, he knew that it would be a long sentence. My
children will be mortal, though, just like Lilith's. Stupid, too. I think
I'm going to be lonely."

"But it was the fruit of the *other* tree that you tempted me to eat,
"Eve said, stubbornly following her own line of thought, "not the
one that Lilith ate. Why was that?"

"I wanted to figure out whether I'd taken them in the right order—whether eating the fruit of the tree of knowledge of good and
evil first might have given me a different perspective on the virtue
of the fruit of the tree of life. As things are, you see, I can only look
back. When I ate the fruit of the tree of life, I didn't have the faintest
idea whether it was a good or an evil thing to do. I have an opinion
now—but I can't tell whether it's the same opinion I would have had
if I'd eaten the second fruit first. What do you think?" While it
spoke, the serpent had succeeded in moving a little way along the
branch, and back again. It seemed pleased with its modest achieve-
ment.

"I think it might depend," Eve said, "on where one might have
to live after eating the fruit of the tree of life. Not than it matters to
me, given that the flaming sword has taken the option away. What's
your opinion?"

"My opinion," the serpent told her, "is that it all depends on how good a liar you are. To live anything like forever, and find more good than evil in the experience, I'll probably need to be a very good liar indeed. It'll require a lot more practice than I'll need merely to be able to get around—although I seem to be mastering the intricacies of arboreal movement. You wouldn't care to lift me on to a branch nearer to the ground, I suppose? The height of this one's making me rather nervous."

Eve picked the serpent up, and put it down in the grass by her feet. "Take one step at a time," she said, not without a certain ironic vindictiveness. "You have to learn to walk before you can run, metaphorically speaking."

"That's the fruit talking," the serpent said. "You wouldn't have been able to try to hurt my feelings two days ago. Aren't you glad I happened along?"

"Yes, of course I'm glad," Eve said, suspecting as she said it that she might be lying. "With enemies like you, who needs friends?" If it was a lie, she wondered, ought the lie to be reckoned a mere reckless folly, or an expression of some kind of existential triumph? There was, she realized, a certain aesthetic satisfaction in twisting and turning, even for someone incapable of swallowing her own tail and disinclined even to put her foot in her mouth.

"Where are you going?" asked the serpent, as she turned on her heel.

"To see the Lord God," she replied. "I think he's hesitated long enough. It's time to go."

"Will I ever see you again?" the serpent asked, hopefully.

"Not if I see you first," Eve assured it—honestly, this time. "Once we're outside the garden, the enmity will kick in. It's nothing personal."

* * * * * *

When Eve arrived in the settlement Adam was pleased, partly because he was glad to see her and partly because he thought her presence might make Lilith jealous. He was still undecided as to which of them he wanted to be with, but he certainly wanted to have the choice. He took her into the reed hut, apologizing for the appalling stink, but he wasn't surprised when she decided that she'd rather sit out in the open, by the fire. They had no privacy there, but Azazel sat down on Eve's far side while Lilith sat on Adam's, so the imitations that Azazel had forged faded into the background of shadows.

Adam commiserated with Eve over her expulsion from the garden, and explained that he would have waited by the hedge had he not been so certain that the Lord God would forgive her and let her stay. "It wasn't your fault, after all," he told her. "I was the one who should have known better, having had so much more experience—it was my responsibility to protect you. You were weak; that's the way the Lord God made you. He made me strong, and I should have been strong enough for both of us."

"The Lord God would have let me stay if I'd approached him the right way," Eve assured him, "but I couldn't bear to be alone in the garden, without anyone of my own kind. He refused to make me a new partner, on the grounds that He'd already tried that, so I eventually had to ask Him to let me go. He was grateful, in a way, because that was the only way the terms of His curse could take full effect, and He hates inconsistency, even in Himself. He warned me that you might not want me, because you would surely have found your first wife, just as young and beautiful as when you last saw her, but I had to take the risk."

Eve was looking past Adam at Lilith's firelit face while she said this. Lilith, in her turn, was studying her. Adam was studying both of them, although he had to twist and turn in order to look in both directions alternately. He felt a distinct thrill as he tried to imagine what each of them must be thinking.

Lilith was the taller of the two, by far the stronger, and arguably the more beautiful—but Eve was more delicate as well as softer, and arguably the prettier. Adam purred like a lion, and blinked away the smoke that was teasing his eyes.

"You're very welcome, Eve," Lilith said to the newcomer, "and you may set your mind at rest. I never was Adam's wife in any meaningful sense, and never wanted to be—but you were his wife from the moment of your creation, and that's certainly your destiny now."

"There's no need to be hasty," Azazel put in. "Eve's still a stranger here, and it would be unwise of her to rush into anything. She must be very hungry and thirsty, as well as tired. We must give her meat to eat, and something pleasant to drink, before we start settling anyone's future."

There was a whole lamb rotating on a spit over the cooking-fire, and the scent of its roasting was as exhilarating as any perfume in Eden. Eve paused to savor it before accepting Azazel's invitation to take her aside and give her something pleasant to drink. Adam got up too, but only to draw Lilith away in the opposite direction.

"He's not going to take you with him," Adam said, when they stopped at the edge of the village compound, where the bare ground gave way to a thicket of brambles and thistles. "It won't matter what you say or do. Making a show of giving me up won't help. He might flirt with Eve for a while, just to make both of us jealous, but he'll fly off in the end as a beam of light, to explore the stars alone. He's not like us—and not like the Lord God, either. He doesn't need company—not any more."

"I know that," Lilith said. "But I'm not like you, either, Adam. I ate the fruit of the tree of life, and never tasted the other. There's a sense in which I'm more like him than you, and meeting you again has only served to emphasize that fact."

Adam shrugged his shoulders, with calculated effrontery. "It's your decision," he said, disingenuously. "If you want to leave me to Eve, you can. She wants to be with me, it seems—even though she could have stayed in the garden." Adam did not believe that Eve really could have stayed in the garden, but he was willing to appear to believe it, if it would serve his purpose.

"Apparently so," said Lilith, "but is that what *you* want?"

"I might not have a choice," Adam parried, feigning regret. "I'm carrying the burden of the Lord God's curse, alas. On the other hand, I have a responsibility to you, too."

At that moment, a snake reared up from a tangled clump of thorns and thistles beside them, and made as if to strike at Adam's heel. Lilith, however, grabbed the creature behind the head and cracked it like a whip, breaking its back. She took three paces back the way they had come, and threw the corpse into the fire.

Adam went after her, but she turned her back on him and went into the reed hut. Adam hesitated for a moment, but then turned round to greet Azazel and Eve, who were returning to the fire holding bowls full to the brim with foaming liquid.

"It's rather bitter," Eve opined.

"Yes," said Azazel, "but I think you'll find its after-effects amusing."

* * * * * * *

When Adam awoke the next morning, Lilith had gone, and so had Azazel. Adam was quite certain that they had gone their separate ways—and he remained certain until his dying day, even though he never saw either of them again, at least in human form.

"The settlement is ours now, wife," he said to Eve, when his loyal follower eventually awoke, groaning and nursing her aching head. "It's our legitimate inheritance, and we'll be its king and queen. We'll found a dynasty, and our children's children will rule the world, for ever and ever. Our life and theirs will be hard, to begin with, but they'll make progress enough to exceed the wildest dreams of the Lord God, and the boldest experiments of demonkind."

"Yes, husband," Eve replied, without the least detectable hint of insincerity. "God's kindness will surely balance out his curses in protecting us and guiding us, and nothing can prevent us henceforth from knowing good from evil."

* * * * * * *

And Adam knew Eve his wife, and she conceived, and bare Cain, and said, I have gotten a man from the Lord.

[*Genesis* 4:1]

THREE VERSIONS OF A FABLE

In the first version of the fable, which was prepared for human contemplation by Oscar Wilde, a lovesick student laments his inability to find a red rose, which has been demanded as the fee for a dance with a lovely girl. A nightingale, understanding the nature of his desperation, implores the rose-trees in his garden to provide a single red rose, so that the student might pursue his courtship.

The only tree capable of producing such a rose asks that the nightingale press her breast against a thorn, so that her life-blood might supply the necessary color. She complies, singing all the while in order to force the blood from her reluctant veins, but the effort leaves her dead and drained.

When the student finds the unexpected rose he is ecstatic, and he carries it triumphantly to the girl. Alas, she has already received a gift of jewels from a wealthy suitor and she is no longer interested in roses or in students.

The student draws the conclusion from this unfortunate episode that love is silly and impractical, and that he would do better to devote himself to the study of philosophy. This is not, however, the lesson which the reader is intended to draw. The reader is supposed to appreciate the awful tragedy of the nightingale's sacrifice, born of her admirable but foolishly optimistic conviction that love is better than life, and that the heart of a man is worth far more than the heart of a bird.

Were nightingales actually capable of the powers of thought and judgment that the fable credits to them, they would surely tell the tale differently. No true nightingale, however noble her sentiments might be, would ever be so foolish as to think that the heart of a man held anything uniquely precious. Were nightingales to incorporate some such fable into their plaintive songs, they would surely equip their sister with a much more relevant motive. Perhaps they would not let her die at all, but, if they did, they would want her to die for something more worthwhile than a stupid student's fatuous love-life.

The nightingale version of the fable might credit the initial capture of the bird's attention to the student's mournful lament, but it would be the melody of his mourning rather than its content that would intrigue her, and give her pause to wonder what difference it might make to her own song were she to suffer as he seemed to be suffering, for lack of a red rose. It would not be for his sake that she would press her breast to the thorn, but for her own, and for every drop of blood she gave to the rose she would receive a full reward of inspiration. She would sing as no other nightingale had ever sung before, although each and every one had nurtured the passionate desire.

The nightingales might not care overmuch what became of the rose once the nightingale had finished her work of art, but they would probably want the girl to receive and cherish it even though she sent the student packing. In all likelihood, the nightingales would end the tale with the observation that the girl pinned the rose to her own breast, and that, until it withered, her head was filled with an inaudible song, whose wonder and beauty could never be recalled to her mind by any of the jewels she was later to wear in its stead.

Were rose-trees actually capable of the powers of speech and decision that the fable credits to them, they would undoubtedly tell the tale differently again. No true rose-tree would suck the life out of a nightingale for no better reason than to provide a love-token for a human being. From the viewpoint of the tree, the only possible motive for its action would be frankly vampiric.

The rose-tree version of the fable would make the nightingale a hapless victim of a cunning and convoluted snare, and she would not be the only victim of the scheme. The rose-trees would begin the story at any earlier point, crediting their own kind with the suggestive whisper that first inspired the girl to state her fee. The student's lament, and the nightingale's response, would be intermediate stages in the plot, which would come to its climax when the girl accepted her bribe. Her cruelty in spurning her lover would then be mirrored by the triumph of the vampire rose as it grasped her breast with its avid thorns, and drew new life from her heart.

In the rose-tree version, of course, the rose would not begin to wither until the girl had withered and died herself. Even then, it would probably be plucked from her breast by some other romantic fool, incapable of realizing that beauty is essentially a snare, which tempts the unwary to clasp savage thorns to their innermost souls.

Fortunately or unfortunately, nightingales and rose-trees are devoid of intelligence; for them, at least, there is no such thing as a moral or an immoral tale. As for humans, they are free to shape and reshape tales to every purpose and meaning they can contrive to imagine.

THE TITAN UNWRECKED

or,

FUTILITY REVISITED

Having narrowly avoided an iceberg on her third return trip, the *Titan* had fulfilled all the expectations entertained of her. She had, as anticipated, established the promptitude and regularity of a railway train in shuttling back and forth between New York and Southampton, making the distance between Sandy Hook and Daunt's Rock well within her six-day schedule almost without fail. When she set out westbound from Southampton Water on the evening of Boxing Day in the year 1900 she carried a full complement of passengers, whose expectations of celebrating the dawn of a new century on the night before their disembarkation in New York generated a mood of unparalleled cheerfulness and hopefulness from the moment she slipped anchor.

The *Titan*'s passenger-list was the customary deep cross-section of Anglo-American society, ranging from a duke and several millionaires in the finest staterooms to two thousand hopeful emigrants in steerage, but the significance of the voyage—the last Atlantic crossing of the nineteenth century—had attracted an unusually high proportion of romantics of every stripe, including a large company of Frenchmen who had come from Cherbourg to join the ship, and a considerable number of writers—true literary men as well as newspaper reporters—in search of inspiration.

Certain elements of the *Titan*'s cargo were equally exotic, or so it was rumored. In addition to the usual mundane treasures, her secure hold was said to contain the entire contents of a recently-looted Egyptian tomb, and an exotic biological specimen of mysterious nature and origin had allegedly been brought from the Isle of Wight with only hours to spare before the hour of departure. Few, if any, of

130

the crew had actually see these alleged marvels, although many more had seen a large collection of coffin-like boxes that had been stowed in the main luggage-hold, and a series of crates containing an elaborate array of what appeared to be electrical and acoustic apparatus, which had been carefully packed away in the space reserved for fragile items.

Because the purser had a mischievous sense of humor, almost all of the writers found themselves seated at the same table in the first-class dining-room for the evening meal whose serving began while the ship was rounding Land's End. The main course was the breasts of pheasants and partridges shot in the run up to Christmas Eve and hung over the festive season; the legs were, as usual, directed to the second-class dining room, while the offal was added to the sausage-meat reserved for steerage rations. The writers eyed one another suspiciously, all of them anxious for their relative positions on the highest literary ground, and each one wondering who among them would be first to describe the *Titan* as a "ship of fools."

"I, for one," said Mr. Henley, seemingly by way of breaking the tension, "will not be sorry to see the very end of the so-called *fin de siècle*. I have had my fill of decadence, and I feel sure that the new century will be a vigorous and prosperous era, in which there will be a new alliance between the manly and aesthetic virtues—an alliance that will revolutionize moral and intellectual life, and quicken the march of progress."

This bold assertion caused some offence to M. Lorrain, whose consumptive cough suggested that New York might be only a stopping-point for him, *en route* to the warm, dry air of Arizona or Nevada. "The century may change," he said, softly, "but the faltering steps of civilization will not recover their sturdy gait by means of optimism alone. We are products of the nineteenth century ourselves; there is a sense in which the *Titan* is already a ghost-ship, whose parody of life is but painted artifice."

M. Lorrain's immediate neighbors, Mr. Huneker and Mr. Chambers, nodded in polite but half-hearted assent, but stronger support was provided by Mr. Vane. "We are indeed ghosts without knowing it," he said, dolefully, "sailing to judgment while in denial, afraid to confront our sinful souls."

"Well, I feel perfectly fine," said a reporter from the *Daily Telegraph*. "And I'm with Henley. The Boer War is won, the siege of the Peking legations is lifted, the Empire is in the best of health...."

His colleague from the *Daily Mail* took up the refrain: "Oscar Wilde's rotting in Paris; Lillie Langtry's on her way to New York aboard this very vessel, without her new husband in tow; Sherlock Holmes is busy investigating the robberies at Asprey's of Bond Street and St. James's Palace, and all's right with the world."

"Is Miss Langtry really aboard?" asked Miss Lee, who was the only woman at the sixteen-seater table. She had to turn around to squint myopically through her eyeglasses at the captain's table, some twenty yards away.

"If it was my fellow Frenchman who robbed Asprey's," M. Apollinaire observed, "your famous detective will be frustrated for once. Arsène Lupin will show him a clean pair of heels."

"Was it Lupin who looted Asprey's?" said M. Jarry. "If so, then it must have been Fantômas who burgled St. James's Palace. The principle is the same, of course; they will both be safe in Paris by now, drinking absinthe with dear Oscar."

"I fear that you are wrong, *messieurs*," said M. Féval *fils*. "The unprecedented nature of the double crime strongly suggests that neither Lupin nor Fantômas—nor even the two of them in combination—could have planned and executed it. The *coup* was undoubtedly the work of the brothers Ténèbre."

"The brothers Ténèbre have not been heard of since your father's time!" Apollinaire protested. "And they were English, in any case. They merely masqueraded as Frenchmen."

"Not at all," said M. Féval. "They are such masters of disguise that one must penetrate far more layers than that to reach their true identities. At bottom, they are personifications of sin itself, just as Mr. Holmes is a personification of intellect, while d'Artagnan and Cyrano de Bergerac are personifications of gallantry."

"We shall not see *their* like again," murmured Mr. Huneker, not entirely regretfully.

"Don't you believe it!" said the man from the *Daily Mail*. "There's a personification of gallantry sitting not twenty yards away, right up there at the captain's table between Mr. Edison and the foreign fellow."

"Count Lugard," supplied his colleague from the *Telegraph*. "A Transylvanian, I believe. Old Hearst seems to have taken a dislike to him—can't think why."

"I recognize Tom Edison, of course," said Mr. Robertson, "but I don't know your paragon of gallantry. Who are the four young ladies lined up with them, though? They seem to be putting old Rockefeller and his chum Carnegie in a very sweet mood, and poor Lillie in the shade."

"Three of them are the count's daughters, I believe," M. Féval said. "The fourth is traveling with Quatermain—his ward, I presume. Her name is Ayesha."

"Ah," said Mr. Chambers. "So the *Mail*'s model of gallantry is Allan Quatermain, the legendary discoverer of King Solomon's Mines. I thought he was dead."

"The rumor was exaggerated, apparently," Mr. Twain put in. "Happens all the time."

"Didn't he claim to be something of a coward in his account of the Kukuanaland expedition?" Huneker asked.

"Typical British modesty, my dear sir," said the *Mail* reporter. "Being American, you wouldn't understand that. The man's a shining example to us all—the perfect embodiment of the Imperialist creed."

"With men like him at its beck and call," the *Telegraph* man added, "who can possibly doubt that the Empire is destined to rule the world in the twentieth century as it has in the nineteenth?"

"Every last one of us," murmured M. Lorrain, too softly to be heard by any but his immediate neighbors—who were, of course, in complete sympathy with his judgment.

* * * * * * *

Meanwhile, at the captain's twelve-seater table, the alleged hero in question was looking around in all apparent satisfaction, while the count from Transylvania was whispering confidentially in his ear.

"My friend," the count was saying, "I cannot thank you enough for directing my attention away from Carfax Abbey towards the farther horizon. You are absolutely right—to take a creaky sailing ship for a port like Whitby would have been utter madness, when there is a vessel like this to carry my precious cargo. It was well worth the wait—and there are two thousand peasants down below, you say, crammed into their bunks like veal in crates?"

"No trouble at all, my dear chap," Quatermain replied, magnanimously. "Had it not been for your suggestion of the ingenious trick of carrying the soil of our homeland with us, carefully secreted in the hold, Brother Ange and I might have been anchored to the Great Hungarian Plain indefinitely. You and I have given one another the precious gift of liberty, whose torch-bearing statue and glorious motto we shall salute side by side as we sail into New York while the century fades into oblivion."

"What motto is that?" asked the count, curiously.

"Do as thou wilt," Quatermain replied. "It is the American Dream."

"Your charming ward assures me that you're an excellent story-teller, Mr. Quatermain," Captain John Rowland broke in, as he re-filled his whisky-glass. "Not just the tale of how you discovered Solomon's mines, she says, but any number of other ripping yarns. I hope you'll entertain us with a few of them during the crossing."

"Ayesha flatters me, as always," Quatermain told him. "I'm afraid that my accounts of elephant-hunting and the many lost races of Africa's dark heart have grown a little stale by now. They are un-able to compete, in the nascent modern era, with Dr. Watson's ac-counts of the amazing ingenuity of Sherlock Holmes—not to men-tion those delightful ghost stories Mr. James tells. Ah, if only they were with us, we should certainly be obliged to rescue them from the oblivion of the writers' table! Perhaps we should invite Mr. Twain to join us one evening—he's said to be a dab hand with a tall tale, I believe."

"If we ask Mr. Chambers nicely," Mrs. Hugo de Bathe—the former Lillie Langtry—put in, "he might revert to his old self and favor us with another account of *The King in Yellow*."

"We don't allow fellows like that on *this* table, Miss Langtry," Andrew Carnegie said.

"Not our sort at all," echoed John D. Rockefeller. "Two of them are newspaper reporters, you know."

"If there were one of *my* reporters on board," said William Randolph Hearst, "I'd make damn sure that he traveled second class, but these British journalists are too genteel by half. If you want good stories, it's no good looking at them."

"I fear that I'm only a humble white hunter myself," Quater-main said, with a sigh, "but I've been fortunate enough to lead an adventurous life, and to see some passing strange things. If they make good stories, it's generous fate that must be credited with their authorship. I couldn't make anything up to save my life."

"You're not so humble any more," the Captain observed. "You've as many diamonds as were stolen from Asprey's and St. James's put together, so they say. The produce of King Solomon's Mines has made you rich."

"I'm just one more soldier of fortune living on my capital," Quatermain said, with a sigh of regret. "There was one haul and one only—and I still feel guilty about having the monopoly. Such a pity that Good and Curtis never made it back! I might never have made it myself, if not for the loyal devotion of dear old Gagool! I can't compare with people who make money day by day by means of their industry and ingenuity, like Mr. Rockefeller, Mr. Carnegie, Mr. Hearst, and Mr. Edison."

"Money makes itself, dear chap," Rockefeller assured him, "if you let it have its way. Hard cash does hard work."

"That's the wonder of Capitalism," Carnegie added.

"With a little help from the ads," Hearst supplied. "You have to maintain demand to keep the cash registers ringing—but they'll ring in the new century with a mighty peal."

"I'm just a humble inventor," Edison assured the hunter. "Haven't a penny by comparison with these chaps. The utility of my inventions is its own reward. I'm content simply to have given the world such electrical wonders as the incandescent light-bulb, the phonograph, the telephone, the perfect woman and the chair, not to mention the machine for communicating with the dead. I need no more financial reward than is adequate to fund my further experiments."

"A machine for communicating with the dead?" the count queried. "We have not heard of that device in eastern Europe."

"It's still in the last phase of its development," Edison confessed. "I have the pieces of the prototype carefully lodged below, with all the fragile goods. I put the final touches to the design in London, but I didn't have time to assemble the demonstration model. I thought of taking it to the exhibition in Paris, but I'd rather give the first glimpse of it to American eyes."

"There's no need to wait until New York, then," said Hearst, who had leaned forward attentively as soon as Edison had mentioned his new machine. "You have a better audience in this dining-room than you could hope to get in any exhibition hall in Manhattan. Even if we have to let the British reporters in, they won't be able to get their copy home before my papers hit the streets. Why not bring the machine ashore to a real blaze of publicity?"

"So that Mr. Hearst can steal yet another march on Joe Pulitzer," Rockefeller murmured to Carnegie.

"Be a damn sight more amusing than tales of shooting lions in Africa, at any rate," was Carnegie's whispered reply.

"Well, I don't know about that," Edison said to Hearst. "I'm not sure that the mid-Atlantic's the best place for that kind of chat. I've an idea that the dead might prefer to hang out in cities, just as we do."

"Do you really think so, Mr. Edison?" Ayesha asked, sweetly. "One hears as many tales of haunted wildernesses as of haunted houses—and there's no shortage of tales of haunted ships."

"If they're just like us," Captain Rowland put in, after taking another draught from his whisky-glass, "they'll probably love the *Titan*. Give them a change of scene, what?"

"Absolutely," Quatermain put in. "We have four more nights at sea ahead of us, and I doubt that my meager ability to emulate Scheherazade can possibly keep a company like this on tenterhooks for all that time. I'd dearly like to see Mr. Edison's machine in operation."

"I'd prefer to see his perfect woman!" the Duke of Buccleuch muttered.

The remark did not seem to be addressed to anyone in particular, but Edison heard it. "That was a private commission," he said, frowning. "And besides, we have five perfect women of flesh and blood seated at this very table, have we not?"

"You're far too kind," Ayesha said—although Mrs. de Bathe, who was now forty-seven years old, merely acknowledged the compliment with a slight nod of the head. The count's companions, who did not seem to have a word of English between them, smiled vaguely as they were carefully surveyed by seven pairs of male eyes.

"Well, I guess it *might* be a good idea to try the machine out before we reach New York," Edison said. "It'll take some work, mind—I'll need to borrow a couple of your crewmen, Captain Rowland."

"Granted," Rowland said, generously. "I'll instruct them to set it up in the first-class saloon—under your supervision, of course. When can you have it ready?"

"Not tomorrow or the next night," Edison said. "It's a very tricky assembly. Might be ready on the twenty-ninth, I suppose."

"Excellent," said Captain Rowland, refilling his glass yet again. "What a fine voyage this promises to be!"

* * * * * * *

John Rowland was sleeping dreamlessly, as only a hardened drinker can, when he was awakened by his first officer, Mr. Hodgson.

"I'm afraid there's trouble in steerage, sir," Hodgson reported.

"There's always trouble in steerage," Rowland growled. "Anybody dead?"

"Five, sir—and talk of worse than murder."

"Five!" Rowland sat bolt upright in bed. Deaths in steerage were not uncommon in the course of a westbound journey, because the wretches that huddled into the accommodation in the lower decks by the thousand were often suffering from malnutrition and disease—conditions frequently exacerbated by the sacrifices they had made to purchase their tickets to a new life. To make things worse, the Irish, in particular, tended to be exceedingly quarrelsome. To lose five on the first night out was, however, highly unusual. "And what the devil do you mean, *worse than murder?*" Rowland added, belatedly.

"Three of the victims are young men, sir, and two of them young women. All were said to be in relatively good health before boarding, although they looked damnably thin to me—but the point is, sir, that they've been exsanguinated."

"What on Earth does that mean?"

"It means they've been drained of all their blood, sir. Each of them has a ragged wound in the throat, in the vicinity of the jugular vein and carotid artery. There's talk of vampires, sir."

"Bats?" said the befuddled Rowland.

"No sir—human vampires, like Sir Edward Varney, who was said to have been hanged several times over, or that Hungarian countess who cut a swathe through Paris when Napoleon was first consul."

"Five bodies, you say?" Rowland repeated, pensively. "Do they think we have five vampires aboard?"

"Yes sir, that's the theory," Hodgson confirmed. "There are vigilantes roaming the lower decks already, sir, saying that if the vampires can't be caught, staked through the heart and beheaded today there'll be five more bodies tonight, and five more every night till we reach New York."

"Staked through the heart and beheaded? What kind of barbarians are these people?"

"Mostly Irish, sir. In fact, that's the moderate view. Some are saying that the five victims will rise from the dead to become vampires themselves, so that there'll be ten victims tonight, twenty tomorrow, forty on the twenty-ninth, eighty on the thirtieth, and a further hundred and sixty on New Year's Eve. If we were to be delayed at sea until the second—which isn't so very improbable, if the weather report is to be trusted...."

"Nonsense," said Rowland. "Storms in the Atlantic are water off a duck's back to the *Titan*. We'll be in New York shortly after dawn on New Year's Day, come hell or high water!

"Well sir, even if that's so, the total casualty figures calculated by the alarmist faction would take a fair bite out of the number of steerage passengers, even though we're riding full. Even if the numbers turn out to be a wild overestimate, there's another kind of alarmist wondering what might happen if the monsters were to turn their attention to the upper decks—in which case there might be a real tragedy, if, in fact, there really were any vampires aboard."

"Which there aren't, of course," said Rowland, confidently. "What have you done so far to quell the panic?"

"Mr. Black tried to reassure the frightened emigrants by pointing out that we'll be burying the five bodies at sea, and that it'd take a damnnably clever vampire to find its way back to the *Titan* from the bottom of the Atlantic," Hodgson reported. "That might have been a mistake, in retrospect, because it seemed to concede the possibility that there might actually be vampires involved, which it might have been wiser to deny point blank. Sorry about that, sir."

"That's all right, Hodgson," Rowland said, as he pulled on his uniform. "Black was only doing what he thought best, although they're hardly likely to take such assurances seriously from a second mate. It needs a captain's authority to make such things clear. Hand me that bottle of Scotch, would you? I need a nip to clear my head. Tell Mr. Black and the purser to meet me on the bridge—and find that fellow Quatermain. We may need help on this one, and he's a heroic sort, if what they say is true."

Mr. Hodgson hurried off to execute these orders. Rowland finished off the bottle and then made his way forward, lurching slightly in spite of the state-of-the-art stabilizers with which the luxury liner was fitted. Hodgson was already on the bridge, with the second officer and the purser, young Kitchener—but it was to Allan Quatermain that Rowland turned first.

"There's trouble afoot, Quatermain," he said. "Five people dead—steerage people, but paid for their passage nevertheless—and wild talk about vampires. It needs to be nipped in the bud. I'd like you beside me when I go down there to address the mob, if you're willing. It'll give them extra confidence, you see, you being a big game hunter and all. I'll tell them you'll look into the matter personally, if I may."

"You certainly may," Quatermain said. "I'll do everything I can to help, of course."

At that moment, the door burst open. A young man pushed his way past the sailors stationed beside it, muttering what Rowland assumed at first to be "murder," before he realized that this was one of the French contingent who had come over from Cherbourg on the *Deliverance* to meet the *Titan* at Southampton.

"Monsieur," said the Frenchman, "I am Edward Rocambole, the grandson and heir of *the* Rocambole, and I have come to offer my services as a detective!"

"I never heard of anyone called Rocambole," said Rowland. "Did you, Hodgson?"

"No sir," said Hodgson.

"Nor have I," Black chipped in.

"Nor I," added Kitchener.

"Damn cheek, in any case!" said the captain. "This is a British ship and I've already recruited the best possible assistance in Mr. Quatermain here." He leaned over to whisper in Quatermain's ear: "We don't need any help from some jumped-up Frog who thinks he's Paris's answer to Sherlock Holmes, do we Mr. Quatermain?"

"I think we can handle the matter between the two of us," Quatermain murmured. "Bud-nipping's a job best left to expert fingers, in my experience. Too many hunters frighten the game, you know."

"Exactly," said Rowland. Then he raised his voice again to say: "Won't be necessary, thanks all the same, Monsieur Cricketball."

"But I am the grandson of Rocambole!" Edward Rocambole protested.

"And I'm very probably the bastard grandson of King George IV, as is every dissatisfied soul in England," Rowland countered. "Not that it matters, given that we're in mid-Atlantic. On the *Titan*, I'm master regardless of my ancestry, grand or humble."

"If I might be so bold as to ask, Mr. Rocambole," Quatermain chipped in, "Are you by any chance a second class passenger?"

Edward Rocambole's face went scarlet—a sight that would surely have stirred the spirit of any vampire—as he seemed to realize, belatedly, what he was up against. He muttered what might have been an apology, despite featuring the words *sang, cochon*, and *chien*, and hurried away.

"Right," said Captain Rowland. "I'll just take a little nip of whisky, and then we can go below and pour oil on the troubled waters. Meanwhile, Hodgson, better get those burials organized. Don't want dead bodies cluttering up the *Titan*, do we."

"Can't you store them in the refrigeration hold?" Quatermain asked. "They are, after all, the *prima facie* evidence of five heinous crimes.

Rowland exchanged a furtive glance with Hodgson and Black before saying: "No, we can't. All the available space is taken up by provisions for the voyage. We can't put dead bodies in with the food, can we? The *Titan* is famous for her standards of hygiene. Anyway, if we keep the bodies on ice we'll only feed anxieties about their rising from the dead."

With that, the captain led Allan Quatermain away, thanking him profusely for his kindness in offering support and protection.

Quatermain stood silently by Rowland's side, posing impressively, while the captain made his speech to "the rabble in steerage." The captain's judgment was proved correct; thanks to the weight of his authority and Quatermain's reputation, the mob's leaders were cowed into submission, and were, in the end, meekly delighted to be reassured that there were no vampires aboard the *Titan*.

* * * * * * *

At dinner that evening there was a certain gloom at the writers' table, in spite of the fact that there was Dover sole fried in butter for the fish course, venison pie with roast potatoes for the main course, and spotted dick for dessert. "Three Irish and two cockneys," the man from the *Daily Mail* complained. "Where's the news value in that?"

"Couldn't agree more," said his colleague from the *Telegraph*. "What vampire worth his salt would go after scum like that, when there's flesh of the highest quality on offer." He was staring across the room at the count's three daughters, who were looking even lovelier tonight than they had the previous evening.

"Do vampires take salt with their blood?" M. Apollinaire enquired.

"Sir Edward always had a taste for serving-wenches," Miss Lee pointed out. "If he'd only stuck to them, he wouldn't have been hanged nearly as many times as he was."

"In any case," said M. Vane, "we're all sailing to judgment— what does it matter if some of us get there a day or two ahead of the rest."

"If I were a vampire," M. Lorrain observed, "I wouldn't bother with the likes of the count's daughters."

"Nor would I," said Jarry. "I'd take out Rockefeller, Carnegie and Quatermain. Three vast fortunes to be redistributed at one fell swoop! If they've only had the decency to make substantial bequests to the Arts in their wills...."

"Not likely," said Mr. Huneker, mournfully. "Rockefeller and Carnegie have heirs avid to inherit, who won't let a penny get away if they can help it. Hearst would be a better bet. I don't know about Quatermain, though—does anyone know if this Ayesha's in line for Solomon's diamonds if the old braggart croaks?"

"If there are five vampires aboard," Mr. Twain pointed out, "they could dispose of her too, and the Duke of Buccleuch to boot—and that's just for starters. If the other gossip is reliable, though, they'd all be back again the day after tomorrow to lodge their complaints via Tom Edison's machine."

"It'll never work," Mr. Henley opined. "I knew a man one that tried to sell me a time machine, but it turned out just to be a bicycle with knobs on."

"That Ayesha's a queer one, though," Mr. Chambers said. "Came up to me while I was playing deck quoits his afternoon and asked me if I had a copy of the *King in Yellow* I could lend her. Said she'd always wanted to read it."

"Can I have it after her?" M. Apollinaire put in, swiftly.

"There's no such book, damn it!" Chambers said. "I made it up."

"That's what Dad used to say about vampires," said M. Féval *fils*. "But the bodies keep turning up, don't they?"

"It was probably a fight, a suicide pact and an overdose of laudanum, not necessarily in that order," Henley opined. "It all happened in steerage, after all."

"I'm astonished that the captain decided not to preserve the bodies until we reach New York, though," said Mr. Robertson. "Dereliction of duty, in my opinion. One way or another, those five people were murdered. There ought to be an investigation."

"There's some chap in second class pretending to be a detective," the man from the *Mail* chipped in. "One of your lot, I believe." He was looking at M. Lorrain.

"What do you mean, *my lot*?" Lorrain demanded.

"French, of course," supplied the man from the *Telegraph*. Name of Rocambole."

"Isn't he dead?" asked Mr. Huneker.

"The report was probably exaggerated," Mr. Twain put in. "Happens all the time."

"He's the first M. Rocambole's grandson, Edward," Féval *fils* supplied. "Not a bad chap, really. He's been asking questions in the refrigeration hold."

"Probably after some food," said the man from the *Mail*. "If we're only getting venison pie on the second evening out, they must be getting sausages—and what that leaves for steerage, I can't imagine."

"Faggots," said the man from the *Telegraph*.

"What the hell do you mean by that?" demanded M. Lorrain.

Miss Lee put a soothing hand on M. Lorrain's arm. "It's a form of English *cuisine*," she explained.

"There's a phrase to make the blood run cold," M. Jarry observed. "*English cuisine.*"

"I rather like venison pie," M. Apollinaire confessed.

"It could have been worse," Miss Lee explained to her neighbor. "It might have been black pudding."

"I thought Britain had put an end to the slave trade," Mr. Chambers said, with ill-disguised irony.

"If we hadn't," Mr. Henley said, dryly, "there might have been a different result to your Civil War.

* * * * * * *

Meanwhile, at the captain's table, John Rowland was beaming at Ayesha with eyes softened by a delicate whisky glaze. "You really are the most beautiful woman I've ever seen, Miss Ayesha," he murmured. "Do you have another name, by the way?"

"She-Who-Must-Be-Obeyed," the coquette said, seeming to misunderstand his question. "But I'm a bit of an old dragon, I fear, beside Mrs. de Bathe and Count Lugard's daughters. Now they really *are* lovely. I could almost fancy them myself."

"Not as lovely as you, my dear," Rowland insisted.

"Damn it, Quatermain," John D. Rockefeller said to the great white hunter, "I'd rather listen to one of your blessed stories than watch Rowland make love. No lions, though. Ever encountered a vampire, by any chance?"

"As it happens," Quatermain said, "I have." He had not spoken loudly, but such was the authoritative tone of his voice that the other murmurous conversations ongoing around the table immediately died. All eyes turned to the alleged paragon of gallantry.

"It wasn't reported in any of my newspapers," Hearst said, skeptically.

"Ran into Varney, did you?" asked the Duke of Buccleuch, effortlessly exceeding the American's skepticism.

"No," said Quatermain. "I encountered the Brothers Ténèbre. The younger one is a vampire, you know."

"I thought the younger of the two so-called Ténèbres was a thief named Bobby Bobson," said Buccleuch. "Teamed up with William something-or-other. Weren't they hunted down in Hungary way back in the 1820s?"

"They have been hunted down many times," Count Lugard put in, "but they always return, with new names befitting every new era. Always different, and yet always the same: one tall and manly, the other short and gentle. They are English, as you say, but also French, German and...let us say, *cosmopolitan.*"

"Not American, though," Carnegie put in.

"We'd soon put a stop to their antics," Rockefeller agreed, "if they actually existed, and weren't just phantoms of the Old World's imagination."

"Wouldn't last five minutes in the land of the free," Edison agreed.

"Wouldn't last two in your electric chair, Tom," Hearst added.

"Hold on a minute," said Captain Rowland, banging his glass on the table to call his guests to order. "I want to hear Mr. Quatermain's story. If he says that he's met these two characters, I'm inclined to take is word for it. Was it in Africa, Mr. Quatermain?"

"It was on a ship," Quatermain said. "Not such a fine vessel as this one, of course, but a neat enough rig in her way—the *Pride of Kimberley*, a cargo vessel with two dozen passenger cabins. I came up from Cape Town to Lisbon in her a few years back. First night out, a body turned up, in much the same condition as those we buried at sea today. Just one, mind—a young woman. No one suspected a vampire, at first, until a second body turned up in much the same condition, when the crew started muttering. That was three nights later, mind—if it was a vampire, it wasn't so very hungry. Probably on rations, given that we only had eight women aboard, only three of which could be reasonably described as young. I'm getting ahead of myself, though. Like Captain Rowland, the skipper turned to me for help as soon as the first body was found, and I promised to look into the matter."

As he paused to chew a mouthful of spotted dick, Carnegie whispered to Rockefeller: "Fellow can't even get his plot in the right order."

"Unlike Rowland, who can't get his *hors d'oeuvres* in the right plot." murmured Rockefeller. "He'd do better to set his cap for one of the Count's daughters—at least they wouldn't understand what he's saying."

"Not suspecting a vampire at first," Quatermain went on, "I figured that any skullduggery aboard a ship like the *Pride of Kimberley* was bound to concern diamonds. On a ship like the *Titan* there must be rich and various pickings for any thief clever enough and bold enough to try his luck, but the *Kimberley* was outward bound from Cape Town. I wasn't the only passenger carrying a few stones to cover my traveling expenses—in fact, it would have been hard for a flying fish to skim the deck without hitting someone with a few sparklers stashed away in his luggage.

"At first, when I began asking my fellow passengers to check up on their hidden goods, they all reported that everything was in its place—but within twenty-four hours of my asking, they began coming back to me to say that they'd checked again, with much less happy results. Nearly half of them had lost their secret savings, and most of the losers were in no position to complain to any authorities in the Cape or England, because the stones were being smuggled. They'd never have confessed it to me if I hadn't shown them my own stones, and explained to them that I reckoned that old King Solomon had probably imposed his duty at source, so I didn't see why Queen Victoria should get a second cut.

"Then the second body turned up, and the third chap who had a daughter in tow started worrying about losing more than his half-dozen second-rate gems. Even the men who only had wives got a little distracted, by hope if not anxiety. The blood-sucking seemed to me to be a strange business, because I couldn't see why a vampire would get on a boat where he'd be out at sea for days on end, and where his predations would stick out like a sore thumb. You could see why one might get on a great ship like this, I suppose, where there are three thousand potential victims at sea for less than a week, but the *Kimberley* was another kettle of fish. I decided soon enough that the guilty party couldn't have come aboard in search of blood, and that taking the blood he needed to sustain him was just a matter of necessity while he carried out his intended plunder—which meant, I figured, that whoever had taken the diamonds must also be taking the blood.

"Now, one of the first passengers to complain that the secret compartment in his trunk had been emptied was a tall German fellow who clamed to be the Baron von Altenheimer, who was traveling with his brother Benedict, a Catholic priest—a Monsignor, no less. I was suspicious of the Baron from the very beginning, because he claimed to have been at Heidelberg, although didn't have a single dueling scar and never mentioned G. W. F. Hegel in casual conversation. I set myself to keep a very close watch on the pair of them. He fancied himself a story-teller, but I noticed that his brother kept slipping away when he was telling his tales, protesting that he had heard them all before. I followed the Monsignor the very next evening, and caught him rifling the lining of a three-piece suit hanging up in one of the cabins—which turned out to have seven rough-cut stones sewn under the collar.

"I managed to knife him between the shoulder-blades while his back was still turned, but it wasn't a mortal blow. Actually, he made quite a fight of it—he was a wiry little chap, and he certainly didn't have muscles like a priest—but I turned the tables on him after he'd chased me up on deck and eventually managed to throw him overboard. Not a moment too soon, either, seeing that his brother, having delivered his punch line, immediately came at me with a saber. The baron was a much bigger fellow than the priest, with quite some reach, but I'd had the presence of mind to secrete one of my hunting-rifles in the scuppers, just in case, and I got to it before he sliced me up. I let him have both barrels, and he went over the side too. He was probably dead before he hit the water, but it wouldn't have mattered if he wasn't. The sharks were all around us by then, having been attracted by the younger one, who was bleeding like a stuck pig from the wound in his back.

"We went through their luggage of course—that's how we discovered who they really were—but we didn't find a single diamond. Even the stones that Brother Benedict had snatched from the loaded suit must have gone over the side with him. The sharks must have scoffed the lot—but at least the third young lady was saved from becoming a vampire's victim, much to her relief. She was very grateful to me, but as she was much the ugliest of the three, I didn't take advantage of the poor child."

"Ayesha wasn't with you on that trip, I presume?" Captain Rowland asked.

"No, she wasn't. This is her first time out of Africa. It's all a great adventure for her."

"Actually, my dear," the young woman drawled, "it's been a bit of a drag so far. No disrespect to your marvelous ship, captain, but I'll be glad to get back on dry land, where I can be myself again."

145

"Meaning no disrespect myself, young lady," the captain said, "but I'll be very glad to have four more days of your company before you do."

"You don't suppose *we*'re in danger, do you, Mr. Edison?" the former Mrs. Langtry said to her neighbor.

"I doubt that I am," Edison replied, a trifle ungraciously. "These ancient monsters never attack men of science."

Andrew Carnegie, meanwhile, leaned over to whisper in John D. Rockefeller's ear: "Didn't believe a damned word of it myself," he said. "Made the whole thing up, I shouldn't wonder."

"I don't know," said Rockefeller. "If he were making it up, he'd surely have painted his fighting skills in a kinder light—and he'd have added a love interest too. You can be sure that's what Mr. Chambers would have done—or even that Twain fellow. Didn't I read that he was dead, by the way?"

"I read that too," Hearst put in, "in one of my own papers—so it must be true. We won't have far to look for our vampire, if any more poor folk turn up dead, will we?"

* * * * * * *

Captain Rowland was woken again shortly before dawn on the twenty-eighth, this time by Mr. Black. Rowland had been dreaming about chasing a sea serpent, desperate to be hailed as a hero by Mr. Hearst's *New York Sun* and to win the love of the fair Ayesha.

"What is it now?" he demanded.

"Five more dead, sir," Black reported. "Three young men, two young women. Only one Irishwoman this time, though, and two Americans on their way home."

"Americans? Not...."

"No sir—steerage, like the others. Mormons, I believe."

"That's all right, then. Can't imagine Hearst getting excited about that. More rumors, I suppose?"

"Yes sir. They're not going to be fobbed off by a speech this time. And there's been a leak."

"A leak! Which compartment? How bad is it?"

"Not in the hull sir—I mean that someone in the crew's been letting out information about the cargo."

"You mean..."

"No sir, not that. The sarcophagi in the secure hold."

"Damn! That *will* make Hearst excited, for all the wrong reasons. He's very secretive, for a newspaperman. Still, I suppose it's not every day one gets a chance to pick up the contents of a freshly-looted tomb on the cheap while passing through Cairo. You can't blame the man, given that he has the money to spare. So the steerage mob has got the idea that we've got a gang of Egyptian vampire mummies aboard, has it?"

"Yes sir."

"Very well. You know the drill. Meeting on the bridge. Send for Quatermain—and Hearst too, I suppose."

Black hurried off and Rowland got dressed, cursing his luck. By the time he arrived on the bridge, Hearst was already berating Hodgson, Black and Kitchener. "When I say absolute secrecy, I mean absolute secrecy," the newspaper magnate was shouting, at the top of his voice. "If I wanted people to know my business, I'd print it. I want an armed guard placed on the hold with my treasure in it—a dozen men, the very best you have. If anyone comes near it, they shoot to kill."

"We'll do everything necessary to protect your property, sir," Rowland assured him. "And yours too, sir, of course," he added, turning to Allan Quatermain."

"Oh, don't worry about *my* luggage," Quatermain said. "I don't have any precious stones stashed away in my boxes—just some interesting fossils I picked up in Olduvai Gorge."

"Precious stones!" howled Hearst. "Who told you I had gems? Do you think I'm some kind of smuggler? Why, I'll bet that Carnegie's bullion is worth five times as much as my few trinkets—and as for Rockefeller's suitcase full of bonds...."

"Excuse me, Mr. Hearst," Rowland said, soothingly, "but none of us is supposed to know about any of that. I don't think Mr. Carnegie and Mr. Rockefeller...."

"Don't be an idiot, man, I'm not going to print it. I've got *real* news to print, about preachers' love-nests and actresses' bastards."

"Guards with guns aren't going to quiet rumors, sir," Hodgson said. "If anything, they'll just inflame them further. Will you try to talk to the people in steerage again, captain?"

"If you'll pardon the suggestion," Quatermain put in, "I think it might be a good idea to change our tactics. Instead of going down to the steps of the third-class deck to talk to anyone who cares to listen, perhaps we might invite a few of the ringleaders up to your stateroom—sit them down, offer them a cigar and a few bottles of champagne, talk about the situation like civilized men. I'm sure we can make them see sense and convert them into ambassadors of reason. Especially if Mr. Hearst can promise to give due acknowledgement to their contribution in the *Sun*. Perhaps Mr. Carnegie and Mr. Rockefeller might offer their services in finding the anxious gentlemen employment, when they reach New York."

"That's exactly what I was about to suggest," said Rowland. "A capital plan, worthy of a true naval strategist. Organize it, Hodgson. Put the extra armed guards on the hold anyway, though. Can you see to that, Black? As soon you've arranged for the disposal of the bodies."

"Yes sir," said the two mates, in unison.

"Have you really got *fossils* in those boxes of yours, Quatermain?" Hearst asked, in the meantime, having evidently calmed down. "Dinosaurs, do you mean?"

"Not dinosaurs, Mr. Hearst," Quatermain said. "I've seen a few dinosaurs in my time, but I never managed to bag one, worse luck. These are humanoid bones. I intend to make a gift of them to the New York Museum of Natural History?"

"Who told you about that, damn it?" said Rowland, whose attention had only just returned to his passengers' conversation.

"I didn't know it was a secret," Quatermain said, equably. "Surely everyone knows that New York has the second best Natural History Museum in the world?"

"Not for long," Hearst assured him. "It'll be the best soon enough."

"It certainly will," Rowland agreed, in spite of being an Englishman.

"It would be if we could catch one of these vampires for its exhibition halls," Quatermain said. "Especially if it turned out to be a mummy. Two attractions for the price of one!"

"If anyone touches one of my sarcophagi," Hearst said, darkly, "they'll end up wrapped in bandages themselves."

* * * * * * *

By mid-afternoon on the twenty-eighth, Allan Quatermain's plan seemed to have worked like a charm. Harmony had been restored to the lower decks, and everything was running smoothly on the Titan, in spite of the worsening weather. The vessel was sailing into the teeth of a force nine gale from noon till six o'clock, and the rain was torrential, but the wind slackened in the evening and the deluge relented. As the crew were about to go into dinner, Black reported that a good proportion of the steerage passengers were dreadfully seasick, and that more than one had expressed the thought that exsanguination by a vampire would be a mercy.

There were a few absentees from the first-class dining-room too, but the writers' table was full. Several of the faces on display were a trifle green, but these were men with nibs of steel, and they were not about to let a little nausea prevent them from enjoying a meal whose price had been included in their tickets. The fish was only cod, but the main course was roast lamb with mint sauce, with prune flan to follow.

"You don't suppose that Hearst's mummies are really rising from their coffins by night to steep their bandages in blood, do you?" said the man from the *Telegraph* to the man from the *Mail*.

"Who cares?" said the man from the *Mail*. "It'd be a great story if we were ever able to print it, but your editor wouldn't wear it any more than mine would. We could try hawking it to Pulitzer, I suppose."

"He wouldn't touch it either," said the *Telegraph* man. "The good old days are long gone; it's all one big cartel now. These other chaps might make something of it, though—benefits of poetic license and all."

"I'm afraid not," said Mr. Twain. "The trouble with being an honest liar is that you have to maintain plausibility. A Yankee at King Arthur's Court is one thing—vampire mummies on a transatlantic liner is another."

"Perhaps so," said M. Féval *fils*, regretfully. "Although...."

"I do hope there isn't going to be a mutiny," said Mr. Henley.

"Really?" said M. Apollinaire. "Why?"

"A mutiny might be quite amusing," M. Jarry agreed.

"There isn't going to be a mutiny," Mr. Huneker said, "unless the vampires start picking on the crew. The passengers might let off a little steam, but nobody with an ounce of common sense goes in for serious rioting on a ship in mid-Atlantic, especially in the dead of winter."

"We shall meet our fate soon enough," opined Mr. Vane.

"You talk like a one-book writer, Mr. Vane," said Mr. Chambers, a trifle snappishly. "Think of the delights awaiting us in New York. Think of the romance of America, and the new-born century!"

"We've got to get to New York first," Miss Lee pointed out. "Have you been out on the promenade deck today?"

"Certainly not," said M. Lorrain.

"We'll get to New York all right," said Mr. Robertson. "A little late, perhaps, but we'll get there. I trust this ship implicitly."

"Everyone trusts his ship implicitly, until it starts to sink," M. Jarry observed.

"An allegory of life," said M. Apollinaire, with a sigh. "I must mention it to Mallarmé when I get back."

"Didn't I read that he was dead?" Mr. Henley put in.

"Probably an exaggerated report," said Mr. Twain.

"Happens all the time," fifteen voices chorused, before Mr. Twain could draw breath.

"The deaths in steerage weren't exaggerated, though," said Mr. Chambers, pensively. "We've another four nights at sea yet—maybe five if the storm sets us back a long way. That's twenty or twenty-five more bodies, at the present rate."

"Enough to devastate the whole of our table," Mr. Huneker agreed, "if the vampires get tired of slumming. Except, of course, that we all have ink in our veins instead of blood."

"There might be worse things aboard than vampires," said Mr. Twain, who had recovered quickly enough from his momentary embarrassment. "I talked to your friend Rocambole today, M. Féval, and he dropped a few dark hints about secret lockers in the refrigeration hold. Now, it happens that I was also talking to the crewman who's in charge of the refrigeration unit—that Kitchener fellow—and he jumped like a jackrabbit when I asked him what he had in his secret locker. Denied everything, of course—just ice, he said—but one of his kitchen staff muttered something about monsters of the deep that never really died, even if they were cut to pieces."

"Sea serpents, you man?" said the man from the *Mail*.

"Not likely," said the man from the *Telegraph*. "I heard a rumor about that ship that went down in the channel last week—the *Dunlin*, I think it was, or maybe the *Sandwich*. There was talk of that being sunk by a monster that should have been dead but wasn't."

"There can't be any sea serpents in the Solent," Mr. Henley put in. "they'd never get away unobserved in Cowes week."

"That's just the point," said the man from the *Telegraph*. "This was something tinged with a far more sinister superstition than any mere sea serpent."

"Like vampire mummies, you mean?" asked Mr. Chambers.

"Something of the same order, I suppose," the man from the *Telegraph* admitted, "but there was talk of Madeira...."

"Rowland's favorite tipple seems to be Scotch," M. Jarry put in.

"Mine's absinthe," M. Apollinaire added.

"*I* heard a rumor that these sarcophagi in the hold don't actually have mummies in them at all," the man from the *Mail* told his colleague, competitively. "They're actually stuffed full of gems, bullion and bonds. All shady, of course—but that's how these millionaires stay ahead of the pack, isn't it?"

"Let's hope it's all still there when we reach New York," said the *Telegraph* man. "I'd hate to think of those French bandits who robbed Asprey's and the palace making off with it, wouldn't you?"

* * * * * * *

Meanwhile, Allan Quatermain was responding to a query from the Duke of Buccleuch as to whether he'd ever encountered a mummy."

"Several," Quatermain answered. "But only one that was given to wandering around."

"And was it a vampire, too?" inquired Hearst, sarcastically.

"Not at all. He was a rather plaintive chap, actually, animated by the desire to be reunited with his long-lost love, Queen Nefertiti. He choked a few people to death, but only because they got in his way. I had to do something about it, though—the business was getting out of hand."

"Blew him away with your elephant-gun, I suppose," Carnegie observed.

"I did try that," Quatermain admitted, "but the bullets went clean through him, and the dust they blew out simply spiraled around for a few minutes before getting sucked back into his body. I could have been in a sticky situation myself then, but he wasn't much of a runner."

"How fortunate," murmured Mrs. de Bathe.

"I had to set a trap for him instead," Quatermain went on. "Happily, he was none too bright—the ancient Egyptians used to take a mummy's brain out through the nostrils with a kind of hook, you know, and put it in its own canopic jar—so he fell right in. I'd filled the pit with oil, and laid a gunpowder fuse, so it seemed like a mere matter of striking a match and retiring to a safe distance."

"Seemed?" said Rockefeller. "You mean that it didn't work?"

"Oh, he went up like a Roman candle. The resin Egyptian mummifiers use to stick the bandages together is very flammable, and what was left of his body was as dry as a stick. If anything, the operation was a little too successful. It turned him into a cloud of thick black smoke in a matter of seconds. The trouble was that the trick he had of sucking back his dust after bullets went through him worked just as well on smoke. One minute there was nothing but a cloud settling slowly to ground-level, the next he was reformulating, a little larger than before and in a far darker mood."

"How terrible, my dear fellow!" said the count. "What on Earth did you do next?"

"Ran like hell, old man. He was a little nippier on his pins now, but I still had the legs of him. I needed to rethink the whole problem, but once I'd figured out what was what, it wasn't too hard to come up with a new plan. Given that fire hadn't worked, the logical thing to try seemed to be water, for which he seemed to have something of an aversion—but transporting water from the Nile is a tricky business, and he wasn't about to be lured into the stream."

"So you buried him, did you?" Hearst suggested. "Got him back into his pyramid and slammed the door behind him."

"That might have worked, I suppose," Quatermain said, judiciously, "but it didn't seem to me to qualify as a final solution. Besides which, I already knew that he was a sucker for pitfall traps—so it was just a matter of figuring out what kind of filling might work better than oil." He paused for dramatic effect

"What did you use?" Rowland asked, impatiently.

"Molasses," Quatermain said. "Nice, thick, sticky molasses. After a couple of days of impotent struggling, he'd virtually dissolved in the stuff. After two days more it had set rock hard. We broke up the mass and sold the pieces in the souk as dark candy. I didn't eat any myself, but those who did said it was delicious. I think I've got a few pieces left in my cabin, if anyone wants to try some."

"Doesn't that qualify as cannibalism?" Edison asked.

"No more so than enjoying this delightful repast," Quatermain said, indicating the lamb shoulder on his plate. "Or, for that matter, breathing. Where do you think the carbon in our bodies goes when it's recycled? Julius Caesar's atoms have been redistributed so widely by now that there's one in every mouthful we eat, another in every breath we take. And Attila the Hun's too, of course, not to mention Cain and Solomon, Herod and Apollonius of Tyana. There's a little of everything human in every one of us, gentlemen—and a little of everything unhuman too. Cats and bats, mice and elephants, snakes and dragons. Everything circulates—except wealth, of course. Wealth always flows uphill, from the pockets of the poor to the coffers of the rich. Isn't that so, Mr. Rockefeller, Mr. Carnegie?"

Hearst burst out laughing. "I concede, Mr. Quatermain," he said. "You're a cleverer storyteller than I thought. Except, of course, that you're contradicting yourself. The story you told last night, about the infamous brothers Ténèbre, suggests that wealth sometimes vanishes into the maws of sharks."

"Was that really the moral of my story?" Quatermain said. "Well, perhaps—I'm just a humble white hunter. If you know anything at all about the brothers Ténèbre, though, you'll know that they're infinitely more skilled at self-reconstitution than any mere mummy. They always come back, and they always have another robbery to execute—but they're just fleas on an elephant's back when it comes to questions of serious wealth. I'll wager that they could clear out the hold of this ship—and the first-class cabins too— without putting any one of you gentlemen to any serious inconvenience, even though your luggage would seem a fabulous fortune to any of those poor folk down in steerage. They'll have little chance in life but to be vampires' victims, I fear, even if they reach New York with the blood still coursing in their veins."

"Not so," said Edison. "Were your immortal bandits to make off with my machine for communicating with the dead, I'd be the loser and so would the world. It's irreplaceable. Light-bulbs, phonographs and electric chairs can be mass-produced; once you have the trick of their making, it can't ever be unlearned, but the machine for communicating with the dead is a different thing altogether—a radically new departure. Its operation isn't based on the laws of physics, but the principles of pataphysics."

"What on earth is pataphysics?" demanded the Duke of Buccleuch.

"It's the scientific discipline that deals with exceptions rather than rules."

"It sounds more like scientific indiscipline to me," said Carnegie.

"In a manner of speaking, it is," Edison admitted. "It's a tricky basis on which to build a technology. Every fugitive principle of pataphysics is good for one unique machine, but mass production is awkward. The factory principle doesn't apply, you see—every one would have to be hand-crafted."

"Sounds un-American to me," Rockefeller observed.

"Is it really unique?" Quatermain asked. "I had not imagined that we might have anything so rare and priceless aboard. What about you, my dear? Had you any inkling of this?"

"No," said Ayesha. "I had not. And yet, we are to be privileged to witness the machine's debut tomorrow night, are we not?"

"I'm afraid it won't be tomorrow, ma'am," Edison said, sorrowfully. "The crewmen Captain Rowland lent me are doing their best, and the ship's stabilizers are working wonders, but the storm is making things difficult even so. It'll be the thirtieth now, I fear."

"What a pity!" said the count.

"I have no doubt that it will be worth the wait," said the former Lillie Langtry, "And the pleasures of anticipation will be all the more piquant."

"I'll drink to that," said Rowland.

"We shall all look forward to it immensely," Ayesha assured the inventor.

* * * * * * *

Later that night, when the last of the first-class passengers had retired to their cabins, Ayesha came into Allan Quatermain's cabin. Once through the door she changed her stance slightly, and when she spoke her voice seemed a good deal deeper than it had in the dining-room.

"You can steal Edison's machine if you want to," she said, "but we have to take the rest too. I'm not going without the gems from Hearst's treasure-trove, Carnegie's bullion, or Rockefeller's bonds just so you can tinker with some idiot machine. What would we want with a machine for communicating with the dead, anyway? It's not as if we haven't been dead often enough ourselves—if our peers had wanted a chat, they could have dropped in on our graves then."

"It would all depend on which dead people we'd be able to talk to," Quatermain told his companion, stretching himself out on the bed as he spoke. His Africa-tinged British accent had vanished; one might almost have taken him for a Frenchman by the timbre of his voice. "Some dead people—the aristocracy of the astral plane, you might say—must know many interesting and valuable secrets."

"You want us to go hunting buried treasure under the advice of ancient pirates and plunderers?"

"The more recently-dead have their secrets too. I've always thought that blackmail is a more civilized crime than burglary—and so much more modern. We ought to move with the times, Brother Ange, lest we make strangers of ourselves in a world we no longer comprehend."

"I comprehend Carnegie's bullion as well as he does, Brother Jean," the false Ayesha said. "Nor have I the slightest difficult in comprehending Rockefeller's bonds. No matter how the world changes, there'll always be money, and where there's money, there'll always be thieves. We are timeless, brother; that is the very essence of our nature. We are the shadows of the love of money that is the root of all evil, and we shall never lose touch with the world, no matter how many times we are banished from it, only to return."

"The love of money is not the only kind we shadow," the false Quatermain observed. "You might consider leaving your grosser appetite unslaked tonight. Exsanguinated corpses are a trifle conspicuous on a ship, even one of this gargantuan size."

"Have you mentioned that to the count and his harem?" the cross-dressing brother retorted. "They've been starved too long to be moderate in circumstances like these. And I've been hunting alone for far too long not to enjoy the company. You should come with us tonight, you know—you're supposed to be a great white hunter, aren't you? Stalking Irish colleens is so much more fun than stalking elephants, and one can take so much more pleasure from them, even before one drains them dry."

"*Chacun a son goût*," said the false Quatermain. "I am the Chevalier Ténèbre; I treat courtship in a very different fashion."

"More fool you. Given that the count's ladies are spoken for and Lillie Langtry's past it, there's nothing in first class worth making your kind of effort for, but the lower decks are full of girls who fondly imagine that there's something better awaiting in New York but whoredom. Think of the disillusionment I'm saving them! Anyway, it's the swordplay that attracts you to the knightly life, not chaste courtly love. You must be aching for a good fight. You might try picking one with one of those frightful writers—the world could do with a few less of their kind."

"Once we're in Manhattan," the pretended Quatermain said, "you can gorge yourself to your heart's content. It won't do you any harm to go easy for a couple of nights."

"It's a couple now, is it? And I expect you want me to talk to the count and his brides, vampire to vampire?"

"If you wouldn't mind. If we stir up a hornet's nest here, it'll be that much more difficult to lay our hands on the loot, and I'm sure that the count would rather not advertise his arrival in New York too loudly. I know that we're not much given to virtues, but a little patience might help our cause here. If you explain it to the count, he'll keep his brides in line. He doesn't tolerate disobedience."

"Neither do I," said Ayesha, reverting momentarily to her role. "I'll do it—but only on the understanding that we take every last penny of whatever Hearst, Carnegie, and Rockefeller have stashed away. If Edison's machine is heavy, it goes on to your share of the load, not mine."

"Agreed," said Allan Quatermain.

The fake white hunter turned over on the bunk then, intending to go to sleep—but five minutes after Ayesha had left, there was a knock on his cabin door.

At first, Quatermain did not recognize the man who entered in response to his invitation, but after a few moments he remembered where he had seen the other before. "Mr. Rocambole," he said. "What can I do for you?"

"I came to see you, Mr. Quatermain, because I don't trust that drunken fool of a captain," Rocambole said. "It seems to me that you're one of the few men on this damned boat with a head on his shoulders. I've been carrying out some investigations down below, and I'd like to share my findings with you, if you don't mind."

"Not at all," said Quatermain. "I'd be interested to hear what you've found out. You decided to inquire into the murders in spite of the captain's rude refusal of your help, I presume?"

"I did. I've conducted more than a hundred interviews with relatives and friends of the murdered individuals, and people who were close to the locations in which they were killed. I've got some pretty good descriptions of characters who had no reason to be around on the nights in question. I'd have taken the information to the captain in spite of the way he treated me, but...well, they're first class passengers, you see."

"Ah," said Quatermain. "That would make the matter rather delicate."

"They're not British, though," Rocambole added. "Or French, of course. Would that make a difference, do you suppose?"

"I don't know. Who are we talking about?"

"Count Lugard and his three daughters, and a man I haven't been able to identify—short, slim and fair-haired. I've asked Féval and Apollinaire to see if they can spot him in the first class dining-room, but they both said that the description doesn't ring a bell. The count doesn't have anyone else traveling with him, I suppose, except for his daughters."

"I don't believe so. Are you actually alleging that the count and his three daughters are vampires?"

"Of course not—that would be preposterous. My grandfather told me some tall tales, but he always told me to leave the impossible out and stick to real possibilities, however unlikely. I suppose they might be members of some secret society of assassins, but I think it far more likely that they're gathering blood for some kind of medical research. I think they're experimenting with blood transfusions—or, rather, preparing to carry out such experiments when they reach New York. Surgeons are attempting to use the technique to compensate for blood loss during amputations, I believe."

"It seems rather far-fetched," Quatermain observed, "but it does have the virtue of avoiding the supernatural. Where do you suppose the count and his assistants are storing the blood?"

"In the refrigerated hold. It's the logical place. I bribed one of the cooks to let me check out the food storage units, and I couldn't see anything suspicious there, but I'm there's a secret compartment or two behind one of the bulkheads. If I could get hold of a plan of the ship, I might be able to figure out where they are."

"And you think that I might be able to obtain one from the captain or one of the mates?"

"The purser, Kitchener, might be your best bet—but you'll have to be careful. I don't want to arouse the suspicions of whichever crewman is in on the conspiracy."

"Are you sure that one of them is?" Quatermain asked.

"Yes. Someone's responsible for the captain's churlish attitude to my offer of help. He's just a drunken dupe, of course, but one of the two mates must be pulling the strings. That Hodgson's a rum chap—has a camera, you know, takes pictures up on deck when there's no one there to take pictures of. Scribbles, too. On the other hand, Black's got political ideas. I never trust a man with political ideas. I like a straightforward man like yourself, sir—a man who faces his problems squarely, with an elephant gun. Grandfather would have approved of you."

"The feeling would have been mutual, I'm sure," Quatermain said. "Very well, Mr. Rocambole—I'll try to get you your plan, and I'll make some enquiries of my own. Can't let a gang of blood-runners operate unchecked on one of Her Majesty's merchant ships, can we? You can depend on me."

"Do you know who the other man might be, Mr. Quatermain? The short one, I mean."

"I'll enquire into that too," Quatermain assured him. "Can't say I've noticed him, but he may be a crewmen or a second-class passenger. Villains of the count's type always have minions, in my experience."

"Thank you, Mr. Quatermain," Edward Rocambole said, stepping forward to shake the hunter's hand before withdrawing.

"If I were you," Quatermain said, "I'd keep a very careful look-out tonight."

"I will," Rocambole promised. "Not a wink of sleep for me. If I catch a glimpse of any one of them, I'll find out what they're up to."

* * * * * * *

By the time the captain was woken by his cabin-boy on the twenty-ninth the sun was over the horizon and his hangover had taken so strong a hold that he had to quaff half a bottle of cognac to bring it under control.

"Nobody died, then?" he said, as soon as his tongue was unfurred.

"Nobody drained of blood, sir," the cabin-boy reported. "Last night's only casualties were two old men who died of hypothermia for lack of decent overcoats. Nobody's panicking over that, sir."

"Excellent! Tell Black to heave the bodies over the side forthwith, and let's hope for a day's plain steaming. How's the weather?"

"There's a lull at the moment, sir, but the bo'sun says that there's another storm-front visible in the south-west, heading our way. Going to be a rough afternoon."

"Damn. Passengers are always in a better mood when they've chucked a few deck quoits around. I suppose it'll still be blowing this evening, so the orchestra in the ballroom will be playing so many extra notes that every waltz will turn into the Gay Gordons. Never mind—there's still the casino."

By the time the captain had refreshed himself and climbed up to the bridge the storm-front was almost upon the vessel, and the sky in the south-west was very dark indeed.

"Wouldn't have fancied that in the old days, Hodgson," Rowland said to the first mate. "Enough to put a sailing ship's schedule back two days, and fill the bilges with vomit. Nothing to fear here, though: the *Titan*'s unshakeable and unstoppable as well as unsinkable. No icebergs in sight, I hope?"

"None, sir," Hodgson confirmed. "May I take my camera out on deck to photograph the storm?"

"If you like. Silly idea, mind. Where's the fun in looking at postcards of clouds and corposants when you can have French whores in any pose you fancy?"

"It's a hobby, sir," the mate said.

The captain's excessive claim regarding the unshakeability of the *Titan* proved woefully unfounded, especially when her second funnel was struck by lightning. The bolt burned out the wires of the ship's internal telegraph, causing all kinds of problems in the transmission of orders. By the time he had to dress for dinner again John Rowland felt that he had been run ragged, and he was direly in need of a stiff drink. When he descended to the dining-room the meal was in full flow, and he was forced to bolt his mock-turtle soup in order to catch up with the next course. It wasn't until the halibut had been cleared away and his roast beef and Yorkshire pudding arrived that he began to relax, aided by his eighth glass of claret.

By this time, Allan Quatermain was reaching the conclusion of yet another story. Popular demand seemed to have dragged him back to the subject of King Solomon's mines. "Yes," he was saying, in answer to a question from the count. "Old Gagool was with me for a year or two after we got back from Kukuanaland. She was a fount of esoteric knowledge. It was she who told me where I could find Kôr, in fact, where I met Ayesha. It was a crying shame that she was immolated by that pillar of flame—but she was very old, you know, and she really did believe that it would rejuvenate her; that was the whole reason she guided me there. I admire the way that natives place such tremendous faith in their superstitions, though. Humans ought to live according to their beliefs, don't you think? We need to be true to our nature, or we're guilty of a terrible cowardice."

"Don't like all this talk of true nature," Carnegie said. "People decide for themselves what they want to be. I'm a self-made man, through and through."

"Me too," said Rockefeller. "What about you, Hearst?"

"Can't see the difference," Hearst growled. "If your nature's to be a self-made man, that's what you'll be. If not, you'll be what other people make of you.

"Sophistry," said Carnegie.

"Not at all," said Count Lugard. "Mr. Hearst is right, and so is Mr. Quatermain. We do not come innocent into the world; we are what we are. Some are shaped to take destiny by the horns and transform themselves, thus entering the next phase of human progress. Others are shaped to submit, and thus to slide back towards the animal. Most people, thankfully, are cattle with delusions of grandeur."

"Thankfully, Count?" Edison queried.

"But of course. Life is a struggle; for the few to succeed, it is necessary that the many must fail. Power is, by definition, power over others; the more one many has, the more his underlings must be deprived of it. Those of us who have it can only be glad that the majority of humankind is submissive, eager to be led...and bled."

"The man has a point," Rockefeller admitted.

"A very good point," the Duke of Buccleuch agreed.

"It's a very harsh way of thinking," Mrs. de Bathe objected.

"It's a very obsolete way of thinking," Edison put in. "Power is no longer limited to the authority to command the muscles of animals and men. Power nowadays is oil and coal, electricity and steel. Power nowadays is *machinery*. In the twentieth century, all men will be better able remake themselves, by means of their technology. Nor will it be merely a matter of their material conditions; with the assistance of a vast array of instruments of discovery whose nature you can hardly imagine, men will become a greater deal wiser. Knowledge is power too, and the twentieth century will be an era of information. We ought to envy the generations that will come after us, gentlemen."

"A little knowledge is a dangerous thing," Buccleuch muttered.

"And too much is a truly terrible thing," murmured Count Lugard. "Mankind cannot bear overmuch enlightenment."

"We invariably do envy the generations that will come after us, as we gradually grow older," Carnegie said, in a louder voice. "And when we die...ah, how envious the dead must be of the living!"

"We'll have a chance to find that out, won't we?" Hearst said. "This time tomorrow, eh, Mr. Edison? No further delays, I hope?"

"Everything will be in order by the time we have dined tomorrow, Mr. Hearst," Edison confirmed. "We shall give the dead yet another opportunity to envy our repast before we consult their wisdom."

"If this storm doesn't let up," Hearst muttered, "we'll probably give them the chance to envy us queuing on deck to throw up over the side. Are you sure this beef hasn't spoiled, Rowland?"

"Perfectly sure, Mr. Hearst," the captain said. "We have excellent refrigeration facilities in the hold behind the galley. Nothing ever spoils aboard the *Titan*."

"The perfect place to store fresh blood," Quatermain whispered in Ayesha's ear, "if one were a clandestine medical researcher devoid of ethics."

"Or any other kind of uncanny flesh," Ayesha whispered in her turn, "if it so happened that all the blood had been quaffed by more scrupulous predators."

* * * * * * *

Coincidentally, the conversation at the writers' table had reached exactly the same topic. "Searched the refrigeration hold, did he?" M. Jarry said to M. Apollinaire, while he contemplated a slice of Yorkshire pudding impaled on his fork.

"Yes," said M. Apollinaire, "but he thinks there's a secret compartment there, where the blood's being carefully stocked up."

"For transfusion, you say?" Mr. Robertson asked.

"We don't say anything," M. Féval *fils* corrected him. "We're merely repeating what he told us. According to him, it's definitely a matter of transfusion. He might be right. He's the detective, after all."

"It's disgusting," said Mr. Henley. "I don't know how people come up with these ideas. I used to like horror stories when they had ghosts and natural monsters, but I don't approve of this *medical* horror. It's all mad scientists and gruesome violations of the body—practically pornographic."

"And M. Rocambole thinks that Count Lugard and those three lovely girls of his are the blood-burglars?" Mr. Chambers asked, seemingly anxious to get back to the point.

"Yes," M. Apollinaire confirmed. "Transylvanian, you see. No reverence for the Hippocratic Oath. Very amusing, isn't it?"

"He isn't spreading this around the lower decks, I hope," Mr. Twain put in. "We don't want mobs of unruly peasants marching into the ballroom with torches and pitchforks, demanding that we hand the count and his daughters over to them, do we?"

"Don't we?" said M. Jarry. "Why not?"

"Because we're English gentlemen, you oaf," said the man from the *Telegraph*. "We'd be obliged to defend the honor of the three young ladies—and their lives too of course—even if they are dagoes. We'd be obliged to wade in, even at the risk of our lives. By the way, do you mind my asking why you're wearing bicycle shorts?"

"Because I make thirty circuits of the promenade deck on my velocipede every day, *monsieur*, even when it is raining," Jarry informed him.

"It's all blown over now, anyhow," the man from the *Mail* put in. "There might be a few more deaths from hypothermia tonight, and if another funnel gets struck by lightning we could all wake up with a shock, but the vampire business seems to be over and done with, more's the pity. If only the count's daughters had been victims...*that* would have been a story."

"Not unless old Buccleuch turned out to be the vampire," his colleague from the *Telegraph* put in.

"Ayesha would make a far better vampire than the duke," Miss Lee suggested.

"Except that female vampires don't usually target female victims," Mr. Henley observed.

"They do in le Fanu's story," Mr. Huneker corrected him. "And there was that poem of Coleridge's...."

"*Is* there a secret compartment in the refrigeration hold?" Mr. Vane interrupted. His face was so drawn and haggard that he might have been intending to crawl into it and die.

"Oddly enough," said Apollinaire, "I believe that there's more than one. After I'd talked to Rocambole, I took a look myself. There's definitely one extra locker down there—he didn't notice it because it's behind a stack of herring-boxes. I couldn't tell how big it might be just from looking at the door, but I bumped into Mr. Kitchener, who was taking a plan of the ship to Quatermain's cabin, and he let me take a quick look at it. It's there all right—and another one whose door I hadn't spotted. Of course, they might be ice stores—but if so, why does the one I noticed have such a huge padlock on it?"

"You don't suppose it's the safe where old Rockefeller's bonds are stashed?" Mr. Huneker suggested.

"Not unless the guys with guns are a bluff," Mr. Twain said. "They certainly act as if the bonds and Carnegie's bullion are exactly where you'd expect them to be, in the secure hold along with Hearst's Egyptian loot."

"What did Quatermain want with a plan of the ship?" Mr. Robertson asked.

"I think Rocambole asked him to get it," M. Féval answered. "Quatermain's the man who can get things done, it seems. He has the captain eating out of his hand."

"Not a pretty image," Mr. Chambers observed. "To have Ayesha eating out of one's hand, though...."

"It works the other way round, according to rumor," Mr. Twain told him. "Her name means She Who Must Be Obeyed, supposedly.

"Whatever," said Mr. Chambers. "So, if there are two hidden chambers in the refrigeration hold, and one's full of pirated blood, what's in the other one?"

"Did you know," Apollinaire said, "that the *Titan* has nineteen watertight compartments, with a total of ninety-two doors, all of which can be closed within half a minute if the hull's breached. It was all on Quatermain's plan."

"I think you mean *could*, not *can*," Mr. Robertson put in.

"What's that supposed to mean?" Miss Lee asked.

"It means that they *could* be closed within half a minute before the funnel got struck by lightning," Mr. Robertson told her. "Now that the internal telegraph system has been damaged, though, they probably can't. If we were to be holed tonight—by hitting an iceberg, say—the subsequent flooding might not be containable. Or, indeed, if we were holed tomorrow or the day after, unless the crew can make adequate running repairs."

"We're all sailing to judgment," groaned Mr. Vane. "Soon, we shall be face-to-face with God. And how shall we answer, when he asks us whether we have sinned?"

"Well, I for one," said M. Jarry, "shall say *mais oui*."

"May we what?" asked the man from the *Telegraph*.

"We certainly may," said M. Lorrain, as the dessert arrived. Every eye on the table regarded the ice cream with slight suspicion, but the heroes of letters raised their spoons as one, and set to work.

* * * * * *

On the morning of the thirtieth, Captain Rowland was woken by Mr. Hodgson, who informed him that eight bodies had been discovered during the night, of whom only three were victims of hypothermia and poor clothing."

"Not vampires *again*?" the captain wailed.

"I'm afraid so, sir," Hodgson replied.

The obligatory meeting on the bridge was called.

Allan Quatermain was late arriving at the meeting, having been buttonholed *en route* by Edward Rocambole, who had explained regretfully that he had tried with all his might to stay awake all night for a second night running but had proven sadly unequal to the task.

"But now we know about the hidden compartments," Rocambole had said, as Quatermain hurried off, "we'll be sure of finding the secret blood bank! The scoundrels won't get away with their nefarious scheme!"

"We'd better have the ringleaders up to my stateroom again," Rowland told Mr. Black, when the council was finally complete. "This time, I suppose they ought to have brandy with their cigars."

"That might not be enough, sir," Mr. Black opined.

"On its own, no," Quatermain agreed. "We should invite them to return later, as guests in the first class saloon, when Mr. Edison demonstrates his machine for communicating with the dead. They won't want to miss an unprecedented demonstration of that sort. We can even suggest that the occasion might be an opportunity to solve the mystery—that the dead with whom we communicate might be able to tell us who the guilty parties are."

"Excellent thinking, Quatermain," said Rowland. "I'm extremely glad that you're with us this trip."

"A further suggestion, if I may," the hunter added. "It might be worth including Mr. Rocambole in the party. He's been doing a little investigating on his own behalf, and it would be as well to put a lid on any rumors he might be spreading."

"Damned Frenchman!" said Rowland. "Oh well, if you think it advisable, we'll do it. Take care of it will you, Black. How's the work on the internal telegraph coming along, Hodgson?"

"Not terribly well, sir. If Mr. Edison hadn't tired himself out working all night on his machine I'd have asked for his assistance, but he's put the DO NOT DISTURB sign on his cabin door. The weather's no better, alas—but they do say that lightning never strikes twice in the same place, so we'll probably be fine."

"Actually," Quatermain said, "I remember once...."

"Not now, Mr. Quatermain," said the captain. "I'm sure that your story is an excellent one, but please save it for dinner. We need to get to work."

"One more point of information, if I may, sir," said the hunter, meekly. "What *is* in the two storage lockers connected to the refrigeration hold?"

Silence fell upon the entire company, as the captain and his two mates exchanged uneasy glances.

After a few seconds silence, Captain Rowland said: "Ice, Mr. Quatermain. Just ice."

"That's what I thought," said Quatermain, mildly. "I'll pass the information on to Mr. Rocambole, just to set his mind at rest."

* * * * * * *

That night, at dinner, Allan Quatermain held the captain's table enthralled with his account of multiple lightning strikes on an unnamed peak in the Mitumba Mountains, which had fortunately put an end to a number of hideously grotesque multitentacular creatures that had been directing a murderous native cult for centuries.

"I don't understand what a gang of whistling octopi were doing up a mountain in darkest Africa in the first place," Carnegie muttered to Edison, as fluttering hearts slowed in their paces and the members of the audience began to breathe more easily again.

"Actually," said Edison, "the plural of octopus is *octopodes*, and the creatures described by Mr. Quatermain appear to have had more than eight tentacles in any case. There've been rumors of such creatures from a dozen different parts of the world. Traces of them have recently been discovered at several archaeological sites, but they don't appear to have been bony enough to fossilize conveniently, so their taxonomic status remains dubious, and it's difficult to tell how long they've been around—millions of years, probably. Some of their relatives still live in the sea, apparently; while I was at the Royal Society in London I heard a rumor that some body-parts had been caught in the net of a vessel fishing off Madeira. The locals were terrified, for some reason—said they weren't really dead, even though they were mere fragments, and that they were inherently evil. They were dispatched to London for examination, but they never reached England, alas—they were aboard the *S.S. Dunwich*, which sank off Selsey Bill the week before Christmas."

Meanwhile, Ayesha was saying: "The lightning was a blessing. We had heard rumors of these creatures and their unspeakable depredations even in Kôr. The natives who worshipped them as gods—or as the petty representatives of gods even more unspeakably dreadful—had become excited of late, anticipating the imminent return of some ultimate horror that would put an end to man's dominion over the Earth."

"Savages believe all kinds of weird things," said Rowland, staring into her wide blue eyes. "Mind you, we old seamen know better than to laugh at all their superstitions. We've encountered monsters in our time, haven't we, Mr. Hodgson?"

"We have indeed, sir," Hodgson said.

"Hodgson could tell you tales of the South Seas that might even startle Mr. Quatermain," the Captain went on. "Mind you, you don't have to go as far as that to find bizarre creatures nowadays. The beaches on the Isle of Wight...." He stopped suddenly as Hodgson put a hand on his arm. "Oh, of course," he said. "Sorry."

"Horror stories are all very well," the Duke of Buccleuch opined, "but I'm not sure they're fit accompaniment for roasted mallard and baked Alaska, especially when there are ladies present. I can see why a fellow's mind might turn to morbid matters when we've got Mr. Edison's phantasmagoria show to look forward to with our brandy and cigars, but I think a little self-control's in order while we're eating. Don't you agree, Mrs. de Bathe?"

"I don't mind at all," the former Lillie Langtry hastened to assure Quatermain and Edison.

"I am not a stage magician," Edison said. "My machine is not a phantasmagoria. What you will see tonight is one of the greatest experiments in history, more important by far than Roentgen's games with X-rays or Marconi's attempts to develop wireless telegraphy. When my machine is connected up to the ship's generators, everyone present will be privileged to witness the dawn of a new era in human history. It will advance the cause of Enlightenment by an order of magnitude."

"Don't know about that," Buccleuch muttered. "Damn spiritualists have been pestering the dead for years, and all we have to show for it is stupid gossip."

"The duke has a point," said Hearst. "If you're aiming to horn in on the medium business you'll have to be careful of your overheads. It's a limited market, and the clients aren't big spenders, for the most part."

"The marketing strategy will be a bit awkward," Carnegie agreed. "A machine for talking to the dead isn't like the electric light-bulb—something that every home needs and has to buy repeatedly because of built-in obsolescence. Do you envisage it as a domestic appliance, like your phonograph, or will it be an institutional sort of thing, like the electric chair?"

"I've already explained that the machine isn't amenable to mass production," Edison said. "I envisage it as a wonder of the world, which might be placed in its own custom-built building as a modern oracle."

And what will it actually *do* for us?" Rockefeller wanted to know. "When you get down to the nitty-gritty, what'll the news be *worth*?"

"I think that rather depends on exactly what the dead have to say for themselves when Mr. Edison opens his channel of communication," Quatermain interjected. "Even if spiritualist mediums are honest—not that I doubt them all, mind—their links with the world beyond seem to be tenuous and discontinuous. If Mr. Edison can open a channel capable of carrying much heavier traffic for sustained periods, the dead may become a good deal more voluble."

"That is my hope," Edison confirmed. "At present, our forefathers can only communicate with us, if at all, in fragmentary whispers. My machine will hopefully give them the ability to speak clearly, at far greater length and in far greater detail."

"But it might not work in the way you envisage," Count Lugard suggested. "And even if it does...it has occurred to you, I suppose, that at least some of the dead may bear us some ill will—and that they might be at least as prone to mendacity, malice, inarticulacy, false belief and insanity as they were when they were alive."

"Come now, Lugard," Quatermain said. "Even aristocrats like yourself and the Duke of Buccleuch, who are heirs to centuries of feudal oppression, surely have nothing to fear from the bitter slanders of a few wretched peasants? Why, I dare say that there are hundreds of elephants, dozens of lions and not a few giraffes whose souls might harbor resentments against me, but I'd be willing to face them all as squarely now as I did when I gunned them down."

"And what about the unspeakable *octopodes* from the Mitumba Mountains?" Carnegie asked. "Are you willing to hear what *their* immortal souls have to whistle in your ear?"

"Of course," said Quatermain. That would be a small price to pay for such opportunities as the privilege of meeting up with my old friends Curtis and Good again."

"You don't think they might be a little envious that you walked away with all King Solomon's treasure while they stayed behind to feed the vultures?" Hearst suggested.

"They have the treasures of Heaven now," Quatermain said. "They were virtuous and generous men, and I cannot imagine that they would bear me any grudge."

"They're likely in a very small minority, then," Hearst said. "What about the majority whose members are suffering the torments of Hell and the rigors of Purgatory? Shall we hear their screams of agony when Edison switches on his machine, do you think?"

"My machine will hopefully put an end to all such idiot superstitions," Edison said, stiffly. "I am confident that it will demonstrate the infinite mercy of God—or His utter indifference to the condition of the dead, whose echoes beyond the grave must be natural phenomena, like electricity and X-rays, waiting to be revealed by the march of progress."

"And exploited, of course," Carnegie added. "After discovery comes utility."

"Just so," said Rockefeller. "Still can't see exactly how you'll make your money, though."

Edison raised his eyes to the heaven in which he did not seem to believe, but he remained silent. Presumably, there seemed to him to be no point in correcting the millionaires' misconceptions yet again.

"I'll drink to that," said Captain Rowland, although it was unclear to his eleven dinner companions exactly what he meant by "that."

* * * * * * *

At the writers' table, the talk was similarly dominated by Mr. Edison's impending demonstration.

"It will be interesting to converse with Shakespeare," said Mr. Huneker.

"Chaucer and Malory," Mr. Robertson speculated.

"King Arthur himself, and Sir Perceval too," suggested Mr. Twain.

"Plato, Aristotle, and Epicurus," added Mr. Chambers.

"Charles Baudelaire and Villiers de l'Isle Adam," M. Lorrain put in.

"Sappho and Catherine the Great," mused Ms. Lee.

"Napoléon Bonaparte and Georges Cadoudal," was M. Féval's slightly mischievous suggestion.

"Horatio Nelson and the Duke of Wellington," countered the man from the *Telegraph*.

"Walter Raleigh and Elizabeth I," supplied the man from the Mail.

"Simon Magus and Apollonius of Tyana," said M. Apollinaire.

"Attila the Hun and Genghis Khan," M. Jarry contributed.

"All mere flights of destiny's fancy," Mr. Vane opined. "We shall all meet the Lord, whether Mr. Edison's machine works or not, and we shall all be judged.

"Percy Shelley and John Keats," Mr. Huneker went on, blithely.

"Samuel Johnson and Jonathan Swift," Mr. Robertson added.

"George Washington and Julius Caesar," said Mr. Twain.

"Homer and General Custer," added Mr. Chambers.

"Salomé and Cleopatra," was M. Lorrain's second contribution.

"Michelangelo and Leonardo da Vinci," Ms. Lee suggested.

"Fra Diavolo and Cartouche," said M. Féval *fils*.

"Jack Sheppard and Dick Turpin," riposted the man from the *Telegraph*.

"Richard III and Henry VIII," said the man from the *Mail*.

"Merlin and Morgana la Fée," said M. Apollinaire.

"Gilles de Rais and Jeanne d'Arc," said M. Jarry.

"If the lines of communication remain open, of course," M. Féval observed. "We'll have some stiff competition in the new century. If every home in the world acquires one of Mr. Edison's machines, Father will want me to serve as his amanuensis, I'm sure. Now that we have the electric light-bulb and the typewriter, the transcription of the deads' pent-up literary works could become a long and arduous task."

"It could be worse," said Mr. Twain. "We might be historians."

* * * * * * *

When the dining-room had emptied again, the gentlemen reassembled in the saloon, where they brought out their pipes and cigars, as usual—except for those who preferred a glass of absinthe, with or without a dash of ether.

Mr. Edison's machine had already been set up, and connected to the ship's generator. In appearance it was somewhat reminiscent of a cross between a telephone exchange and a church organ, its manifold pipes being tuned to catch and amplify the voices of the dead, while its multitudinous switches were designed to secure and facilitate connections between the mundane and astral planes.

There was a stool at the front, from which all the indicators were visible and all the controls accessible, but Edison did not take his seat immediately; he busied himself checking the various connections for a full fifteen minutes, during which interval his audience—augmented now by Edward Rocambole, a select handful of his fellow second-class passengers and an equal number of representatives of the third class—shuffled for position. Almost all of the watchers were standing up, the seating in the saloon being arranged about the walls, offering a very poor view. Thanks to the *Titan*'s stabilizers, the waiting men were only swaying gently from side to side even though the storm outside was raging as never before.

Finally, the moment of truth arrived. Mr. Edison turned to his audience, bowed, and opened his mouth to make a speech.

"Oh, get on with it, man!" said the Duke of Buccleuch, rudely. "We all know why we're here. Let's hear what the dead have to say, if anything."

Edison was obviously not pleased by this demand but he scanned the faces of the crowd, as if in order to measure their opinion. What he saw there evidently disposed him against further delay, and he sat down. He reached out his right hand to take the lever that would activate the machine's electricity supply, and pulled it down decisively.

The machine crackled and hummed. The pipes emitted eerie sounds, reminiscent of harp strings stirred by a wayward wind—but then the voices began to come through.

They *were* voices—no one in the saloon could have any doubt about that—but it was quite impossible to distinguish what any one of them might be saying. There were thousands, perhaps millions, all attempting to speak at the same time, in every living language and at least as many that were no longer extant.

None of the voices was shouting, at first; they were all speaking in a conversational tone, as if they did not realize how much competition there was to be heard. As the minutes went by, however, this intelligence seemed to filter back to wherever the dead were lodged. The voices were raised a little—and then more than a little. Fortunately, the volume of their clamor was limited by the power of the amplifiers that Mr. Edison had fitted to his machine, and he immediately reached out to turn the knob that would quiet the chorus—with the result that the voices of the dead became a mere murmurous blur, denied all insistency as well as all coherency.

Edison's own voice was clearly audible over the muted hubbub when he turned to his audience to say: "If you will be patient, gentlemen, I am certain that our friends on the Other Side will begin to sort themselves out, and make arrangements to address us by turns, in order that each of them might make himself heard. It is just a matter...?"

He was interrupted then, by an unexpected event.

Allan Quatermain, who happened to be looking out of one of the portholes, observed four bolts of lightning descend simultaneously from widely disparate parts of the sky, converging upon the funnels of the *Titan*. All four struck at the same instant, each one picking out a funnel with unerring accuracy.

The cables connecting the ship's internal telegraph system had been imperfectly repaired, but there was nevertheless a continuous circuit running from the bow to the stern, and from the crow's nest to the keel. It ran through every bulkhead and every compartment, every cabin on every deck, every hold and locker, every davit and stanchion, every rivet and joint. The lightning surged through the hull, possessing every fiber of the vessel's being.

The *Titan*'s wiring burnt out within a fraction of a second and Mr. Edison's machine collapsed in a heap of slag, although it left the man himself miraculously untouched, perched upon his stool. So diffuse was the shock, in fact, that the men standing in the saloon, their womenfolk in their cabins, and even the masses huddled in steerage felt nothing more than a tingling in their nerves, more stimulant than injury.

Nobody aboard the *Titan* died as a direct result of the multiple lightning strike, but the flood of electrical energy was by no means inconsequential. Communication between the *Titan* and the world of the dead was cut off almost instantly—but *almost* instantly was still a measurable time, and the interval was enough to permit a considerable effect.

Exactly what that effect was, no one aboard the *Titan* could accurately discern, and the only man aboard with wit enough even to form a hypothesis was Jean Ténèbre, who had briefly borrowed the identity of the elephant-hunter Allan Quatermain.

If the real Quatermain had made any posthumous protest, his voice went unheard.

What the Chevalier Ténèbre hypothesized was that by far the greater portion of the power of the multiple lightning-strike, which had so conspicuously failed to blast the *Titan* to smithereens or strike dead its crew and passengers, had actually passed through the ship's telegraph system and Mr. Edison's machine *into* the realm of the dead, where it had wreaked havoc.

What the realm of the dead might be, or where it might be located, the chevalier had no idea—but he supposed that its fabric must be delicate and that the souls of the dead must be electrical phenomena of a far gentler kind than the lighting of Atlantic storms.

Thomas Edison had presumably been correct to dispute William Randolph Hearst's claim the Edison's machine might only enable the *Titan*'s passengers to hear the screams of the damned in Hell— but if the souls of dead humankind had not been in Hell when Edison closed his master-switch, they obtained a taste of it now.

And they screamed.

They screamed inaudibly, for the most part, because the pipes of Edison's machines had melted and their connections had been dissolved—but there was one exception to this rule.

The brothers Ténèbre and Count Lugard's party were not the only individuals on board the *Titan* who might have been classified as "undead." The fragment of the creature that had washed up on the beach at Nettlestone Point, having earlier been found by a fishing-vessel off Madeira and lost again from the *Dunwich*, also had an exotic kind of life left in it. Like many supposedly primitive invertebrates, the part was capable of reproducing the whole, under the right existential conditions and with the appropriate energy intake.

When this seemingly-dead creature screamed, its scream had only to wait for a few microseconds before it was translated back from the fragile realm of the dead into the robust land of the living.

It as a strange scream, more sibilant than strident, and it was a strangely powerful scream.

As Edison's machine had briefly demonstrated—confounding all the skeptics who had refused for centuries to believe in spiritualists and necromancers, ghostly visitations and revelatory dreams—the boundary between the human and astral planes was not unbreachable. When the unnamable creature, whose close kin had died by lightning in the Mitumba mountains, was resurrected by lightning, its scream tore a breach in that boundary, opening a way between the worlds—and through that breach, the newly-agonized souls of the human dead poured in an unimaginable and irresistible cataract.

The breach, Jean Ténèbre subsequently decided, could only have lasted for a few microseconds more than it took to make the scream audible in the first place—but while it lasted, the souls of the dead had a chance to assert themselves in the world of the living, of a kind they had never had before—not, at any rate, in such quantities.

The souls of the dead vied with one another to dispossess the souls of the living: to claim the bodies of the *Titan*'s three thousand passengers for their own use and purposes.

The competition was understandably fierce.

There were eight people aboard the *Titan* whose souls could not, as it turned out, be dispossessed. The two brothers Ténèbre, the count who had inverted his name, and his three lovely brides were six of them. The seventh was Edward Rocambole, whose opinion of his own heroism was so unshakable that he simply could not be persuaded to vacate his mortal habitation. The eighth was an eleven-year-old girl in steerage by the name of Myra, who was just lucky.

* * * * * * *

As the thirty-first of December 1900 whiled away, Jean Ténèbre made some slight attempt to figure out who might now be inhabiting the bodies of his fellow passengers and the *Titan*'s crew. He spoke seven languages himself, so he made a little more progress than another man might have, but it was still an impossible task. The dead turned out to be very discreet, and they clung to their assumed identities as stubbornly as the chevalier had ever clung to any of his multitudinous pseudonyms.

By the time he had to dress for dinner, Jean Ténèbre had found some reason to suspect that Captain John Rowland might once have been a Dutchman named Vanderdecken; that Mr. Hodgson might once have been an American gentleman named Edgar Poe; that Mr. Black might once have been Edward Teach, nicknamed Blackbeard; that William Randolph Heart might once have been Judas Iscariot; that John D. Rockefeller might once have been Nebuchadnezzar; that Andrew Carnegie might once have been Cyrus the Great; that the Duke of Buccleuch might once have been Wat Tyler; that Edison might once have been Daedalus; and that the former Lillie Langtry might now be the former Catherine de Medici; but he could not be sure.

The one thing of which he *was* sure was that, in the struggle for repossession of the Earth, the meek had, in general, not prevailed.

That night, however, dinner was served as usual, although the only meat left aboard was chicken, all the remaining pork and beef having mysteriously vanished into one of the storage-lockers adjoining the refrigeration hold.

At the writers' table, the conversation ran along lines that were a trifle unusual, but nevertheless perfectly civilized.

"Are you going to stay in the writing game?" Mr. Robertson asked Mr. Twain.

"I doubt it," said Mr. Twain. "Not unless Edison hurries the development of moving pictures. That's where writers will make money in future—that and broadcasting, Marconi-style. How about you, Chambers?"

"I'm heading for Texas," Mr. Chambers said. "Going into the oil business, I think. The twentieth century is going to need power, and there's an ocean of black gold lying around just waiting to be sucked out. Are you with me, Huneker?"

"All the way," Mr. Huneker agreed. "But I might just get into automobiles. They're not much to look at just now, but I have a feeling there's scope in them—and a market for your oil, Chambers."

"You're staying with the *Mail*, I suppose?" said the man from the *Telegraph* to his friend.

"Just for a while," his colleague agreed. "Provided I make editor within two years. It shouldn't be difficult. Within five I'll have middle England eating out of my hand. You?"

"I fancy that I might found a tabloid of my own. The *Daily Mirror*, say—or *The Sun*, if I could be sure that swine Hearst wouldn't sue me. I'll not be in competition with you, mind. Wouldn't want to confuse the poor lambs with debates or the truth, would we?"

"Europe," Jarry said to Apollinaire, "is ripe for looting. England and Germany will be at one another's throats even if we don't stir the pot, with France caught between them. Given that the sun never sets on their various imperial adventures, that puts the whole world up for grabs or very nearly."

"There's going to be big money in armaments," opined M. Féval. "Bigger and better guns, tougher and thicker armor. Civilians won't be able to stay out of twentieth century wars, with fleets of airships raining down bombs on cities."

"And big money in medicine too," M. Lorrain put in. "It always pays to have both sides covered in a major conflict—killing and healing always go hand in hand. There'll be fortunes to be made out of any method of combating infection and syphilis. Armies are wonderful instruments for spreading the plague—all that camaraderie and rape."

"High explosives are passé," Apollinaire mused. "Poison gas is the way forward. Atom bombs, maybe a little further down the line. Germ warfare too, if your medicines can provide the means to protect the folks at home."

"The long-term future's in morphine and human trafficking," Ms. Lee opined. "Even if populations aren't displaced *en masse* by wars, there's bound to be migration on a scale that beggars the imagination, and even the people who aren't physically wounded in your universal wars will be in dire need of pain relief."

"We shall be judged by our actions," Mr. Vane asserted, cheerfully. "Let's make sure that we make better use of our second chances than we ever did with our first."

* * * * * * *

The following morning, shortly after dawn, the *Titan* steamed past Sandy Hook and soon came within sight of the Statue of Liberty.

"It's going to shake things up when this lot get ashore,", said Ange Ténèbre, still playing the role of Ayesha, as he/she drank in his/her first sight of the home of the brave and the land of the free. "You now, if I weren't so incorrigible, I might have thought twice about stealing the bullion and the bonds, let alone Hearst's antique gemstones."

"They're too busy making future plans to care overmuch about minor inconveniences," his brother said. "As for shaking things up, I doubt that America will notice anything out of the ordinary. It's always been a land of opportunity."

"Aren't you forgetting the thing in the storage-locker? The people from the New York Museum of Natural History are going to get a shock when they open it up."

"I expect it'll slip over the side and head for Innsmouth," Jean Ténèbre said. "One shoggoth more or less isn't going to disrupt the flow of history any more than adding an extra ounce of rapacity to the characters of men like Hearst and Rockefeller."

They were joined then by Count Lugard and his three delectable brides.

"Did you dine well last night, Monsieur Ange?" the count asked, politely.

"Yes indeed," said Ange. "Poor girl seemed a trifle disconcerted, not having expected her second term on Earth to be terminated quite so rapidly, but her blood hadn't curdled at all. You?"

"Likewise—and my three lovelies had a good time also. Irma was a trifle reckless, descending no further than the second class cabins, but she says that it was worth it, just to see the expression on Monsieur Rocambole's face when he realized that there was, after all, no gang of technicians aboard covertly collecting donations for medical research."

"The world is full of such misconceptions," Ange lamented. "The only things in life that are dependable are lust and avarice."

"Do you not mean death and taxes?" The count asked, laughing to emphasize that he was joking. They were, after all, surrounded by evidence of the evitability of death, and they both knew perfectly well that only little people paid taxes.

"Aren't you afraid that the sunlight will shrivel you up and make you burst into flames?" Ange riposted, laughing just as merrily.

The count looked up into the brightening sky, then down at the sunlight reflected in the myriad windows of a host of skyscrapers. "I shall love it here," he said. "And my brides will have the time of their unlife. We'll soon make ourselves felt in Manhattan. Things will never be the same again."

"Not according to Jean," Ange told him. "He doesn't think the arrival of the *Titan* will change anything."

"That's not what I meant, Brother," the chevalier corrected him. "I meant that no one will understand *why* things have changed. They'll be expecting change regardless, and our contribution to it— not to mention that of the three thousand reanimates—will seem to be nothing more than the mundane surge of history. This is a new century, Brother Ange; even if the *Titan* had hit an iceberg and gone straight to the bottom, you and I would still be living in interesting times."

"Always assuming that we could still come back again, if our graves were lying on the ocean floor," Ange said.

"For the likes of us," said Jean, "fate will always find a way."

ABOUT THE AUTHOR

BRIAN STABLEFORD was born in Yorkshire in 1948. He taught at the University of Reading for several years, but is now a full-time writer. He has written many science fiction and fantasy novels, including: *The Empire of Fear*, *The Werewolves of London*, *Year Zero*, *The Curse of the Coral Bride*, and *The Stones of Camelot*. Collections of his short stories include: *Sexual Chemistry: Sardonic Tales of the Genetic Revolution*, *Designer Genes: Tales of the Biotech Revolution*, and *Sheena and Other Gothic Tales*. He has written numerous nonfiction books, including *Scientific Romance in Britain, 1890-1950*, *Glorious Perversity: The Decline and Fall of Literary Decadence*, and *Science Fact and Science Fiction: An Encyclopedia*. He has contributed hundreds of biographical and critical entries to reference books, including both editions of *The Encyclopedia of Science Fiction* and several editions of the library guide, *Anatomy of Wonder*. He has also translated numerous novels from the French language, including several by the feuilletonist Paul Féval.

Made in the USA
Lexington, KY
13 December 2009